PRAISE FOR *FROM O...*

"John Kelly's novel is inventive and inten
reader's point—it's luxuriously involving." **—Richard Ford**

"A big rip-roar of a novel: deeply nuanced, authentic, madcap, and very, very funny indeed. *From Out of the City* subverts itself and diverts us at the very same time: a wonderful new Irish novel." **—Colum McCann**

"Wild and fresh and invigoratingly demented—this is a fierce-ly funny novel that will bring to mind the glorious excesses of writers like J. P. Donleavy, John Kennedy Toole and Thomas Pynchon." **—Kevin Barry**

"John Kelly has pulled Dublin out from under our feet and with surgical precision, dexterity and wit, he has dissected it, then reassembled it, before hurling it into the future. *From Out of the City* has all that is required of good satire: humour, truth and above all the ability to make us more than a little afraid." **—Christine Dwyer Hickey**

"*From Out of the City* is intricate, outrageous, sophisticat-ed, funny and wonderfully entertaining: what more could a reader ask?" **—John Banville**

PRAISE FOR JOHN KELLY

"John Kelly is an immensely gifted writer—he can do things with the spoken language that are rare to behold and behear." **—Tom Paulin**

"Rampant wit and a deft and elegant control of language . . ." **—*The Times***

"Witty, inventive, exhilarating . . . " **—*The Guardian***

FROM OUT OF THE CITY

FROM OUT OF THE CITY

John Kelly

DALKEY ARCHIVE PRESS
Champaign / London / Dublin

Library of Congress Cataloging-in-Publication Data

Kelly, John, 1965-
   From Out of the City / John Kelly. -- First edition.
   pages cm
   ISBN 978-1-62897-000-5 (pbk. : acid-free paper)
   I. Title.
   PR6061.E4935F76 2014
   823'.914--dc23
                     2014001018

This publication was partially supported by the Illinois Arts Council, a state agency, and the University of Illinois (Urbana-Champaign).

From Out of the City received financial assistance
from the Arts Council of Ireland.

www.dalkeyarchive.com

Cover image: *Visitor*, by James Hanley. The owners have granted permission to use this work but wish to remain anonymous. We thank both parties for their generosity.

Design & composition: Mikhail Iliatov
Printed on permanent/durable and acid-free paper

for DH & SH

Mali corvi malum ovum

WE ALL KNOW what happened. A small bang. More of a pop than anything and the Commander-in-Chief of the Army and Navy of the United States, and of the Militia of the several States, slumped sideways onto the deep blue carpet of St. Patrick's Hall. Crimson soaked purple into black and dignitaries screamed at the sight of presidential brains lashed across the broad white britches of George III. There were summer blossoms on the tables, potatoes in their jackets and shattered stars of crystal in the Wicklow lamb. All in all, it was a shocking Smörgåsbord of blood, liquor, mint sauce and bone and many were sorry they missed it.

After the hopes of the third decade and successive Presidents of relatively benign sensibilities, Richard Rutledge Barnes King had been the unimagined throwback, poking at every vipers' nest on Earth until the air had once again been filled with the almost-forgotten dust of skyscrapers. A proud Memphian, he was a cigar smoker, a pill popper and an alcoholic. His favourite actor was Ernest Borgnine, he played poker with his bodyguards, and he loved his dog – a malodorous, retromingent cockapoo called Elvis. In fact those close to President Richard King might argue that he was, as extremely powerful people go, by no means the worst. Some may even have loved him.

And perhaps it was darling Princess who loved him best of all. Princess King, the bright young thing who never once stopped calling him Dad and who was, at the time of the shooting, a student at Trinity College and the real reason for the visit in the first place. She was the Presidential daughter, a beauty and a brainbox, said to have fallen so far from the tree as to be interested in literature, fashion, fire music and wine. A high-flier academically and a comet in the Creative Writing course, she paid for her dedication by being permanently locked up, for her own security, along with the Book of Kells, Beckett's cricket bat and a phalanx of heavily armed men with thick arms and pimply necks. It was no life for a young one but there it was. We don't choose our fathers or, for that matter, the class of enemy they make.

According to Channel NB1, Princess was not present at the Castle on the night her father fell. It seems she got the news while relaxing in her bomb-proofed rooms, quietly reading Sheridan Le Fanu and sipping Merlot. And just as well. A mercy surely for Caesar's daughter not to see his body at its end, fanned by the bloodstained hands of bodyguards and rushed by a copter as if to the Underworld itself – in this case the Phoenix Park, not named for the fabulous bird which might renew her Daddy's life, but for *fionn uisce* – clear water which might merely bathe his wound. A single wound by all accounts. A bloody exclamation mark. To the head.

And so, quite oblivious in Trinity, perhaps Princess had been expecting a call from Dad at any moment. News of when they might meet for a catch-up and a hug. Later that night perhaps. Or, same as last time, a few moments grabbed at the airport in the morning. But of course, when that shot was fired and Richard King tumbled to the Castle carpet, nobody was thinking much about daughters and dads. Already, in the commandeered bunker of Áras an Uachtaráin, it was all motherfucker this and motherfucker that as the American brass glared at a blinding hologram of Planet Earth so lit with data that it looked like a glitter ball. And then, sometime close to dawn, that doctor with the buzz cut appeared live on Channel NB1. He was red-eyed and shaking and he mumbled into a mixed bouquet of microphones that the President was dead and that everything possible had been done.

The versions of these events are many. Variations on a theme. Conjecture, propaganda, conspiracy theory, misinformation and ballyhoo. The official account, repeated almost daily and which now seems to intersperse the very movements of orchestras and the lulls in sporting occasions, amounts to nothing but pronouncement, obfuscation and spin. The unofficial accounts – the work of hustlers, shysters, speculators and hacks all trying to make a buck on the back of it, are more insidious still. And then of course there are the fantasists, less damnable in many ways but peddlers all the same and their lies, dark and intimate as death, are no different from the rest. Until now I have remained silent, watching the lot of them – the officials, the P. T. Barnums and the basket cases alike, all crawling like maggots from the corpses, munching hard on some class of fiction, non-fiction or script. It has not been, I must say, the most edifying of sights – a nation drowning in the self-serving guff of snake-oil salesmen and government-approved gobshites pimping out what's left of its suffering soul. But now here at last is *my* version and any invention lurking here, however bespoke, is informed, considered, and earned. I am an old man, I am a clever man. I have been doing what I do for a very long time and this, my disquisition, is grounded in observation, surveillance and analysis. It is therefore definitive and reliable and serves nothing but itself. It contains therefore the truth. *Verum ipsum factum*, as per Vico of the Vico Road, Killiney, County Dublin.

So yes, there may well be gaps in the narrative but I can assure you now that such matters as I cannot know for certain, verifiable by notes both taken and purloined (from sources both peccable and im), I have filled in for myself with rigor and skill, just as a singer might reconstruct a ballad, with accuracy, from whatever fragments he has – the right and proper method by which any ruined song is resurrected. And while the verses it contains may never tell us exactly what happened, they will tell us precisely how people felt. Otherwise how might it ever survive to be sung in human hearts, even in a ragged form, in the shades of subversion and despair?

Of course I shall do my very best to make it readable, digestible and tolerable but that said, I cannot promise same. For this is no thriller or makey-up tale of suspense. Nor is it some titillating, investigative reconstruction of events which may or may not have happened. It is, rather, an honest and faithful record of breakage and distress at a time when dysfunction – personal, local, national, global, cosmic and whatever lies beyond that again, beyond even the farthest pricks of our increasingly desperate little probes – pervaded all. A time when everything was already broken and when, in many ways, the shooting of a President (the actual detail that is) was neither here nor there.

After all, Richard Rutledge Barnes King was not the first world leader to be taken out by a single silver bullet. Nor was he the first, for all the power and protection of his office, to meet a violent death while travelling in foreign lands. He was, however, the first to die in the old spawning grounds of Ireland and this is the angle which made things rather more intimate for the country's eight million citizens and especially intimate for me. Otherwise the actual assassination does not especially concern me. My preoccupation here is not so much the end of life but, rather, its continuance.

It occurs to me also (and I'm writing this first part last) that if this published testament is now in your hands, then as per my clear instructions to Blood, Tobin & Fry Solicitors, I too must be dead. Deader than dead. And dead, I trust, from nothing more sinister than senescence.

ONE

THE FEAST of St. Isidore of Seville and I awoke to the sound of rain. It panicked me briefly – that old spurt of fear that I'd been transported through the night to some foreign land where summer downpours are still imaginable. I thought perhaps that I was in Iceland or Nova Scotia but a quick scan across the yellowing sweep of my pillow was enough to assure me that my *locus* was as was – my own country, my own house, my own room, my own scratcher. Which was very good news. And what's more, there had been no bad dreams, it seemed, from which to thrash awake. No twistings of the limbs, no tightenings in the chest, no pulses in the lumpy baldness of my head. An erection too no less. On this unexpectedly wet morning of my eighty-fourth birthday, lo and behold, a boner of pure marble. Happy Birthday to me, I whispered to myself. For I'm not a squishy marshmallow. We'll roast you on a stick. Bum-tish!

Eight tumbling decades since I first landed at the South Dublin Lying-in Hospital, Holles Street named for Denzille Holles, Earl of Clare – a place now infested with cut-throats, brigands, smackheads and rats but still serving then, at the hour of my arrival, as The National Maternity. A very palace of human nature.

– What kind of a name is Monk? asks the midwife.

– Named for Thelonious, says my father, his eye on the clock.

– Felonious?

– θ, says my father, Thelonious with a θ.

– Oh right, says the midwife (a culchie). Little Thelonious.

– Yes, says my father, as in Thelonious Sphere.

– You have me there again, says the midwife (Roscommon).

– Thelonious fucking Monk, says my mother with a sigh. A fucking trumpet player.

– Piano, says my father, buttoning up his coat. And celeste on *Pannonica*.

– I see, says the midwife, not seeing at all (Boyle).

– At one stage, says my mother, this prick was pushing for Stock-hausen.

– Stock what? says the midwife (somewhere out beyond Boyle).

– And Suk, says my mother. That was another one.

– It's pronounced *Sook*, says my father, and I never once suggest-ed Suk.

– Stockhausen, says my mother. For fucksake. Stockhausen or Suk.

And so this is the pair – Bleach and Ammonia – who gave me life and this grand ruin of a house in which to enjoy it. 26 Hibernia Road, Dún Laoghaire. Three-storey, over-basement, Victorian residence c.1850, features including original fireplaces, quality cornice-work, centre roses, panelled doors and five generous bedrooms of proportions considered gracious. From the street, it resembles every other house in this section save for its evident security apparatus – a multitude of surveillance cameras perched like blackened gargoyles on the walls. All of it necessary alas as we live in changed times and while Hibernia Road, leading to Britannia Avenue, now Casement Avenue and named for Sir Roger, was once an address considered salubrious (c.1850), it's now no more than a desolate trench of dereliction and crime. Burned-out, sea-blown, not altogether inhabited and shoved well back from the main strip, Hibernia Road is, these days, neither visited nor travelled. Not by citizens. Not by Guards. Not even by the gentlemen and ladies of the military. Ours or theirs.

In fact the whole town of Dún Laoghaire, named for a 5th-century king of Tara, is now largely defunct and undesirable. Like a mouthful of rotten teeth it grins ever more grotesquely into the swill of Dublin Bay – *Cuan Bháile Átha Cliath* – polluted beyond all salvage by plutonium, uranium and flesh and where sits, in apparent permanence, a Brobdingnagian aircraft carrier, named not for Kevin Barry, just a lad of eighteen summers, or Maggie Barry who sang "The Flower of Sweet Strabane", or James J. Barry of Barry's Original Blend Corkonian Tea, but for Commodore John Barry, the Father of the American Navy, born in Wexford in 1745. The thing has been sitting there for so long now that people don't even see it any more. And if they do they pass no further remarks. And in any case, don't all the nice girls love a sailor?

Dún fucking Laoghaire. Where I have lived all my life. Dún Laoghaire, Dún Laoire, Dunleary (briefly Kingstown) where the monks of St. Mary's caught their shoals of herring. In the 17th century it was a landing place for big-shots and men-of-war and in 1751 a shark was hauled ashore. In 1783 an African diver disappeared under the waves iin a diving bell, and in 1817 the first stone of the East Pier was laid and all those virgin tonnes of granite were dug out of Dalkey Hill and dumped. Otherwise there's not much to commend the place at all. Not now anyway. Dún Laoghaire. 9.65 km ESE of the metropolitan hub – the very spot where the Millennium Spire used to be and, before that again, an effigy in Portland Stone of Lord Horatio Nelson, Viscount and Baron Nelson of the Nile and of Burnham Thorpe etc., etc. The Pillar blown to smithereens of granite and black limestone in 1966. Granite from Kilbride. Pedestal, column and capital. His nibs on the summit, myopic, head lathered in the guano of herring gulls. Vice Admiral of the White and my two uncles that did it. Maguire and Patterson. And Clery's Clock stopped dead at 1:31 AM. *Faoileán scadán.* The colony. The colonized. Nelson's blasted colon : the colonoscopy for fucksake. And I'm sleepy now. Might roll over yet and perhaps some dreams will come. And snooze. And slumber. And I might as well. Only young once. Snuggle and snooze.

But of course this rain was wrong and I raised my head to check once more that this really *was* my room. And surely it must be. The goose-down duvet, grey and unstained, the clock and the Glock, the empty glass still fragrant with dusty Hennessy, the ancient maps of Paris and the Dingle Peninsula, the curling snaps of smiling people long dead, and the sideboard with the stolen bust of Berkeley fitted with old wraparound shades, now a bookend for the little concertina of Sci-Fi paperbacks all read so eagerly when I was a boy so happily in love with the future. Berkeley, Bishop of Cloyne, nicked sixty years ago from the Long Room of Trinity College and taken out the front gate in a wheelbarrow. So yes, I assured myself once more, with an element of certainty now, that this was, surely to goodness, my room. My own *leaba* in number 26 and I had not, unless I was grievously mistaken, been kidnapped or otherwise rendered in my sleep. And it was my birthday too. And in Dún Laoghaire, as if to mark the occasion, there appeared to be actual precipitation.

These thoughts, such as they were, uncontrolled, semi-conscious and leapfrogging each other, were suddenly interrupted by a most extravagant yawn. My jaws shifted and cracked and a pain shot through my skull like a little private bullet of my own. And then there followed the long slow-motion masticatory shimmy in order to correct the jawbones again and with that second crack there came a certain peace, not so much a click this time as a clock, and I could relax again, still alive, glubbing now on my pillow like an old lippy cod. *Gadus morhua*. Extinct source of vitamins A, D, E and several essential fatty acids. And what a treat that would have been on my birthday. Cod and Chips from Burdock's of Werburgh Street, named for the church of St. Werburgh, named for Werburgh of Chester, a Benedictine abbess, prophetess and seer of the secrets of hearts. And Burdock's had haddock and ray and lemon sole and scampi and goujons – until that final scare, that is, and everyone stopped eating fish. Even the cormorants in Dún Laoghaire stopped eating fish and they all died away with the seals. The Germans call it *Seezunge*. And the Spaniards too. I do miss a bit of tongue, says Missus McClung. *Lenguado*. All things lingual and gustatory. *Larus argentatus*. And that terrifying colony ensconced in the ruins of Liberty Hall, dive-bombing all who might chance it on foot across the Tara Street Bridge. Screeching. Wheeling. Plummeting. And the best of it all is that it's more than likely that I know every last one of them – both chancer and gull – by name, reputation and record. Because nothing gets past a man as invisible as me. Oh where oh where is that gallant man? Eighty-four today.

But now on this unexpectedly wet morning in my gargoyled

house on Hibernia Road, my sub-duvet reverie at an end, I finally manoeuvred myself to the edge of the bed, gripped my thighs and pressed down hard, the pressure of it translating to push and the body yielding to forces and physics and, whatever the kinetics, whatever the systems and sequences of internal pulleys and cranks called upon so early in the day, my creaking self slowly loomed and my cool morning arse presented itself to the blue grain of the room. I'm up, says I. Another day another dolor – and I announced in the darkest voice of MacLiammóir, *Comedia finita est*. Then chuckling like a changeling in my white t-shirt and flabby boxers I lurched to the window, parted the curtains and peered into the light. Time to think straight now. Time to assess. Time to focus. To get, says you, to the point.

But again I stress that this is not about Richard King or his assassination. Nor is it about how, when they asked me where I was when it happened, the incident in question, that I was able to tell them that I was at home, at number 26, seated on my sofa, a Stoli in a highball, watching the rolling coverage just like everybody else. Or about the fact (and this is something I, of course, neglected to tell them) that I could barely breathe that night as I waited, waited, waited for that newsflash to come, for confirmation from the Castle that the bullet had flown and that ambition's debt had finally been paid. No. Not at all. This is not about any of that. And it never once was. It's more about me and where I live and what I do. And it's also about those people in my care and who will enter soon. But for now this is just me, on my birthday, eighty-fourth, out of bed and at my bedroom window in my boxers and my vest.

And so what did I see? One of my foxes, soaked and muddy, was dragging a blue hula hoop across what used to be a flowerbed and I immediately pictured what I must have missed – the moonlit fox gyrating like a pole dancer and counting out the revolutions. The thought of it made me giggle and I decided that perhaps this really was a very good day in Dún Laoghaire. There hadn't been rain in months and now here it was at last. Real dancing rain just like the glorious downpours of my childhood and I could smell within it some strange hint of the perpetual. Pandiculation followed. A temporary deafness. Then elbow pain and recovery. I placed my pistol in the drawer, closed it tight and then, and only then, I began to pad the bare boards to the bathroom. I take no chances now, ever since the time I found myself half asleep at the sink, putting toothpaste on the barrel, about to scrub my thirty-two teeth with a loaded weapon. I'm far from doddery but even so.

The electric is erratic these days, water even more so, and so I showered for the thirty-second legal max. Then I dried myself off, dressed quickly in a clean white t-shirt, shorts and sloggy bottoms and descended to make myself a camomile tea with honey substitute. Lots of men my age couldn't manage these stairs at all but I'm as supple as I ever was, my joints constantly swimming in fake fish oil. Thanks to the good folks in Nippon my bones are fortified by every available mineral, vitamin, and dietary silicon smoothie, and once I'm up and about I have neither ache nor pain. Not physical pain at any rate. Jesus, Mary and Joseph where would we be without the synthetics? And without the Japanese? Dab hands the Japs and we'd be lost entirely without them. But fuck it I do miss the bees. I wish the Japanese would sort the bees. And the bee's knees. For honey, substitute is no substitute. The signs were there for years and nobody lifted a fucking finger. It wouldn't have happened in Japan. Only it did. World without bees. Amen.

From the kitchen window I watched the fox, still tossing the hoop, and although I always hate to spook such a scene, the instant I punched in the code, *Vulpes vulpes* shot off like a brushstroke and the hula hoop rolled, keeled and settled on the burning grass like a portal. Sorry Foxy Loxy, I muttered as I put on my trainers and stepped out into the air, raising my face briefly to the skies for the wet of the rain, the actual rain, and I walked briskly, swerving around my dripping barricade of dumped antiques, down to the tumbledown shed which, these days, leans drunkenly against the sycamore. I took my tea with me. The rain was warm and syrupy and it plashed with pleasure in the steaming mug.

There was a wood pigeon balled up in a beech (I have the eyes of a raptor) and a blue-tit was hanging on the giant echium – the self-seeding, tit-feeding echium growing about a foot a day like some slow-motion purple firework. There were wrens up until about fifteen years ago. *Troglodytes troglodytes*. And blackbirds too. And I used to see them run low across the lawn like infantry out of their trenches and I loved to listen to them sing, watching them snuggled in the holly bush, thinking themselves well defended in the jags. These new alien finches can be unexpected company at times, but it's not the same. And the shrikes I can do without. Butcher birds. Cruel impalers. *Cracticus* something and there's always one on the shed, eyeing me up, a shrew in its bill, or some supersized beetle which arrived in a suitcase from West Africa.

The shed (the dacha I call it) is warped and narrow and it houses century old, half-empty buckets of paint, an original mountain bike, an axe, bits of obsolete surveillance equipment and sheetweb spiders the size of kittens. I love it in there. Most especially in the rain. As a child, the sound of rain always soothed me and I used to hunker in this very same shed, watching the showers lash the cordylines in scenes which seemed tropical. For a moment, I felt like I was the same child again, sheltered in my hidey hole, enjoying the thrilling little shivers which enveloped me – Bleach and Ammonia back in the house arguing about the nap of the lawn or the pressure in the tap. Heavenly, I told myself, perfectly at peace and in the shed, and then with an almost overwhelming sense of liberation, I lowered the front of my sloggy bottoms and pissed with panache from the dacha porch. Breathing deeply like some ancient God I targeted the agapanthus with my jet.

On my first day as sole owner and occupier of number 26 Hibernia Road, flush with freedom and possession, the very first thing I did was relieve myself in this very garden. As the Gods made Orion. The second thing I did, and just as symbolic, was remove most of the contents and dump them outside. Bedsteads, mattresses, tables, chairs, sideboards, china cabinets, Ottomans, bedside lockers, standard lamps, carpets, rugs, mats, holy statues, vases and assorted prints by late 20th-century racketeers. These I piled on the flowerbeds before going back inside to lie on cushions on the floor and crank up the thumping Hi-Fi. Compact discs in those days. My preference then was for bands like New Order, Pere Ubu, Suicide, and The Fall. My father's study, with its CDs of Bartók, Stravinsky and Stockhausen, I locked up and left alone. He was a vulpine man, my father. Vulpecular. But he liked his music, eschewing the wigs for the moderns and enjoying it in his own way. I liked it well enough too, but I was never in the mood for it. Not in those days anyway.

By four in the morning, I had begun to realize my actual discomfort and I returned to the barricade to strip it of essentials – one sofa, one rug, one kitchen table and one chair. These I reinstated in the house while everything else was left bewildered to the elements, where it lies to this day, piled up and creaking, providing shelter and security for generations of scraggy Dún Laoghaire foxes, all of them, including the one with the hula hoop, born and bred within its labyrinthine heap. Otherwise the place hasn't been touched at all and number 26 has somehow distilled with natural precision to the point of being quite perfect for my purposes.

On two floors, front and back, the rooms full of boxes (cereal and shoe) stuffed with photographs, files, scribbles, cuttings and notes, now packed almost to the ceiling, decades of profiling stacked in dense little cities of leaning piles of paper and card. Priceless material all of it, of course, and a fire hazard beyond all imagining, but if it goes up, it goes up. It's no use without me anyway. Without meaning. Like a web without a spider.

At the very top of the house, with a dormer window facing the street, is the actual HQ. On one side of the room, under the plunging slope of the ceiling, is a bank of monitors, permanently on, which links me to the city and beyond. The rest of the space is commanded by a high-back swivel chair of distressed black leather and a fold-out single bed covered in notebooks, orange peel, pencils and sharpenings – the never forgotten stench of desk – all laid out on a carpet so grey and so stained with decades of spilled coffee as to resemble, with some accuracy, a map of the surface of the moon. And this is where I do what I do. And I do it without cease. It takes sustained and careful husbandry but I'm able for it still. There's divinity in it. And a modicum of love.

TWO

SCHROEDER IS a name we all know. Anton James. Lived next door to me, adjacent to the right, and one of those I monitored. In fact I had been watching Anton Schroeder extremely closely, on an almost daily basis, for a very long time. This is all new information but I'm saying it now in as clear a manner as possible. From his very first days to his last I was a constant and, for the most part, unseen presence in that young man's life – not a guardian angel as such, or a spirit guide, but more of a whisper, a benign and focussed energy willing him to move in this way or that.

For the purposes of these pages perhaps the best place to start is the break-in. It's as crucial a junction as any and while it contains comedic elements, thanks to the pantomime policemen, this is no joke. What happened, for all its quirks of language, action and coincidence was serious stuff and I'm not making it up. Even if I wanted to, I wouldn't have the skills.

Schroeder and Francesca had been drinking in Heffernan's. Pints of Weißbier in those days and Dunkelweißen now and again, until herself was diagnosed as coeliac and they both took to the Stoli. They got back around midnight, the pair of them hammered, and Schroeder went straight to his office to make rapid notes on whatever he had been talking about earlier, still believing that one day he might transform such blootered insights into some miraculous art. And while he was up there scrawling in the margins of a vintage New Yorker, Francesca discovered that the envelope left out for the cleaner was no longer on the sideboard. The sound system was missing also, along with a Rickson's flying jacket which had been an early present from Schroeder.

By this stage Schroeder too had realized that something had happened. The four shirt-boxes which contained the notebooks, diaries, drafts and discs he had tended since the age of nine had all vanished and he suddenly felt as if a circular saw was at work in his gut. All he could say to Francesca was fuck the sound system, fuck the Rickson's and fuck the fucking cleaner, they've taken all my stuff. And then as he staggered around the house, massaging his own head like a bystander caught in a bomb, Francesca, for all the good it would do, rang the Guards. They told her that it sounded like junkies and then, a week later, they were on the doorstep with the very same baloney. A big Guard and a small Guard who seemed, as a result of some locker-room prank, to be wearing each other's uniforms. And again I must stress. This is no comic interlude. And the following is exactly what was said. Verbatim.

– Good morning sir, says the big one. We've come about the break-in.

– More or less definitely junkies sir, says the small one. More or less.

Schroeder could see that this was all just a procedural matter. Just blame some anonymous druggie and forget about it. They weren't even slightly interested. He hadn't expected much else but even so.

– You can't be up to them fellas, says the big one.

– What kind of junkie, Schroeder asks, steals notebooks and diaries?

The small Guard consults his notebook.

– It says here they took a sound system and a quantity of cash. And an item of clothing.

– They took the first drafts of three novels, says Schroeder. I'm asking you, who would steal the first drafts of three novels?

The small Guard pretends to perk up.

– Jaysus, this looks like a case for Sherlock Holmes.

The big Guard looks away, smiling to himself.

– A comedian as well as a Guard, says Schroeder.

The small Guard has cheeks like raw bacon and the only thing keeping his cap from falling down around his shoulders is his massive set of crimson ears. A country-cute hoor all the same and, pretending to be oblivious to Schroeder's glare, he holds a smile like a First Communicant.

– Do you write much, Mr Schroeder? Books is it?

Then the big Guard's shoulders begin to quiver and Schroeder strains to stay calm. He knows that while this pair may be attached to the more benign wing of the law and order system, they are, by blood, related to the nasties. He would therefore be wise to keep this in mind in whatever way he reacts.

– Well, he says finally, and in neutral. This is very important to me. My house has been broken into. Items have been stolen.

– Sir, sighs the big Guard, we have drug gangs, prostitution rackets, assaults, armed robberies and crack houses coming out of our arses. And that's just in this street. If you understand me.

Schroeder snorts in defeat. With that tired outburst, the big Guard has revealed himself the typical quagga of jaded public servant – a wolphin, a jaglion or a mule – half man, half filing cabinet. He is someone who has all the information but cares little for any of it. And even though it's first thing in the morning, he already sounds like someone very much finished for the day.

– Yes, of course, says Schroeder.

– You know what this week's delight was? says the small Guard.

– Haven't a clue, says Schroeder.

– Young Miss King out in Sandycove to see the Martello Tower. And it a fecking wreck. Had to seal the whole place off damn near as far as Wicklow. And half the fecking fleet in Dublin Bay.

– Suicide windsurfers maybe? says Schroeder.

– Anything is possible sir. This day and age. Quite the pain in the hole.

– Look, says Schroeder, I just know it wasn't junkies. That's all I'm saying.

Then the big Guard literally groans, giving the very clear signal that his next words are to be final.

– Now sir, there's no point in getting paranoid. That'll get you nowhere.

– No, says Schroeder. Thank you, gentlemen.

– Goodbye sir.

– Goodbye sir. And good luck with the book-writing. The two Guards then take a synchronized step backwards and Schroeder gently closes the door and sits on the stairs.

– Culchie fucks, he mutters to himself. Stupid fucking culchie fucks.

And indeed they were culchies. Fitzpatrick and St Leger. A pair of Norman culchies wouldn't you know, and I kept a close eye on the both of them after that. Fitzpatrick, a time-server straight from a Russian novel, retired soon afterwards on a full pension while young St Leger, he of the bacon face, was later killed outright when his car hit a bus shelter during a chase through Ballybrack. He had been expected to make sergeant at some stage. High hopes for him indeed. Played full forward for Westmeath. Engaged to a nurse in John of Gods.

A few days later I dishonoured my own strictest protocol and turned up at Schroeder's front door. It took nerve but I felt so sorry for him that, having made several copies of everything in the boxes, I walked up the path and buzzed. I was, of course, very well aware that he had never liked the look of me, finding my presence dark and invasive, even from a distance, but he was so relieved to see someone standing on the doorstep holding the missing mother-lode that he actually invited me in. I hadn't planned on this part at all but I remained focussed and took the opportunity to examine him close-up, in the flesh, for the very first time.

I recall that I noted the cragginess, the grey skin, the hair now thinning and barely disguising the ridges which ran like potato drills along his skull. He was wiry and lean, as I was myself on that grim approach to forty, but he seemed far too tired and shaky for a man of his age. No surprise, of course, given his permanent crises and his attempts to deal with them by way of booze, Mahler or both. Usually the Tenth. The first movement. The *Adagio*. Bernstein. Sometimes Rattle. The catastrophe chord at terrifying volume, over and over again, whether for purposes of self-torture or in hope of catharsis, not even I could tell.

– So where did you find everything? he asked, his voice fragile and only slightly Americanized. (That fucking uplift destroyed an entire generation.)

– In a skip, I replied, scoping the room.

– Well, thanks for bringing them back. You want a coffee or something? Tea?

– A coffee would be very nice. Thank you.

He immediately regretted the offer and put the back of his hand to his forehead.

– How do you take it? The coffee?

I saw my chance and took it. I knew that Schroeder was allergic to milk and that he wouldn't have any in the house.

– A little milk, I said. Please.

– I'm not sure I . . .

– Just a drop. And sugar. Two. Please.

And so with Schroeder gone to the store to buy the milk, I photographed the bookshelves, memorized the contents of the medicine cabinet, and bugged the hall, stairs and landing. By the time he returned I had already left, astounded at his carelessness in leaving someone he had previously only grunted at unattended in his home. But then Schroeder is always a piece of cake and he always leaves traces of himself everywhere. Every kick is telegraphed, every swivel is flagged, and I take full advantage with the phantom powers of old age. Anton James Schroeder. My chosen subject. Ask me anything. I know all there is to know.

The early pages of his bio confirm that he crowned during the very last moments of the 20th century, the rest of him following at precisely one second past midnight on day one of the 21st. This landmark nativity, timed to the very second and confirmed by an independent panel of witnesses, marked him as the first crinkled sprog of a brand new Millennium. By all the medical and press reports it was a close-run thing – a sprint finish between the National Maternity and the Coombe (Biddy Mulligan, Pride of) and at one point it was neck and neck. Literally. But in the end it was Baby

Schroeder who slipped out first and the cheer went up in Holles Street and he was held aloft like a gurgling Messiah. The cable was cut and the boy child was bundled up in blue, his skullcap pulsing with compassion, his tiny body already leaking spring water and meconium. Everyone was charmed and before he had even mastered the nipple, little Schroeder was outstaring a barricade of cameras and attempting something like a smile for the old Raidió Teilifís Éireann. Kudos for the hospital and lots of free stuff for Mr and Mrs S.

I was very close that night, sipping Guinness in a jammed bar in Baggot Street, named for Robert, Lord Bagot with g and one t and where I once saw David Bowie and Tin Machine. I got the news within minutes but I didn't linger. There were no taxis that night and so I walked the whole way back to Dún Laoghaire along the old Rock Road, staring up at the sky and thinking about how the world had somehow turned and how this new Millennium Baby would need special minding and care. They brought him home a few days later and Mrs S never once blinked. I could hear everything through the wall. Mr S singing lullabies, Mrs S creaking in the bed and little Baby Schroeder crying like a lion cub all night long.

And yet, the strangest thing of all is this: for the next forty years, myself and Schroeder would only speak once. There were of course the odd muttered greetings over the garden wall but there was only ever one actual conversation and that was when I brought those shirt-boxes to his door. Not much of a conversation, I know. An offer of coffee and a request for milk. But I treasure it all the same. And the more I think about it now the more shocking it is to me that he invited me in at all. As a younger man, he had always been much smarter than that. And as boy he had been a certifiable brain-box. Cautious, rigorous and, school report after school report, always top of the class. Gold star student, his teachers wrote, a pleasure to teach.

At one time it seemed that there was nothing Schroeder didn't know. Capital cities, soccer grounds, makes of car, dates, actors and actresses, historical figures, which river ran where etc., etc. The naming of names was like breath to him – birds, fish, dinosaurs, trees, flags, dogs, herbs and garden plants – all had to be identified and logged. It was the sort of knowledge which kept a boy in control of his world and gave him the steadying sense of being on top of things. I was the same myself. A fact collector.

But then, at some point, everything seemed to change. Borders changed, flags changed, capital cities changed and, in the far north, entire land masses changed as country-sized lumps of ice slipped into the sea. The plastic globe in Schroeder's room quickly became just another curious, spinning thing and his old school atlas might as well have been the work of Ptolemy or Mercator. And then as more and more species became extinct and more and more soccer clubs abandoned their turf, he somehow yielded, let go and wrote everything off as he would later write off his book. Almost overnight he turned into one of nature's rejectors and became a man for cuttings off. Whatever he couldn't master, he spurned.

That said, I knew it still hurt him when he found himself struggling with some television quiz. Questions to which he once knew the answer or, worse again, questions where a once correct answer was no longer so. There was a period when he could beat any television contestant with ease – even in the chosen subject round where you really needed to know your onions. In fact I recall a contestant whose chosen subject really was onions and, even then, Schroeder got six of them right. It was something about onions in the eye sockets of the Pharaoh (I'd need to check my notes) and a line from Shakespeare. Then C. T. Onions. Charles Talbut. Mine eyes smell onions; I shall weep anon.

But by the time King was shot in Dublin Castle, Schroeder no longer farmed such knowledge with any real diligence and had, with actual grief, relegated himself to the second tier. He had allowed himself to slip and to settle, conscious that all his highest hopes (and there were many because of the circumstances) had quietly died alone. Sad to say but Schroeder knew more when he was twelve than he did in his thirties – before all that potential, and that mean-ingless Millennium buzz, had passed into nothingness.

The job at Trinity had not been good for him either. He special-ised in the largely forgotten works of late 20th-century fiction and here again was another trigger for that constant fizz of frustration which one might best read by passing a Geiger Counter across the white knuckles of his writing hand. The book was about eight years ago. *Lucky's Tirade.* The story of a man who dreams the secrets of others and uses this knowledge to make himself as rich as Croesus. But for all its potential (a movie, surely?) and for all the quality of the writing, it had no impact whatsoever. The editor was a cokehead and the publicist was a drunk but that probably made no real differ-ence in the end. *Lucky's Tirade* was verbose, digressive, unconvincing and flawed, and those who read it rarely showed any enthusiasm or, to use a word from the novel, *enthusmiasm.*

And so, in despair and indignation, Schroeder slithered into a burrow of self-loathing and paid a substantial sum of money to have the book removed from the site, hoping that it would simply ex-plode back into nothingness like some unviable planet, blasted into a million smithereens of resentment and defeat. As far as he was concerned, the book was gone. He never referred to it again and he retained not a single copy of his own. As I say, one of nature's rejectors.

But that said, Schroeder never stopped writing and just about everything he pondered and plotted he still hammered out in note form and emailed to himself for safekeeping. Hokum mostly but moved by mood, alcohol, pills and the occasional cigarette, he scribbled ideas and slivers of notions which rarely survived a few hours' sleep. But even so, I intercepted everything and filed it away with especial care, along with the nuked novel which I had printed and hardbound in linen with blind-embossed title in a Pergamenta wraparound. A dozen copies at very great expense. *Lucky's Tirade.* A title which drew negative critical attention from the get-go. Using words like "retromingent" and "Brobdingnagian" brought nothing but further abuse. And, in truth, he really did bring it all on himself.

Lucky raises a buttock and exhales from the depths, producing something rancid and astonishing with all the sonic quality of a knackered bus in deep pneumatic collapse, that sudden relax on its axles over in Dolphin's Barn – the heart-stopping gush of bad air. Hydrogen, methane, oxygen, nitrogen and carbon dioxide coming together in a profound multiphonic honk. It might have been the sad expiration of a beached whale on the rocks of Mayo. It might have been the boat leaving Kingstown in the full fog of Empire. Or even the folk-memory of a Cyclopic New Orleans sousaphone humping up the old streets of Tremé on a Mardi Gras Day.

And all that for a fart. No wonder his readers were pandiculating by the end of Chapter Two.

He's a strange boy, Schroeder. Unmotivated now. And even on this fresh new day of drizzle and possibility, he will be sleeping still, astray no doubt in a vivid dream of Paula Viola – the nation's vamp-on-the-spot, recently voted Ireland's Best Dressed Woman thanks in part to his voting many times over. Schroeder has never actually met Ms Viola, but her nightly appearances on the news and in newsflashes in particular sometimes have him on his knees before the screen in lust and adoration. Even when he makes love to Francesca, she is always somewhere in the room – watching, reporting, the black mic in a death-grip like some high-end dominatrix from Prague. In a PVC catsuit perhaps. Or a transparent raincoat of rose-tinted plastic. Right now she's in a long string of pearls. Eight inch stilettos. Cigarette holder. A black fedora at a dark suggestive tilt. *This is Paula Viola for Channel NB1 News. Dublin City Centre. I like to be watched.*

THREE

THE SCREEN turns itself on (I'm always ahead of my alarms) and the predictable headline is the early morning rain. Then news of unrest in Venezuela, Indonesia, the Sudan and Sweden. Then local titbits – a drive-by, a hospital closure, arrests at Shannon, three fatal stabbings, loose horses on the Tolka Valley Road, Gorczynski out of the Ireland squad and finally more on the rain. I don't dwell on any of it except to witness yet another clip of self-immolation in a Chinese shopping mall. Depressing stuff. Raising my hand, I wave it goodbye and the sudden silence is welcome.

Of course, none of this was ever to have been the future. By this stage of the century the world should surely have overtaken the punts of my old paperbacks and Dublin should, by now, be some Irish Tokyo filled with flying machines, artificial intelligence and a telepathic citizenry. But no. None of it ever happened and our run-down wreck of a capital is now little more than a mix of Camden Market and old Philadelphia, and its citizens can think neither crooked nor straight. In fact, apart from the military, the murders and the feral dogs in the Green, named for a leper hospital, named for the first Martyr, things haven't changed all that much since the year of *Mise Éire* and JFK. And for Ireland to end up as a place neither utopian nor dystopian seems to me to be the worst outcome of all. Neither one thing nor the other and all we have is some kind of stasis. Slow death. And waste.

It all began, if not with the arrival of Richard de Clare, 2nd Earl of Pembroke, aka Strongbow, then with the economic rot which blossomed like an algal mat in the early days of Schroeder's childhood, when the jet stream split for the very first time and there were simultaneous heatwaves in Russia and floods in Pakistan. The IMF, the EMF and Standard and Poor's of 55 Water Street, NYC. It makes me shudder now to recall those years and how they tasted of nothing so much as lead. That overwhelming sense of breakage that was in the air – that stink of falsity and failure. Failed powers and failed priests. Broken systems and broken people. False prophets and false witnesses. False hearts and black arts. Deadbeats and dead ducks. Surfers started seeing the Devil in the skies above Strandhill, the General Post Office went up in flames again, turtles swam in the Liffey at the Strawberry Beds and unholy balls of snakes were found for the first time in the wasted brambles of Glendalough. And these were the days in which I watched Schroeder enter his adolescence and somehow survive without recourse to Australia or the massed regiments of Europe. Depression-era Ireland. Villainy. Treachery. A murder picture which is running still.

I break the fast with naturally cloudy, pressed apple juice, Mocha Sidamo roast ground coffee, two slices of German bread toasted and lightly spread with organic butter, a glass of Marlbank mineral water (still) with one 500mg effervescent lozenge of Vitamin C. Assorted pills, powders and capsules follow, then one potassium loaded banana, another glass of water with a random splashing of Echinaforce resistance drops and finally another camomile with honey. Synthetic but even so. Sweetness is essential. If only the bastards would approve lugduname I'd put it on my pancakes. Then I clear up, do a few stretches, go upstairs and start work.

Each morning, the first thing I do is check everyone's mail. Today it's all official circulars mostly – threat assessments, global security alerts, updates on tropical diseases and then rivers of spam pushing drugs, sex and weapons. No personal stuff for Schroeder yet except for one brief dispatch from Walton.

– *Did you see himself this morning? Taking a slash in the fucking garden? Yuk.*

Walton. Another name we all know. And mid-morning, sore shoulders and down for a tea break, I hear the bored railroad noises of his wheelchair coming from the flat below. Louis Patrick Walton, another one in the orbit of my surveillance and the only one who (sometimes) pays me rent. A complicated character certainly, but as he never goes out the door, he hardly seems like the most thrilling arrival, for our purposes here. Action-wise I mean. But even so, he lives downstairs and so I have my eye on him. Always.

I tap the radiator three times with a spoon – amateur Morse for *good morning you little shit* and the greeting travels downwards. The response comes quickly by way of a sweeping brush poking the floor directly beneath my feet. *Fuck off you old bastard.* And this is about all the direct contact we ever have, other than to deal with matters of rent or small to-be-ignored repairs. The relationship is strictly landlord / tenant and there are never any state visits below. No tea and bickies. No Christmas drinks. In fact, at this point, I haven't seen him in the flesh for six months, three weeks and two days. As I say, he never goes out.

Ever since the accident he prefers to crouch in front of his glowing unit, not so much surfing the net as drifting through it on a rotting, salty raft while permanently (night and day) logged on to the worm-infested website of a ferocious-looking Ukrainian blonde, by professional reputation a black belt in fellatio and a screamer to boot. Her name is Jakki Jack. She's a multi-award winner and Walton worships her. In fact Walton has seen so much pornography that he knows the names of just about every performer in history and can recognise any of them from any angle. He doesn't even need to see their faces to know who is doing what, and to whom. For a party piece he can recite the CV of everyone from the early 1980s onward – what movies she has been in and what her specialties are. Actresses, he gently calls them, and their names all begin with J. To tell you the truth it all makes me a little nauseous. Sometimes it sounds like gangs of drunks are sawing each other in half. Or worse. And his stamina is breathtaking.

That accident I refer to was a bad one. Walton's red Toyota was walloped by a lorry on a roundabout somewhere in the old industrial estate in Sandyford. He wasn't even supposed to be there but he simply took a wrong exit off the Inner Ring and he's still finding it hard to believe his bad luck. From the moment he regained consciousness, it seemed as if everything inhabiting his head was evicted and replaced by an ant colony of relentless questions. Why had it happened? Why had it happened to him? Why not the car behind him? Or in front? What sort of fluke of timing and circumstance had brought about such a catastrophe? He considered all these questions, drunk and sober, for an entire year and came up with nothing. Of course, of the three of us on Hibernia Road – Messrs Schroeder, Walton and Monk – I was the only one old enough to know that such fear of the random is not only deep but incurable. Nothing for that one even in *my* cabinet.

Walton's spin was a good one though. The direct cause of the crash had been, according to him, some kind of high-risk devotion to beauty. The car had been moving so well, so gracefully, that to have given way would have been a crude affront to what he called the "fluid aesthetic of the roundabout." Schroeder saluted him for that theory but he knew that his old friend would never be truly happy again, and had condemned himself to remain henceforth unseen in his curtained, flickering room, insisting that he could live his entire life online, like a pig in shit. Walton thought many such things and he meant none of them. Schroeder worried about him. I worried about him too. But not so much.

In the years before the accident Louis Patrick had been a television presenter on a Dublin-only channel and, despite being thoroughly uncommitted, this made him both a minor local celebrity and a malcontent. His programme *Dinosaur Grooves* (not his title) was basically a string of vintage music clips broadcast to a very small late-night audience, with no other real purpose than to fill dead airtime. Eventually the sheer emptiness of the situation got the better of him and one sub-tropical day in springtime he drove into work, passed through the security gates, went around the block and then drove straight back out again in the general direction of the Wicklow Mountains, where he spent much of the afternoon asleep in a field. When he got back to the flat, his head still full of the sound of rooks, there, stuffed in his letterbox, was a legal document which officially marked the end of his television career.

For a time he enjoyed being unemployed and, at least as far as television was concerned, unemployable. But once he remembered he would need money in order to eat, he began accepting offers to write for all manner of publications. It was all tolerable enough and at least he was no longer defined by a job he had always found more than a little ridiculous. His professional suicide had, it seemed, the potential to be a very good career move. But then came the smash and nothing was ever the same again.

Schroeder helped out at first by getting him what he needed, setting up the basement with the trappings of a changed life, while Francesca visited far too often for her own good. As for me, I did what I could by not pushing for the rent, knowing that Walton just about got by, living as a cipher for his former self, recycling old articles and sending them to editors desperate for content. I monitored all of it but there was never anything of note. Nothing he hadn't said before and said much better. He stayed well clear of current events and apart from one occasion when he battered out a drunken rant about the *USS Barry*, he never really attracted any serious attention. The Embassy checked him out but took it no further.

Schroeder, distressed by the fact that Walton refused to go out, did his best to encourage him but in the end gave up and, for the most part, tried to ignore Walton's damaged presence. The idea of his old friend all hunched in a wheelchair manky with gaffer tape was too much for a man of Schroeder's sensibilities. Yes, Walton could be as pornisophical as he wanted but for Schroeder this was all too dark to even consider. Walton could protest all he liked, but the reality was that there was no drink, no drug, no art, no belief, no politician, no love, no chemical weapon and no masturbatory technique known to humankind that could do a damn thing about what had happened to him.

At times Schroeder feared (a fear not shared by me) that Walton would inevitably mutate into some new strain of computer über-geek – like some nerd in a movie secretly hacking into security systems and planning some murderous attack. Sometimes he pictured

Walton looped in chains, wearing an orange jumpsuit, being led into the arse-end of a transport plane at Shannon and flown off to be tried and fried on *Fox Morning Justice*. An Irish national who, from his darkened (musty) room in County Dublin, had managed to breach Pentagon systems and launch several missiles and a smart but dirty bomb which took the panhandle off Texas, the nose off North Carolina and the knob off Nantucket. He would show no remorse. He would regret none of it. Just as long as the Valley survived.

The San Fernando Valley in the State of Southern California was Walton's spiritual home – or it was until the Morality Act banned the production of pornography on the "homeland territory" of the United States and the entire American adult industry relocated to Europe (including Ireland where the business end of things ensured that the profits, if not the performers, could still go back to California). It was, Walton said, an American solution to an American problem and, he was delighted to report, the new system had impacted in no way whatsoever the quality (his word) or quantity of new releases. The standard of light was different, but that was all.

Francesca was rather upset when Schroeder revealed Walton's addictions. After the accident she had developed a deep and tender sorrow for him and, to some extent, he was all hers to worry about. He was like the sad, special boy in the cellar, living on cream crackers and milk. But once she discovered that he had such a multitude of female friends (after a fashion) and a very special friend in Jakki Jack, for whom he wouldn't leave the house even if he could, she began to feel a little redundant and she stopped contacting him. Her instinct had been to take care of him but Walton's instinct was to take care of himself, no doubt with the aid of all manner of cutting-edge equipment, something which the 21st century had indeed delivered as promised.

And when Walton was asked to state where he was when it happened, the incident at the Castle, he didn't lie. He was where he always was. In front of his unit, high on painkillers and prolonged arousal, communing with Ms Jack and her many fun-loving friends. He might well have added, but thought better of it, that he was also clicking hungrily on ads for drugs, watches, vintage revolvers and Samurai swords and examining, in very dark detail, the endless pop-ups of faces and numbers. Willing partners in the greater Dublin area. Online now. Eager to meet. Every fantasy fulfilled.

Refreshed and back in the attic I find Schroeder's reply to Walton now flashing in the slot. He's asserting that I'm forever pissing in the garden – which is a damned lie – and he refers to me as "a mouldy old bastard" and says he has seen me do far worse. I am understandably hurt and my reprisal is immediate. I download a Chinese short-life virus and prepare its dispatch. A message for Schroeder will appear to have come from Walton and vice versa and once opened, both computers will be knocked out for a full 24 hours. Serve the little fuckers right and I stage-cackle at the thought of Walton apoplectic at being cut off from the screamer. Do him the world of good I reckon. Maybe encourage him to develop an erotic aesthetic of his own? And as for Schroeder, he might even take the opportunity to actually write something longer than a sentence. A short story about a fedora for example. Or the first two paragraphs of yet another novel.

Three screens over I see that Ms Jack is already up and about – a live feed from somewhere in the Alliance, the kitchen-cam trained on her granite worktops as she makes herself a breakfast of yoghurt, muesli and forest fruits. Walton will watch her eat, wash her teeth, shower and then throw a few unconvincing shapes on the bed. I will pick my moment carefully, fire off the virus and then wait with arms folded for Walton to open it and the moans of Ms Jack to cut dead. And then I'll just sit back and listen. Enjoy the outraged wailing of Walton from below.

– *What the fuck! What the fuck! What the fuck!*

I do my shift. I catch up on everyone's correspondence, I tidy up the files and I go through Schroeder's most recent notes. By and large, it's an idle enough few hours and there's little to report until, that is, I make another random sweep through the atmosphere over Dún Laoghaire and I pick up American chatter from what I assume is the *Barry*. I can tell from the tone that they're in preparation for something significant. Nothing specific or obvious is said but when I hear the term "full preparedness" several times over I make the reasonable deduction. Either Ireland is about to be invaded or President King is coming over again. It's starting to look like he's never away. Either he really does love his daughter or, just like his priapic predecessor, he's banging some cocktail waitress from Chucho's of Grafton Street. And I'm right too. The State Visit is announced three days later.

FOUR

A CLASSICAL STATION from Berlin is playing Bach's *Inventionen* and like a maestro myself, I start conducting the throbbing bank of units with my fingertips. Today is a newsflash day. It's a day with ingredients in it. I can tell. Protestors are gathered outside Dáil Éireann, all whistles and roar, cheering like goats whenever a trumpet blurts out "Boots and Saddles" and tattered rags of Rossini. Djembe drums like dark, rolling thunder scatter chaos into a grim mantilla of fumes and Schroeder is standing on an overgrown stoop on Molesworth Street, named for Richard, 3rd Viscount Molesworth of Swords. I'm hooked into every feed I can get – simple enough on a big newsday – and I settle back in my high-backed swivel chair, sipping like some flinty old prophet at a cold ginseng tea.

Of course it's not just me who knows what will happen today. Everybody knows. It's merely a prelude to much more significant events to come but even so. Because Schroeder is present, thinking he's on some kind of date, I'm committed to sticking with it. I hate to leave any of my charges unattended at the best of times, but on a day like today I need to pay special attention. Not since October 1860, when they first scribbled data at Valentia Observatory, has there been a day quite as sweaty as this one. A newsflash day if ever there was one.

Schroeder, of course, loves newsflashes. After my own heart in that way. The interruption. The pumping graphic. The headless ritual of something extremely serious gatecrashing all things domestic and dull. But for Schroeder, however, the crucial element in any such newsflash is a very particular reporter called Paula Viola who goes live at all these events – *all sex-eyed and fresh from the crisp bordello of fact* – as he put it in one of his better lines. For her to speak his name in a newsflash would be, for him, an ecstasy beyond measure. And that's why he needs watching, a particular watching that is, on days like this – a roasting hot day of disruption, disorder and, without fail, bloodshed and grief.

Observe them closely. This dying breed of chanting death-wishers assembled in the sun. A grim bouncing multitude of fists and flags, placards and banners with words like *oil* and *blood* prominent in dripping shades of red as the hardcore rages like an orgy of frogs beneath an enormous tricolour of green, white and orange – *Celtic Poodle* blocked across it in black. And all around, and decades too late, the further flags of Venezuela, Palestine and Mexico. They have come here in such numbers to protest the very notion of the Presidential presence and to jeer, in particular, the sleek as cat-shit slug who keeps inviting him – An Taoiseach, said to be en route in an armour-plated Cadillac donated, along with a new munitions factory (for Limerick of all fucking places!) by that very same President. Richard Rutledge Barnes King. Of the Memphis Kings.

They are, of course, wasting their finite breath. In three weeks' time there'll be marksmen on these rooftops and frogmen in these drains and nothing will be left to lunacy, principle or chance. The most ruthless minds in the country (intelligence, military and show business) will see to it that there will be no incident or blip, and that the ancient sod of Erin will serve with equal parts charm and humility as demanded and already guaranteed. Some tasteless tenor, a fraudulent purveyor of Celtic grotesquerie on demand, is already practicing in the bubble bath, rehearsing the first of a hundred thousand welcomes. Oh, the gruesome thought of it! Some fat, pink man with a twinkle in both eyes, winking at the front rows, soaping the cascading folds of his belly and belting out *If you're Irish come into the parlour, there's a welcome there for you.*

Of course actual Dubliners will simply stay at home that day, content with the booze and the barbecue, ignoring the whole affair with the intense pleasure of total apathy. This new Mojave weather means aprons and sausages and the necking down of Euro-surplus Estonian beer. No excuse needed for anything historically denied the Irish nation, and even this murderous heat remains a novelty. Ancient Ireland is flame-grilling now in some noxious Athenian smog and the old leathery Gael loves it. No more than we deserve after all. Haven't we shivered enough down the frigid centuries of damp and gloom? And aren't we really, at the heel of the hunt, some class of misplaced Moroccans after all? Still making our drums out of dead goats. Still singing unaccompanied in the old swallowed tongue and still wondering why we never have the right clothes for the day that's in it.

I can see Schroeder standing high on a stoop. He's checking the news on his handset – Minister Gibbon confirming that the President will visit Dublin after a stopover at Shannon where he will address US troops. The response arises immediately. A chant. Explicatory. Without lustre or hope. *King not welcome! King not welcome!* But Gibbon is insisting that King will be as welcome as the flowers in May. Then the ad break. Ambulance chasers, dietary supplements, home security firms, erectile dysfunction and cheap flights to Yemen. And then the lunatic trumpet signals again and a line of government vehicles, one of them containing the cloven-headed Taoiseach – Domhnach Cascade TD – passes at speed along the street.

As the Caddy approaches the gates, a protestor breaks through the cordon and hurls himself at the tyres. There are squeals. Then silence. Then more squeals as the Caddy bounces forward and the man dies – his torso crushed like a clove of garlic into the tarmacadam. As the blood spreads with determination on the road, even the Guards turn their faces away. The protestors flare and a megaphone squeals and crunches as Cascade, still talking on his cell, is smothered inside a testudo of waving weapons and led straight through the gates of Leinster House.

Schroeder seems safe enough where he is but I straighten up even so. And, sure enough, the visored Riot Squad soon starts to spill like black mercury onto the street, prodding with stunted weapons at waist height, forcing everyone to retreat to the corner of the National Library where they regroup beneath a flapping image of the young Willie Yeats. As canisters begin to explode, some of the protestors squeeze their faces into gas masks (every household has one) and the huddle seems to mutate into one giant, fantastical creature – a multi-eyed crustacean gesturing in the depths of a spotlit sea. In the rising clouds the studious face of the poet fades in and fades out. He has no words to offer here. No wisdom now in the teeth of brutes.

The stand-off lasts five seconds at most. Then a roar and something soars in a lobbing arc and both Schroeder and I watch it land with a clatter at the security barrier. It's a grenade and Schroeder watches it spin on the road like a foolish avocado. Seconds pass. Then more seconds. Then more. Too many seconds, it seems, and everyone breathes again. A dud. No doubt purchased in some stinking Tallaght lock-up, its provenance a dusty quartermaster in Chad or the Sudan. Dublin is now so full of dodgy ordnance that hardly a night passes without unscheduled pops and bangs coming from the darker districts of the west and north. My eyes flick from screen to screen. And what happens next is a foregone.

A sudden yelp of laughter from within the crowd, perhaps even the one who threw the grenade now cursing his bad luck and trying to laugh it off as if it hadn't really been all that important, as if it was some cheap cigarette lighter typically out of gas. But that laugh is even more significant than the avocado because it's in the script. It's the bit in the script where the script is dropped, which is itself always in the script. Behind their visors, pumped by their own dark capacity for drawing blood, the men of the Riot Squad chew their lips and breathe like heavy horses. They check their straps and scrape their boots on the ground.

Inside the gates of Leinster House, in the middle of the wide car park, An Taoiseach is surrounded by his staff. He finishes his call, fixes his hair, smoothes his silvery jacket and winks. As if in some deep and sorrowful wisdom, he just winks. A sad, solemn and deadly wink and that's the cue. Specials are never loosed for nothing and, seconds later, rapid gunfire stutters across Kildare Street. Pigeons scatter from the rooftops and screams become screeches.

People fall and blood gurgles once more in the metropolitan drains.

And as always after these things, a silence and a smell – chemical, acid and fearful, a smell which gets in the skin and can sicken for hours later, a smell which has travelled already to the Green and has set the dogs a-snarling. But otherwise not much. Just that smell and that silence broken only by the odd chuckle from a Special or the sudden gush of returning pigeons, their pigeon heart-rates already back to normal, their squatters' rights restored.

Schroeder lets out a whispered fuck. She really should be here by now, drilling through the throng, all stilettos and fingernails, the crew following like a caravan of busboys with hoisted cameras and booms. His heart begins to thud as he wills the van to corner the Green at speed, Paula in the back, fixing herself in a mirror – unscrewing the lipstick, tugging her hair and arranging her menacing breasts for maximum impact. All set for a one-take PTC.

He looks a little frantic now, checking both the crowd and the coverage, whisper-swearing like a mad cleric on the roads. She must be here somewhere! She must be! For he has come to realize that it's usually her arrival that actually triggers things, and so she must be here already. But where? He knows that she tends to appear quite suddenly and with such efficient ceremony that it gets everybody rather overexcited and that's usually the moment when the body count tends to rocket. And so he keeps repeating to himself his private, profane office. *Where the fuck is she? Where the fuck is she? Where the fuck is she?*

– Cool it Schroeder. Cool it. You're in the belly of the beast.

But Schroeder, almost as if provoked by my distant advice, suddenly kicks out like a wild horse at the door behind him – something which attracts the attention of a Branchman opposite. Branchman by the name of Pilkington. Kildare. Boozer. Hatchetman. Anglo-Saxon corpuscles. Now thus! Now thus! From Lancashire they say. Originally. Rivington. Then Tore House that was torched in Westmeath. And he's the cut of them too. Derek Pilkington. Detective Inspector now rousing himself to detect and inspect Schroeder "behaving erratically" on the steps.

– Move it Schroeder, I whisper to the screen.

But Schroeder doesn't need to be told this time. Kicking a heritage door is a foolish mistake – a false move in a city where false moves are not encouraged. And so he slips off the stoop and away, heading quickly towards Dawson Street, named for Joshua Dawson, Collector of Dublin, Secretary for Ireland and Member of Parliament for County Wicklow.

– Stay where you are, Pilkington.

Pilkington stays where he is.

– Good man, Pilkington. Good man.

Molesworth Street has been sealed off so Schroeder cuts down Frederick Street, named for Frederick, Prince of Wales, and passes the block-long Evangelical House of God and emerges near Trinity only to find himself completely stuck. Reeking of sweat and cooking oil, the street is Beijing chokka, both ends blocked as far as Grafton Street in one direction and the shell of the National Gallery in the other. Schroeder as usual takes it personally. The leaf on the line, the clog in the pipe, the corpse in the swimming pool, the disruptive act of state or freelance violence to bugger up his day. And so now, here he is, trapped in the once grand gutter of Nassau Street, named for William III of Orange and the Count of Nassau – these days just a fungal thoroughfare of knock-off emporia and only the one pub. He feels stood up. He feels like a bomb.

A helicopter rises up from the rugby grounds and Schroeder watches it head southwards at an angle, like a grim laden bee. Princess King being evacuated as usual. The slightest bit of trouble in the city and she's whipped off to the base at the Park. Thanks to her, Trinity is a fortress now too. Sandbags and razor wire, men on the rooftops with binoculars and rifles. One way in and one way out. Students are strictly vetted and various levels of passes are issued to those deemed appropriate. The rest, those considered a threat for an assortment of bizarre reasons, are required to continue their academic lives at other universities. Worse again, the bar has been closed until further notice and the annual Ball is off.

Schroeder has nothing against her personally. He met her once and liked her, finding her civil, smart and very sexy in that calm and deliberate way that comes with comfort. She was relaxed, confident and funny, and at one point he somehow touched the tanned American skin of her forearm – a breach in security protocol which she didn't seem to mind at all. A jazz fan too – always a good sign in a Yank – and if she hadn't been a student (and the daughter of the man himself) he might have offered to buy her a coffee. But the problem with Princess is this. While undoubtedly charming, delightful, funny and extremely attractive, it's a fact that every place she goes is utterly transformed, in a bad way, by her presence. And of course by the humourless eunuchs of her quite preposterous security detail. No wonder her classmates hate her and, as the helicopter disappears over Westland Row, Schroeder notices a longhair at the railings raising a middle digit skywards, not once looking up from his book. He's lucky he doesn't get it shot off.

Of course I need my wits about me in situations like this. Schroeder is vulnerable now and we all need to concentrate. I lay out a mix of pills on the desk before me and, fingering them like a decade of the rosary, I pop them one by one. Whenever bodies are scattered in the road outside Dáil Éireann a man like me must always try, if at all possible, not to think too much about any of it. Ireland is a very altered place. Everything is broken now and yet most of the Sons and Daughters of Róisín have adapted to these alterations, however inelegant, with remarkable ease. A handy race of people still, we still live on nothing but our wits. And on whatever else it takes. Seven dead that day. Nine wounded. Plus the bloody heap beneath the Caddy. But even so. My sole concern is Schroeder and I attack the keyboard with an astonishing flourish.

FIVE

THE HEAT on Nassau is ferocious and Schroeder, for shade, jooks under the awning of an electrical goods store. A Slavic security guard (technically a giant and swelled even further by body armour) checks him out, inhales hard through his nose and spits out onto the pavement what seems like a live frog. Schroeder gags and sets off in search of some other shelter but is immediately shoved back by a soldier – American – all dressed up for a chemical attack. The over-muscled grunt looks ridiculous but he has a weapon the size of a crocodile and, being virtually obliged to use it, he'll get no argument from Schroeder. Even the Russian giant retreats indoors until the patrol has passed. This end of the street, being on the perimeter of Trinity, is now firmly in American hands and, as their own graffiti has it, they don't fuck around.

I know that Schroeder needs a hit and the only watering hole on Nassau Street is Liddley's – a place frequented exclusively by gobshites, frauds and the operatives who feed off them. If a public house could be a vulgarian's brain then this is it. Scams, schemes, deals, plots and plans are the blood supply of the place and transfusions are available for the price of a drink and an earful of shite. It's nothing but a pumping source of corruption and rot and it's no surprise that of the twenty or so public houses from which I lease security feeds, Liddley's has long yielded the most useful intelligence. The comings and goings, the huddles and the confabs, the flare-ups and rows. In fact Liddley's is priceless in a way its patrons could never even begin to comprehend.

The minute Schroeder walks in he feels that sour buzz of impotence and greed – the rank essence of nothing ever getting done. But then he sees Paula Viola and he's thrown. There are twelve crooked televisions all bunched together, all hanging from the ceiling like the eyes of a giant dragonfly and while it's usually golf or Japanese pop, at this precise moment the screens all star Ms Viola reporting from around the corner. He must have just missed her by seconds and he curses aloud. She's dressed, as seems her current preference, as a tight-skirted lawyer in hidden lingerie. It's a look which Schroeder finds compelling and his fugue is immediate, vivid and detailed. All that perfume and grainy swish. The brand-new bob of damson red holding her cheekbones in its grip. Overwhelming.

– *I'm standing outside Leinster House where just moments ago . . .* I'd give *her* one! somebody shouts from the darkest corner and Schroeder winces and glares. He tries to focus again but the screens then flash from Paula to a podium on the steps of the Government Building and a line of microphones waiting for a voice. A pre-emptive press conference is about to start, the official line about to be fired into the atmosphere like handfuls of ack-ack. Paula will be heading there right now but Schroeder knows he won't get anywhere near her, not a government press conference conducted these days with as many machine guns as cameras. So he decides to stay where he is. Sit in Liddley's and make the most of it – a bar lit like a bubbling antique aquarium. He checks the stock – Seagrams, Kentucky Gentleman, Noilly Prat, English Market Gin, Mr. Boston, Dewar's Blended Scotch, Mount Gay Rum, Stolichnaya and Jameson. Floor to ceiling booze. Paddy the bartender, a notorious grump, is a West African as tall as a baobab and when Schroeder addresses him in French he looks like a man about to murder.

– You speak Wolof? asks Paddy.

– What do *you* think? asks Schroeder.

– Then do not talk to me please.

– Sorry pal, says Schroeder, I mistook you for a bartender. You being behind the bar and all . . .

– I give you a drink. That is all. Then I go home.

Paddy is called Paddy after Patrick Viera, a footballer who once played for Arsenal and, every night without fail, the crowd in Liddley's end up singing, to the tune of "Nel plu dipinto di blu" –

Viera. Oh oh oh oh / Viera. Oh oh oh oh. / He comes from Senegal / He plays for Arsenal.

– You want a drink or not?

But Schroeder persists with the poking.

– So where's home, Paddy?

– What?

– I'm just asking where's home . . . when it's at home.

Paddy glares.

– Phibsboro.

– I didn't mean that.

– You mean Africa?

– Africa's a big place.

– Senegal, says Paddy warily, wiping the bar.

– I've been there, says Schroeder. Dakar. Great music. And there was a brilliant footballer once used to play for Arsenal . . .

Paddy places his hands on the bar and locks his arms straight. It's a silent posture of total confrontation.

– I'm just making conversation, says Schroeder. Everybody I met in Senegal was extremely pleasant.

– This is not Senegal.

Schroeder gives up. The dull sport of disruption running quickly out of steam.

– Just give me a vodka and tonic. No ice. No lemon. *Le do thoil.*

On the dozen televisions Gibbon, the Minister for Justice and Security, is now literally snarling. Backlit by stained glass, like some humourless ecstatic, he's suggesting an absurd alliance of terrorist groups and declaring the dud avocado a direct attack on the democratic values of the State. He will not rest etc., etc. And then, as if to calm the very air in front of him, he raises his hands and grins. President King will be coming to Ireland at the end of the month and he will be as welcome, he repeats, as the flowers in May.

Someone in the bar shouts *Fuck off, Gibbon*! but Schroeder is losing himself in the stained glass. The Four Green Fields of Evie Hone multiplied by the twelve crooked televisions into something kaleidoscopic. It's all far too trippy for Gibbon as he delivers his statement in his usual manner, as if proclaiming a truth from an ancient book, and then says he won't be taking any questions. He never does, and so the press conference ends with the usual shouting and kerfuffle and the Minister somehow seeming to vaporize as the screens quickly switch to oriental strippers. They look young, amateur and very unhappy, and Schroeder turns back to the bar.

A surly vodka and tonic now sits before him on the chrome. It's packed to the brim with ice, a hunk of lemon and a swizzle stick with a shamrock head. Schroeder looks down the bar for Paddy Viera but he seems to be concentrating hard on the till, poking at it with a screwdriver. Schroeder chucks the stick and the lemon onto the floor beneath his feet and, just as he sets about dredging out the infected, cola-coloured cubes, he senses someone right up beside his ear. The accompanying odour is unmistakable.

– Oh for fuck's sake, says Schroeder.

Jules Roark is a yappy little shit from Kerry. He has a face like a Chihuahua and the breath of a humpback whale, and Schroeder reacts as if he has just received very bad news – with a deep sigh of surrender.

– Jays, that's not very friendly, yips Roark. I thought we were close.

– Then you must be on one seriously bad batch.

– Want some?

Roark's mouth opens and closes as he awaits Schroeder's response, thermo-regulating like an infant gharial. The whiff coming off him is making Schroeder ill and so he tries to savour the first hit of the vodka. And it's good. Even in Liddley's, even with tonic in it, even with Roark in his nostrils, the Stoli never lets him down.

– No. I don't want some. I'm just having a quiet drink. On my own.

I know all about Roark. Roark is a dog. He scored heavily some years ago with a non-fiction title called *The Mass Is Over: The Death of Irish Catholicism*, and he was still smugly inhaling the nitrous oxide of its success. Huge numbers of people bought the book, whined about it on talk shows and then went out and bought it all over again. And then fuelled by such brainless outrage, the book sold in numbers and Roark, the scaly little shit, made enough money to quit doing whatever it was he did. On top of that he was a tout for the government (he had most of the attributes and all of the stench) and he was also possibly working low-level for the UIA.

It's ten years ago now, during the Jerusalem War, that the UIA finally displaced the CIA (now largely relegated to duties such as minding people like Princess King while she goes to lectures) and went about its work in earnest. And once the Middle East was truly boiling, they seemed free to do as they pleased and their operations became breathtakingly shameless. Kidnappings, assassinations and the reopening of all the secret detention centres in Poland, Morocco, Uzbekistan and, of course, the not so secret one at Shannon.

I know for a fact that the UIA was involved in what happened in Colombia and it was, without question, up to its oxters in all those African countries which barely lasted long enough to create even the shortest of histories. In fact there has been no world event in the past decade which might not be explained by way of the United Intelligence Agency. And yet, officially, it doesn't exist at all. It's a ghost and a shape-shifter, something which leaves its agents free to operate like phantoms across all borders and jurisdictions.

The only world leader to ever publicly "out" the UIA was President Torres of Mexico. He claimed that only three people knew the actual truth of the UIA's purpose and the full extent of its operations – The President of the United States, The President of the New Republic of China and the President of the European Alliance. And then, barely a month after he made his remarks, he went into hospital for routine surgery and quickly died, all by himself, in the middle of the night. A superbug it was said at the time, previously unseen and especially virulent. He was, they said, killed by a mutating fluke of bad hygiene and nothing more. Of course nobody believed that, especially the Mexicans, who still suspect the real cause of death to have been a lethal syringe under the malicious pressure of a UIA thumb. Almost certainly a member of his own security detail. And of course I concur. *Numquam perit solus Caesar.*

– So Roark, says Schroeder, you still working for them?

– Jays, that's a very rash remark, says Roark. Very rash.

– I'd say you'd be one of their greatest assets.

– There are things one shouldn't talk about.

– Did you ever hear of mouthwash?

– Ah, you're a gas man, Schroeder.

Schroeder groans as Roark attempts to climb the stool, only conquering it at the third attempt, and celebrating his achievement by cramming a wedge of lemon into his mouth and chewing it hard, making a sickening noise, all spittle and juice. Schroeder closes his eyes and tries to make Roark disappear. It doesn't work.

Schroeder had indeed been rash with that UIA remark but he was dead right. The UIA (at bottom-feeder level) is full of people like Roark – enlisted freaks and misfits who can buy drugs, use cash, sell guns and wreck lives without any interference or sanction. They report to everyone and to no one. They're everywhere and all they have to do is finger anybody they want fingered and that's that. Hacks and scribblers are particularly well represented in the ranks, overly keen to have fellow hacks and scribblers under constant scrutiny. Along with schoolteachers, pub philosophers, academics, politicians, pop stars, clerics, workplace agitators and restaurant gossips.

Utterly deluded but totally dedicated, touts like Roark now see themselves as gatekeepers and guardians and are encouraged to think in this way, not just by their handlers, but by the general paranoia now all but pumped into the atmosphere by people like Cascade and Gibbon. But what always remains unclear is what particular gates they are keeping and what precisely they are guarding against, and this makes them all the more lethal. Roark fits the profile perfectly. A cokehead. Vulnerable. Half-a-journalist. And very far up himself. I had long been convinced that he was tailing Schroeder – the way he popped up all over town like his own personal hyena, always trying to sell him charlie and guns. This day was no different. It followed a pattern.

– Bit of bother up the road, says Roark. The chieftain himself got one of them. He sure loves riding in that Caddy.

– Hope they got his insurance details.

– Fuck 'em! They were asking for it! They knew they'd be rounded up. They were just trying to get in early.

– You're a charitable soul, Roark.

– Jays, there'll be none of them left by the time yer man gets here. You know he's a serious alco. Drinks like a fish. Like some kind of especially alcoholic fish. And we already know that Cascade's a total pisshead.

– An alcoholic fish?

– A mullet or something.

– A mullet?

– Yes. A fucking mullet. But with a drink fucking problem.

Roark almost crawls on top of the bar to hook Paddy Viera.

– Hey Pat! Two more vodka and tonics when you're ready, sunshine.

– Not for me, says Schroeder. I'm not staying.

– Insurance details! That's a good one for fucksake. A slippery tit, our Mister Cascade. Tequila slammers by all accounts. King's a bourbon man. Imagine going on the lash with that pair!

The two drinks appear and Paddy, staring at the melting mess of ice cubes in front of Schroeder, snaps the plastic from Roark's claw. Roark winds up for another insertion and finally it comes.

– I'd definitely shag her.

Schroeder exhales.

– You'd shag who?

Roark's eyes widen.

– The President's young one. Princess. What's she like close-up? Dishy huh?

– It was one tutorial. Someone was sick. I filled in. That was the height of it.

– What did you talk about?

– It was the creative writing course.

– Yeah but what did you talk about?

– Creative writing.

Roark clutches his own crotch in a way which greatly exaggerates his potential.

– Character development eh?

– Roark, you're such a swell guy.

Roark falls silent, doubtless some sexual fantasy set in the Long Room of Trinity, but soon he reactivates with an eager jump.

– Did I tell you I was working on a thing about the end of Catholicism?

Schroeder's head sinks between his shoulders.

– Wasn't that your last one?

– This time Schroeder my man, I'm going global. Universal Church, Universal Market. And Ireland is just the same as everywhere else now anyway. More like China than anything, now the lid is off it. Way more like China than America even. Way more.

– Way more.

– And when you think about it. The more China modernizes, the more ancient everything about it seems to become. People are doing stuff which might have seemed normal a thousand years ago but which is just a tad embarrassing at this stage of the century. Mountaintop hermits, levitating priests, horseback bandits, pirates, slaves and warlords. And all those monks setting themselves on fire.

– Fascinating, says Schroeder.

Roark takes another sniffy breath.

– It's like the De Danann, the Fir Bolg, the Celts, the Vikings, the Normans, the English, the Planters, the Poles and the Africans all suddenly turn up here at the very same moment in history, with all of their customs and religions and philosophies and politics – not to mention all their myths and race memories – and they're all trying to get noticed. That's what it's like. Thousands of years all uncorked at once. A time-shattered culture-fuck is what it is. So many people all trying to get heard.

– You don't say.

– Time-shattered.

– You should write that down.

– Total culture-fuck. I just thought of it there now.

– Perhaps you're a genius?

Roark flicks a finger inside his nose. Something flies.

– I'm just saying. It's the reason these monks keep setting fire to themselves. It's the only way to get noticed. The whole of Asia is ablaze with holy men these days.

He swivels away, sipping at his drink and looking at the misery-strippers. But then he swivels back again and angles in close.

– You want to buy a gun?

– Will it work on you?

Schroeder points at Paddy Viera, his index finger aimed right between his eyes. With the same finger of his other hand he gestures at two vacant spots on the bar.

– Two vodka and tonics. No ice. No lemon.

Many drinks and many hours later Roark passes out in the toilets, his nose squashed and bleeding between two broken levees of powder. Schroeder, himself very drunk, tries several times to secure a coffee, but no joy. Finally he asks Paddy (in French) to shout him a taxi and Paddy tells him (in English) that he can get one on the street. Then Schroeder asks him (in Irish) why he is being such a shit and he gets no answer at all.

On the dozen screens a shark seems to be eating a tourist at some marine circus in England. There is blood in the water and the camera is shaking. The great white is chomping and Schroeder is just about to leave when Paddy Viera grabs him by the elbow.

– You think I'm not a Christian.

Schroeder looks at him and tries to focus.

– I couldn't care less what you are, Paddy. Although you'll never, in your fucking puff, win bartender of the year.

– I'm a Christian.

– Well good luck to you. Not many of you guys left.

– And I believe in the Devil too.

– Good man, yourself.

Schroeder is far too drunk for any of this and he panics a little when Paddy suddenly clamps his forearm with his spider-long fingers.

– The Devil he is playing with us. And with God too.

Schroeder pulls his arm away but Paddy leans in even closer.

– The Book of Job.

Schroeder searches his flooded brain for information. He read it years ago. Job. An angry man.

– God, says Paddy, he asks the Devil where he has been and the Devil says, From going to and fro on the Earth, and from walking up and down in it. This is what the Devil says to God.

Schroeder makes another attempt to ease his arse off the stool.

– They play a game, Paddy says. God and the Devil. And the wicked prosper. It is the wicked who prosper.

Then he reaches across and grips Schroeder's face. Schroeder thinks he's about to be kissed. Tiny veins make red rivulets in the yellowy white of the bartender's eyes. There's no life in them anywhere.

He comes from Senegal / He plays for Arsenal.

– Redemption, says Paddy. You will not find it in the place where you look.

Schroeder nods as if in profound agreement and is released. He walks towards the door, upright and breathing hard through his nose. He doesn't turn around when Paddy shouts after him.

– Your friend is a wicked man!

– I know he is, says Schroeder. Somebody should shoot the fucker.

– He is a very wicked man!

– Then you shoot him!

I carefully log the time as Schroeder stumbles back out onto Nassau Street. The traffic is moving again and everything seems reasonably normal, even to Schroeder who is now seeing things in twos and threes. For all the people felled earlier on Kildare Street, every illusion of city life has now been regenerated with every social contract and system newly intact. And so when Schroeder reaches for a taxi as if to swat one, a blurred yellowness stops in front of him almost immediately. It stinks of urine and heat but he gets in anyway and wrestles with the belt.

– Make like a bird for Trinity College.

The driver unplugs an earpiece.

– Say again.

– Dún Laoghaire. Hibernia Road.

– Do I know your face?

– I don't know.

– Are you on the telly?

– Not at this precise moment, no.

Somewhere around Irishtown Schroeder is finally overwhelmed. He feels stressed and nauseous – as if he's losing blood. *Carcharodon carcharias*. He winds down the window, rests his head against the buffeting air and talks frantically to himself, trying to stay conscious, willing the rolling freeway to end and the world to get back on its proper axis, on its proper trajectory around the spinning vault.

– You alright there? asks the driver, nervous of puke.

– No problemo, says Schroeder, his eyelids hanging, his eyebrows at full ascent. No problemo.

Military manoeuvres are taking place on Sandymount Strand and the poisoned sea is lit up like a football pitch. Schroeder conjures Paula Viola to straddle him, all velvety, in the backseat but all he sees is the Taoiseach's wink. And Roark's teeth. And he hears the sound of gunfire. And the screaming on Kildare Street. And then the silence and the blood. And Paddy the bartender and God and the Devil and a great white shark. And after that nothing.

SIX

THE LIGHTS are out again – another in a recent string of power cuts which always results in looting, carjacking and public fornication – and I'm at the barricade, inhaling the smell of Schroeder's king prawn madras laced with garlic and chilli plus an enormous damp naan sweating in a brown paper bag. A 10.50 delivery charge, which Schroeder resents, but is always prepared to pay to avoid that grim trek as far as the Indian and back. He hates that stretch – the fox-proof wheelie bins, the skips, the trolleys and the skeletal bicycles chained to lamp posts, their wheels already plundered by local ratboys all blackheads and bones. I can't say I blame him. Dún Laoghaire's general vapour of heroin and chips is hardly salubrious.

I'm out here because the best thing about the power cuts is that the stars and planets suddenly reappear in the skies. Or at least some of them do, for only the brightest, for all their nuclear incandescence, can twinkle through the dense layers of poisons that float above us now. In fact, with the full glare of the city these days, nobody ever gets to savour even the white light of Venus. When I was a boy I saw its crescent with the naked eye. The morning star. And with binoculars I saw the moons of Jupiter and its Great Red Spot. And then with a telescope I saw the deserts and the polar caps of Mars. I was as good as Galileo in those days, picking out Ganymede, Io, Europa and the other one. Can't think. And tonight, thanks to the outages, I can still spot Venus and Jupiter at the front of the house. Callista! Although Mars has long faded at the back, its orange glow much too perfect a match for the reflected glory of Dublin's grid. And no loss really. What a fucking disappointment that one turned out be. Sitting up there teasing us for centuries. Giovanni Schiaparelli. The *canali*. Percival Lowell in Flagstaff, AZ, *Mars as the Abode of Life*, H. G. Wells and David Bowie. So much hope and so much talk of water and veg and then, in the year I was born, they sent up the Mariner 4. Nix Olympica. The Tharsis Bulge.

And the Vikings. And nothing. And now nobody even mentions it anymore. Nobody even bothers to look up.

And if Schroeder was to enter his garden now, even in this power cut he would see only Arcturus in Boötes and Sirius, the Dog Star. But not The Pup. And never the Pleiades. These I can only trace from memory, these constellations I mapped when I was twelve. Just like 石 中 and the rest of them. Coma Berenices, Cassiopea, Vulpecula. None of this means anything to anyone anymore. Including Schroeder, which disappoints me. He's a man more interested in his naan and only when a text lands from Francesca does he desist from eagerly shining his plate with it. She says she'll be home in a week.

I immediately abandon what stars there are and go inside. I head upstairs (my knee playing up slightly) and I check with the airport. When I see that she's not on any passenger list for the next seven days I get suspicious and, sure enough, when I look into it further I discover that she landed in Dublin two hours ago. She's already back in town and, for whatever reason, she seems to be reserving this starry evening for herself. Not that any of this surprises me. I have always been uneasy about Francesca Maldini. And with good reason too. Firstly she works in PR, secondly she works for the government and thirdly, and most importantly, she reminds me of someone with whom I once had a rash and rather consequential affair. And so for me, this is one of those situations where both observation and instinct come into play.

From what I was able to ascertain from Schroeder's notes, their relationship began when they literally collided with each other outside Holland Park Tube Station in London. Schroeder was then a man afloat and Francesca was an Irish girl with eyes like dark, expensive chocolate who wasn't looking where she was going. Schroeder's throat had tightened instantly and before he had even realised what he was saying, he was suggesting they go for a coffee. She politely declined but when Schroeder persisted, on a very giddy roll in his London bubble, she took a step back and looked at him with the classic flirt face. As he put it, "that omniscient tease of confident availability."

– I've got a boyfriend, she said.

– I'm not surprised, he replied.

And so they met as arranged outside a coffee shop on Kensington High Street. But when Francesca immediately suggested skipping the coffee and going for Thai, it was fairly clear what was in store, something which made the dinner conversation all the more charged. The candles burned in her molten eyes, her knees pressed against his thighs and the talk was all tingling with options. Before long, the Dim Sum bolted and the main course abandoned altogether, they were feasting on each others' mouths in the back of a rattling London cab. Her place was a small flat with a big view somewhere between Holland Park and Portobello and it was there, after several ceremonial shots of vodka, that Schroeder first slept with Francesca Maldini. Next morning, in the Royal Borough of Kensington and Chelsea, a traffic sign near his hotel made him laugh out loud. *Humps for 800 m.*

They next met in Dublin at Christmas time. In the chaos of Grafton Street, all lights, frenzy and cheer, it was, once more, a literal collision. Few words were spoken and they went straight to the new Sofitel and got started in the elevator. Francesca the voracious exhibitionist with the chocolate eyes and Schroeder the connoisseur savouring the pre-kiss silence – that prelude which he then believed to be the most intense moment available to a human being. The split-second preparation, the offer and acceptance, the soft collision and the spinning taste of darkness.

Three weeks later they met once more, this time in an Italian place in Blackrock. And again it was an accident. She was now the laid-back waitress, her hair banded high with velvet, and he was the chippy complainant pointing quizzically at a breast of chicken which was far from cooked. Pretending not to know him, she smiled a professional smile and neatly defined the chef as a "prime asshole," suggesting that Schroeder was lucky the chicken had even been defrosted. She swept his plate away, disappeared through a swinging door and Schroeder could hear voices raised in several languages. Moments later she emerged with such grace and speed that she seemed to be on roller blades. She wore a t-shirt now. Red and yellow, with the words *Santa Monica Boxing* undulating across her breasts.

Seconds later, a man fitting the exact description of a prime asshole came lumbering out with the plate of fluorescent chicken still in his hand and offered Schroeder a complimentary tea or coffee. Schroeder was enjoying himself now and, delivering his lines with skill, he suddenly got up in a wild, exasperated dust-devil of shites and fucksakes and left. It was getting fucking impossible, he shouted, to get a bite to eat anywhere in Dublin – a sure sign of any city's collapse.

Out on the street, Francesca was sitting on a bollard with her back to the traffic. Her hair was loosed and Schroeder noted boot-cut jeans, sandals, a sly Mediterranean smile and once again, the Californian top. He apologized for getting her the sack but she said it didn't matter, that she hated the place anyway and that he could buy her a drink by way of compensation. And so they drank Brooklyn Lager all afternoon in a Blackrock dive which had an old-fashioned CD jukebox playing Nine Inch Nails and Queens of the Stone Age. They talked energetically about Schroeder's preoccupations at the time – celebrity, America, television news, crime, death, himself – all topics which, he believed, seemed to fascinate her. In his mind she was engrossed, seeming to buckle with sheer weakness at his sudden takes, elaborations and slants.

Later that evening they made full use of the bare stairs of no. 28, and even before their shuddering, blasted bodies had finally made it to the bedroom itself, Schroeder had already suggested that she stay the night. He had recognised, even as he lay on the stairs in the stained glass glow of his Dún Laoghaire fanlight, the bruises spreading on his hips and back, that he had not felt this good in a very long time. Some ease had come. Some deep warm excitement had landed.

It seemed that Francesca was feeling something similar for she claimed to be looking for exactly the same thing in life as he was – no more than some manageable blend of comfort and kicks. She had recognised a fellow in this pursuit simply because of the few suggestive jokes he had attempted to tell over their little city of bottles in Blackrock. Plus the fact that she could almost smell the lust coming out of his pores. Sex and laughs were exactly what she needed at the time and Schroeder, not a bad-looking young man in the right light, seemed as good a candidate as any.

I was up all that night running checks on her. And while I allowed them their privacy, neither listening nor recording, it was almost as if I was keeping them company – busy at my work while they were busy at theirs. By morning I had gathered enough intelligence on Francesca Maldini to be seriously concerned for Schroeder's happiness in the days ahead. She was the daughter of the late Bert Maldini of Toledo, Ohio, a former functionary in the American Embassy in Dublin. As a teenager, she had baptised her father The Rattler and had once tried to shoot him with his own personal protection weapon. According to her version of events, he was asleep at the time and snoring like a hog, but nevertheless she missed, hitting the pillow right beside his ear and barely waking him up, leaving the disappointed cells of murder to settle themselves somewhere quiet in the blind cool of her blood. At least we must assume so.

It was shortly after they met that she started work with a PR company called Gandon, Truelock & Bogue, engaged mostly in government work, which is the reason she has since been away so much – three times to China this year alone. Her function, as I have discovered, is to soften up hardboiled industrialists with an advance posse of poets and traditional musicians while, at the same time, escorting a rowdy school trip of journalists to the Forbidden City and the Great Wall and doing her best to keep them away from hookers and drugs and, therefore, alive.

But for the most part, her job was to tell blatant lies about both guest and host and pretend to believe, on behalf of the Irish people, that China, for example, gave two shits about anything, not least lung cancer and climate change. She told Schroeder that she had no real difficulty with it. It was no different, she argued, from the way Dublin accepted Washington's view on everything from breast size to who the bad guys were among the murderous ranks of world leaders. Not to take the Americans at their word, she said, would create complications beyond our comprehension. Not only were we allies, she said, we were blood relatives. The Yanks, she said, were our descendants – an evolved version of ourselves and so the relationship – military, political and cultural – was based on power, weakness and awkward kinship. It must all be considered, she said, by way of the two folk philosophies to which she claimed to be especially devoted – "anything for a quiet life" and "better the devil you know."

But for all the fakery of diplomacy, she had her principles too. She once vomited after meeting a European Foreign Minister she knew for a fact to be a war criminal. Right into a ceramic pot and all over a desert plant in the shape of a succulent hand. But even then, on behalf of the nation, she was a consummate professional. She cleaned herself up and returned to the function with a smile and a mouthful of mints. It's a parallel universe, she keeps telling Schroeder, with either different rules or no rules at all. She can, she tells him, manage to just about hold her own. But then by all accounts, including the official ones, she can do much more than that. She speaks Italian, Irish, Spanish, Portuguese and French and has now mastered basic Mandarin. She's cool, adaptable and in charge of herself. And she can lie through her teeth. Her bosses are well pleased.

Charged now with anticipation by Francesca's text, Schroeder wipes the curry from his fingers and texts a message of urgent desire. Even the architecture of her name arouses him. Italianate. Francesca Maria Maldini back from Beijing via Amsterdam with yet more roots and herbs that'll have him in a permanent state. At the thought of it he stretches out on the sofa with a beer, a comfortable smile spreading on his face. She'll be back soon and reinstated utterly. Showered. In her dressing gown. Reading her dictionary and shaving her shins.

– Tarboosh? she will ask him without looking up.

– A type of hat, he will say.

– What kind of a hat?

– Like a fez.

– Correct!

– Autoassassinophiliac?

– Someone who gets sexually aroused by danger.

– Correct!

And then she'll insert a slip of paper between the wafery pages and close the book.

– Did you miss me? she will ask.

– You look amazing, he will say.

And she will put her arms around his neck and he will press his cheek into her breasts. The red silk and the perfumed heat beneath it. And dampened by his breath, it will slip and slub against her skin and she will move away.

– Don't go Fran, he will say.

But she'll already be up and stretching.

– I've so much to do. Unpack. Put on a wash.

And then she'll breathe in, grit her teeth and dig her nails into his flesh. Then, letting go again, she will ease herself away and open her dressing gown. Out of the blue she will be open-robed and spectacular. Legs and hipbones all carved and smooth. Classic pose. Art nouveau. Breasts like fresh air on the ocean.

– What was that for? he will ask.

– Cheer you up. The oldest trick in the book.

– It's a good book.

And then she will announce that she needs a very long sleep. She will take a 24 hr pill and say that she would be grateful beyond words if he doesn't waken her.

– Not even spoons? he will say.

– I know what you're like. I'll make it up to you I promise. I did some shopping.

And Schroeder will writhe like an eel in her grip and promise to behave.

When she awakes she will find him naked as Narcissus in front of the full-length mirror in the bedroom. He will be enacting that ape to human line-up which tracks the ascent of man from knuckle-crawling to upright and ambulatory and, by that chart, he will seem just about bi-pedal – grunting, slack-jawed and tugging at the greening copper bracelet he wears as some unconvincing defence against science, logic and pain. (Magazine article I think it was. Or just some guff spread in the mush of last year's pub-talk.)

And as he acts out every stage between monkey and man, she will feel a powerful mixture of affection and contempt which, she figures, is the most profound compound in any human relationship. Because in those moments when contempt yields once more to affection, things can still be rather thrilling in their own way. And what could be more like love, she once wrote on a coaster, than to feel such tenderness towards someone you despise more than a little?

– Nice ass, she will say.

And afterwards Schroeder will resume his breathless ape-man pose and there really will be something obscene about him then. Something corrupted entirely. And even though his lower lip will swallow the upper in some pitiable defiance of fact, he will see what looks like a dead thing – spectral, skeletal and reeking of bed, curry and death. There will be something particular and newly wasted about him now, something which seems to indicate nothing other than dull collapse and decline. His stomach will be like some pale dessert. Blancmange, if such a thing still exists. And he will suck himself inwards as best as he can but to little effect. Once he could have sucked back that stomach with such violence that it would have disappeared altogether into a deep and shocking cave; a scaresome darkness which burrowed deep beneath the dark overhang of his birdcage of ribs. But not any more. He is a flabby man. His best days are over. Behind him. If they were ever in front of him that is.

– Was that nice? Francesca will ask.

– Sure it was. Thanks.

And she steps out of bed and hugs me from behind, pressing her cheek hard against my spine. On my skin there is curry and chilli, fenugreek and cardamom, turmeric and cumin and whatever other saucers of pigment which seep so queasily through my pores. Oh Schroeder, you lovely man, she says, and she reaches for Maximillian (a name she herself bestowed in sport and adulation) and I will sniff at my armpits and imagine them as soaking jungles; damp and alive with malaria or Lassa fever. And as she touches me I will open wide the swamp of my mouth and yawn an intense, full-bodied yawn, becoming a sudden Francis Bacon all teeth, flesh, cartilage and bone. It will be a warp spasm of sorts and my head will seem to explode into that of a thylacine; the Tasmanian Tiger, alive in my memory for its disputed extinction and enormous gape. And as my jaws settle again, I will feel her breasts crush against my back and then the hot flutter of her tongue beneath my ear. I will reach back for her, the heel of my hand resting gently beneath the silver stud of her navel and, in an instant response, her fingers will wrap themselves tight around me and all I'll be able to think about is Paula Viola. I will try to batter her image away but I will not succeed. She will be in the room with us. She will be right there. And I will give in to it as I always do. And when the door slams downstairs I'll log on quickly and search for archived clips of Paula delivering newsflashes. I'll settle on my favourite. The night the wave hit Galway. Then I'll open a bottle of hooch and focus hard on the eyes. Maximillian. Maximillian. Always Maximillian. And please, never, ever Max. And certainly not Maxiroony or Mr M. That takes the good out it. And there's nothing funny about any of this. And in the morning, my deals and resolutions made, I will throw back the sheets as if in some grand opening ceremony for myself. I will shower, lather, scrub, renew and wash my teeth with vigour. I will cut my hair and shave my beard and make a bird's nest of the sink.

Sometimes Schroeder wonders if Francesca knows about Paula

Viola – if she can somehow divine even a little of what he's thinking whenever she appears on screen. Can she guess his potent thoughts of a grainy session with someone not Francesca Maldini in a crisp high-rise hotel. In a creamy London flat perhaps? Or on the bare and sacred stairs of number 28. But I can assure you that Francesca knows all about it. Francesca Maldini knows all there is to know about all there is to know. In fact, she spends as much time monitoring Anton Schroeder as I do.

And why am I telling you this? Because as I said at the outset, this is no thriller. This is not, and was never intended to be, an investigative reconstruction of events which may or may not have happened surrounding the assassination of an American President on Irish soil. This is (and in fairness I made this very clear from the beginning) an honest and faithful record of breakage and distress at a time when dysfunction was everywhere and anywhere. At the heart of it are all these people I am somehow bound to know. Schroeder, Walton, Francesca, Paula Viola and, of course, the one I know the least about, Richard Rutledge Barnes King.

But to assume that I can know nothing about him is wrong. You cannot know it yet but a certain accuracy in this regard is, in fact, entirely possible. And I'm not talking about verisimilitude. I'm referring to the actual truth, because the thinkings and doings of Richard Rutledge Barnes King are not at all beyond my ken. I keep repeating it but a man of my age must never be underestimated. Yes I know who was Brown and who was Thomas and yes, I know all about the Palatine Switzers and that Caresse Crosby patented the brassiere. But that's just basic stuff which can be *learned*. There is other stuff which must be *known* and it is my strong conviction that there really is nothing which cannot be known. Apart, that is, from the time of one's own death – something which for all its unknowability has this Quiet Land of Anhedonia entirely hamstrung and helpless with fear. From Bantry Bay up to Derry Quay and from Galway to Dubbelin town. *Bitte für uns Sünder jetzt und in der Stunde unseres Todes. Amen.*

SEVEN

THE PRESIDENT is awake early. Heart-pounding hangover. Mouth tasting like roadkill *mar is gnáth*. From an avalanche of twisted sheets, his two black-socked feet crackle and scrunch and his toes probe for pricks and jags on a floor recently earthquaked in order to rewire the place. He is so very annoyed at the way in which his bedroom floor has been damaged by men with clawhammers and chisels and with so little regard he says for the ethics of good workmanship. These sonsabitches have booby-trapped his very living-quarters and one day he will stand on a spike which might well go through the ball of his heel or the web between his toes. Where would we be then? Where would America be then? The world, for that matter?

It's quite the goddamn mess – mosaics of flattened cigarette butts pressed into his floor, the empty golden packets in the grates of every fireplace along with the mouldy heels of bread all twirled in plastic. And as for the muck and tar they trailed in on merciless boots, there was even, by all accounts, dog shit in the very hall. And everywhere, shards of exploded plaster heaped in little cairns at the skirting boards. Little memorials as if the mice were newly dead. His advisors insisted that the work be done and, in this case, even as President, to mutter aloud and demand rights and entitlements would be to enter into some endless daft discourse of the hypothetical and he would be lost within it without compass or bearings.

And so the sparks had triumphed over Washington and over him. Knowledge was their power and electricity was their knowledge. Their estimate trebled as they farted and sneered and finally left, leaving invisible voltage haring through cables and conduits; wires tangle and plugs dangle and the entire White House fizzes with death, President King in real danger of being fried alive; frazzled like crisp American bacon, identifiable only by his bridgework, his fingertips soldered to a light switch like Adam's to God's. And

JOHN KELLY

so he slips back into bed and turns on the television, flicking at speed to look for Ernest Borgnine. President King has long been reluctant to do anything until he finds him in something and, fortunately, Ermes Effron Borgnino seems to have appeared in almost every movie ever made and so it rarely takes more than a minute to locate him somewhere, smiling on the shoulder of some dullard pretty-boy lead. Sources close to the President say that this began as a game but it is now the most vital ritual of his day and nothing might truly begin without it. It is said that the President will wait for as long as it takes, confident that it will never really take more than a minute of intense flicking. And sure enough, Borgnine appears this morning as Trucker Cobb in *The Flight of the Phoenix*. Ian Bannen as Ratbags Crow.

It's 6:10 AM in Washington. 11:10 AM in Dublin and Schroeder, even more hungover than King, steps over his clothes which lie exactly where he abandoned them last night, on the floor beside the bed. It's as if a someone has died and evaporated – a crime scene pointing to a late night and a lie-in. Fran goes mad when she sees his clothes like this and more than once she has taken them for him. He puts his arms in a dressing gown and feeling as if he may have pushed himself too hard, he takes a seat halfway down the stairs and starts drinking the pint of water he had planned to drink last night. His day, just like that of Richard Rutledge Barnes King, has once again begun with pain and desiccation and the smuts of his soul are not yet showing any signs of returning from that unforgiving place of darkness, sand and dust that both men know so well.

Schroeder has his eyes closed. His head is pressed against the cool of the wall when he hears the sound of footsteps outside – invasive, intimate, louder and louder and climaxing with the heart-stopping clatter of the letterbox. He recoils at what he sees next. A letter is pushed through, the head of the latest British monarch rebelliously askew on what is an envelope of cheap, recycled paper. It lands on the tiles with slap. The handwritten address is in full view and immediately, in Schroeder's ashen brain, a dark panic takes hold.

The postal system is for packages, fliers, and circulars only. Nobody sends epistles apart from retro freaks and people on the insane side of peculiar. Letters are very rare birds and Schroeder guesses immediately. Claude. From across the street. Childhood playmate. Teenage oddball. And even in the throbbing core of his hangover, he can recognise the anxious handwriting of Claude Butler – now an ex-priest living his vacant life in Liverpool. Schroeder shudders at the very thought of him. I shudder too. I never liked Claude Butler. Clueless. Prissy. Claude pronounced not *Clode* but *Clod*. Priest. A prig just like his papa.

And as the President sleeps and dreams of open spaces, Schroeder moves to the high-gloss aubergine of his kitchen and, placing the letter on the draining board, he ties his dressing gown in a petulant knot. He opens the fridge and swears a rapid burst of fucks as a yoghurt falls on the floor and explodes on the tiles. He steps over the splatter, boils the kettle and glances again at the envelope lying face down, just as its author had once prostrated himself before an altar on the day of his ordination – that creepy day when Claude was conferred with sacerdotal powers, making him a priest forever according to the Order of Melchisedech. Another dream betrayed. Another tabernacle raided for what it was worth.

Schroeder swallows two paracetamol and washes them down with a carajillo – the shot of Cardenal Mendoza intended to blitz this granite hangover which will soon demand yet further medication – two ferocious Russian pills and deep massage on the many pressure points of the skull. He knows that any correspondence from Claude can't be good. There has been no communication for years, a situation which seems to best suit their very different lives, and any sudden contact now can mean nothing but grief. Schroeder stares at the envelope as if it is diseased. He'll read it later. Sometime. But not now. Another grim torture deferred.

Unsettled and uncertain, Schroeder heads out early. He pulls the door behind him, pushes it twice to check, and then sets off for town all kitted out in charcoal and black, a grey baseball cap, a messenger bag over his shoulder. The sun, still hanging over Wales, is a white-hot plughole and feeling it immediately roast the bones in his face, Schroeder wrangles from the bag a pair of shades – Italian copies with blue-tinted glass. Also in the bag is an old paperback (always 250 pages max), miniatures of vodka, chewing gum, pills (including Presbutex) and Claude Butler's letter, which somehow seems to crackle every time he thinks of it.

He's just at the corner of Hibernia Road when a car approaches extremely slowly. The window begins to roll down and Schroeder anticipates a silencer pointing in the direction of his forehead. There's a dealer living at the end of the street and he was shot on Christmas Eve – nothing to do with Schroeder but even so. Death-dealing is an indiscriminate business and so he steps back, steadying himself to receive the bloody spurts of pain he is due. But instead of a gun, there's a beckoning finger attached to a sweating, beetroot man with red hair and shades exactly like his own. The man is about fifty years old. Tired looking. Bored. Big fists.

– Branch. What's in the bag? (Derry accent. Donegal maybe. Inishowen. Ballyliffin or Burnfoot. Maybe Muff.)

– Can I see some ID?

– Don't be a prick, Mr Schroeder.

Schroeder hands over the bag with the best look of apathy he can manage. The man shakes the bag in front of his face, then against his ear, then spills the contents into his lap and tosses everything around a bit, flicking quickly through the pages of *Sputnik Sweetheart*, checking the bottles and the pills and briefly holding the letter up to the light.

– Who's the letter from?

– My grandmother. She's in a home.

– In England?

– The homes are better there.

– What's her name?

– I call her Granny.

– Do not be a prick, Mr Schroeder.

He puts everything back in the bag and returns it.
– See much of Mr Walton do you?
– Who?
– Your neighbour.
– No.
– When did you last see him?
– Haven't seen him in months. He never goes out.
– You sure about that?
– Certain.
– Does he ever go out?
– No.
– Never?
– He's in a wheelchair.
– Of course.
– Can I go now?
– On you go now. Mind yourself.

And then the Beetroot Man drives off extremely slowly and Schroeder, his heart pounding, tries to assess what has just happened. Why would a Branchman announce himself in this way? Why the interest in Walton and why make that interest so explicit? All he can think of is that he has just been cruised by a Branchman looking for a tout. An invitation to inform. They were at it all the time with people. Recruiting grasses and stools. And if not that, then why this approach the first place? Why this contact? So public and so upfront.

Meanwhile my prayer is that the Beetroot Man really *is* the Branch. *Just* the Branch, that is. And that, whatever this man is doing in Hibernia Avenue, and whatever his interest is in Walton, that this will all remain a strictly local affair. Because, these days, if things ever go beyond the Branch then you might as well start picking a spot for yourself in Glasnevin, named as we all know for the stream of the Chieftain Ó Naeidhe. That's if Glasnevin will have you. Or if there's even a body to burn. And I too, in the end, settle on the recruitment pitch. The Branchman is looking for a snitch.

He wants scuttlebutt, for whatever reason, on the porndog Walton. But then this is what Branchmen do after all. No need for alarm therefore. But even so, I go for a mild stress buster with a miniscule trace of synthetic morphine, and I chase it with vodka. Neat. Peaty. Immediate.

Presbutex, by the way, is an Alzheimer's "miracle med" only recently available on the black market. It is illegal to possess it but, in the service of ensuring that his mind outlasts his body, Schroeder is well prepared to flout the law and risk prosecution. Indeed I take it myself these days. Otherwise my meds are, for the most part, a balancing act of synthetic hormones, blood thinners, bone preservers and the odd stress-buster as required, but the Presbutex is worth the risk. With about one in three people born at the start of the century now living to at least a hundred, such things have to be taken very seriously. It is also a rumoured cure for any creative mind allegedly blocked or otherwise incapable of telling the truth.

Meanwhile, President Richard King, possibly anxious about his forthcoming trip to Ireland, is dreaming that he is driving a huge shining hearse along the roads of West Kerry. Maybe the road to Baile an Fheirtéaraigh. Or maybe not. Anyway, it's Corca Dhuibhne somewhere and the vehicle has no brakes and is entirely beyond his control as it roller-coasters him along mountain passes of hairpins and hangovers, everything lubricated and fluid as the pedals flop disconnected under his feet. In panic and fear, all he can do is steer in hope as boulders and hedges flash by and swallows unleash themselves towards him like summer harpoons. There is also, in this dream, a talkative man seated beside him in the passenger seat and, as usual, as in all the dreams of President Richard Rutledge Barnes King, that man is Ernest Borgnine. Mr Borgnine is initially trying to reassure the President but the hearse freewheels on and tears begin to ignite in the President's throat. Mr Borgnine, his eyes now frantic with reassurance, begins to talk about a motion picture called *The Whistle at Eaton Falls* but the President begins kicking the dashboard, all the time yelling about not wanting to go to Ireland, referring to it as "a fucking medicine show." Towards the end of that same dream, as the President screams about "Irish bullshit merchants" and how much, as a man of his standing, he resents being on the kerosene circuit, Ernest Borgnine suddenly transforms into the stockade sergeant in *From Here to Eternity* and begins to wave the same switch he once pulled on Frank Sinatra. Mr Borgnine's newly malevolent eyes fix hard on the President and slowly his Borgnine head, in full frame, begins to rotate and accelerate into a raging blur. Then, in what is a common conclusion to Presidential dreaming, King tries to get out of the hearse but the doors, as usual, are locked against all salvation. There are screams and wild tears which only stop when, from the midst of a whirling tornado of himself, Borgnine suddenly punches him hard in the face and the President's nose explodes like a ripe beef tomato.

– Don't go to Ireland, says the Academy Award winner. Don't go near it. That place has been the death of better men than you. And I'm really sorry for hitting you, sir.

EIGHT

AT THE TOP OF THE HOUSE and I'm watching everything on assorted links, breathing through my nose and sipping tea made with fennel ripped this morning from the hedge. Umbelliferous. Carminative. Good for the eyesight of both man and snake. Perfect for the Gestalt and the job in hand.

I locate him, shin-deep in weeds, on the baking northbound platform of the Salthill-Monkstown / *Cnoc an tSalainn-Baile na Manach* DART station. He's well wired by now on miniatures, pills and anxiety and he's watching a new commotion out in Dublin Bay – gannets shafting into the waves like white bolts out of heaven, dozens of them, hurled by Zeus the Mackerel Slayer, the mighty deity of aerial attack. *Morus bassanus* in from the Stack on Inis Mac Neasáin. Erin's Ey. The Garland of Howth.

He barely registers the *Barry*, a marvel dropped in the sea like some magical island but now as normal as the sun. This platform, being a place of daily delay, is both a site of contemplation for Schroeder and the setting for one of the better scenes in *Lucky's Tirade*. The bit where he writes with such extraordinary skill about these very birds.

The gannets plunge on relentlessly, picking off whatever mutated shoals have strayed inshore and brought these giant birds in with them, their jetfighter wings and yellow bills and all that black eyeliner of ferocity marking their faces with efficiency and death. And as I watch them dive and go under, I think of the time I first propelled my bony frame into the Forty Foot and how everything suddenly switched into a silent underwater roar of bubbles and scattering small fry. I still remember the cool shock that took my breath away and stopped my heart in a brief and exhilarating little death, and how I turned myself into something streamlined and for once quite perfect, just like these enormous birds spearing

*fish in the white streaks of Dublin Bay; coming and coming again
in deadly showers, leaving jet trails of themselves in the sky above
Howth Head.*

It's hard to believe the reviews were so bad when you read a passage
like that. Although it didn't take long for him to undo everything
by gratuitously inserting himself just to make a dig at the clergy,
adding, quite unnecessarily, that the birds remind him of *aeroplanes
of precisely creased paper, folded and pressed to the finest points and
launched with hope to seek their own perfection, like the one flung
through a singing church during the dimwit priest's first Mass. And then
when the priest says ah look, it's the flight into Egypt, everybody cracks
up and the flock guffaws. All I can do is examine them all in quiet
despair. These punters easily pleased, I think to myself. This unexact-
ing place where anaesthesia is all.* And then another quite ridiculous
scene about someone about to fall into the path of an oncoming
DART only to be grabbed by yet another priest – this time a Tri-
dentine from New York City wearing a full round collar and Secret
Service shades. He had Claude Butler in his mind when he wrote
that. No doubt about it. *Lucky's Tirade* is a book I can, so to speak,
read like a book.

And then the four depressing bell-rings that always herald some
new announcement of failure on the network. The four ascending
notes that break Schroeder's heart every time he stands on this shattered platform, off on another fool's errand into Dublin City. Yet
more breakdown. Yet more grief.

*We are sorry to announce the late running of the 10:35 train to
Howth. This train is delayed by approximately twenty-five minutes.
This delay is due to . . .*

Public transport in all its charmless decay and Schroeder swears
so loudly that the other people on the platform shift. And they're
right too. Such a violent outburst might well be the prelude to a
shooting spree or worse, and so the alarmed commuters edge even
further down the platform and line themselves up at a safer dis-

tance, staring straight ahead as if they're all about to pee on the tracks. Every fucking day! Schroeder spits again, the Beetroot Man still vivid in his head and the desire to punch something making a hard icy snowball of his fist. He looks for something to thump and when he finds it, he drives his knuckles right into it – the rusting sign for Salthill-Monkstown / *Cnoc an tSalainn-Baile na Manach*. The line of commuters drop their pretence of calm and trot at speed to the very far end of the platform like a little frightened flock of plovers about to fly off, at any moment, in a shower of feathers and shite. Schroeder slinks into the shade.

When the DART finally arrives, the driver looking somehow pleased with himself, the plovers get on at the back and the madman who has punched the sign for Salthill-Monkstown / *Cnoc an tSalainn-Baile na Manach* steps through doors which seem to have opened just for him, the carriage empty but for a small huddle of junkies who slur abuse at each other and look as if their faces are dribbling away into a communal hole. Schroeder steps back out onto the platform again and re-enters the train the next carriage down, this one drug-free but jammers.

Schroeder has written enough about hangovers for me to know exactly how he's feeling. The drilling headache and lurching heart that seems somehow terrified of itself. And he has written enough about these excursions into Dublin for me to know exactly what he's seeing. Free newspapers, in several language editions, trampled all over the floor. Today, it's the official portrait shots of President King standing on a troop carrier dressed as a fighter pilot, his helmet under his arm like a glossy beachball. He has a big grin on his face, all those decades of progress binned and the planet in chaos all over again. An endless orange alert.

There are a few exhausted-looking soldiers in the corner but mostly it's Spanish students, talking at torture-level volume about whatever dramas are taking place on their phones. Schroeder can get through an entire day without saying a word to anyone so he can never understand people who talk like this. And this bunch is talking, talking, talking – the air slippery with the *cedillas* of machine-gun *Español* and he wonders what the little bastards really have to talk about when everything in the heads of youth, even Spanish youth, is misplaced and nothing is understood.

As the train finally cranks away, Schroeder sees the sign for Salthill-Monkstown / *Cnoc an tSalainn-Baile na Manach*, now with its little jelly-mould dent. And cradling one hand in the other he looks down at his knuckles all red, white and blue and puts his forehead to the glass, trying to force assorted thoughts both into and out of his mind. He swallows another pill. That Muff bastard knew his name. And Walton's name. And said he was Branch. And they never say that.

The dust from the seats is blooming in the sunlight and suddenly Schroeder senses the approach of a rangy figure. The air that accompanies him throbs with unease and Schroeder's discomfort deepens when he feels a stare of recognition. He reaches for the book. Murakami (229 pages) and the man – a skinhead – throws himself across the opposite seat, lying there as if expecting to be fed grapes.

– Well? says the skinhead.

Schroeder pretends he hasn't heard. The skinhead persists.

– Did you get it?

– Schroeder looks up from his book.

– Did I get what?

The man looks familiar. Far too cheery for a skinhead.

– Did you get it?

Schroeder decides to move seats but just as he gets up the man reaches out and grabs his leg. Schroeder considers kneeing him in the jaw but instead he glares at the hand and hisses with as much venom as he can manage.

– Do you mind?

It's a poor effort and only makes Schroeder sound like an indignant librarian.

– The letter! says the skinhead. The letter! Did you get it?

– What are you talking about?

Schroeder is shaken, but conscious that people are watching, he sits down again. The skinhead gets excited.

– The letter, man! The letter! It's not like you get a letter everyday!

The other passengers, sensing the unpredictable, gather their bags close and pretend to ignore what's happening. Schroeder stares the skinhead right in the eyes and whispers.

– So you're the Branch too, are you?

The skinhead laughs.

– Not me, mate. I'm better than the Branch.

– Then who the fuck are you?

The man looks around as if he has just heard the stupidest question in the world ever.

– Who the fuck am I? I'm the mailman! Who do you think I am?

Then he laughs like a castrato and Schroeder twigs. It *is* the mailman. Off duty. Unrecognizable in the way a bartender might be. Out of context.

– How do you know I got a letter?

– I'm the mailman. I fucking delivered it.

– I mean how do you know who it's from?

– I checked it. I check all the mail. Not all of it obviously. Just the suspicious stuff.

– Suspicious stuff!

The mailman shrugs.

– I use my discretion.

Schroeder begins to boil.

– You can't read people's mail!

The mailman raises a finger.

– I have to read it. What with the President coming we have to be on full alert.

– I'll report you to the Guards.

– The Guards know all about me.

– I fucking bet they do!

– I report direct to headquarters. I'm their top man.

Schroeder has met fantasists before. The city is full of them – touts and then there are people who think they are touts, the latter often being the more dangerous. But in this case Schroeder fears that this is a mailman who really does check the "suspicious" mail. Believing himself especially anointed for the purpose, he feels obliged to guard the postal matrix, to keep its channels open and keep his eye out for this and for that. His mission is to miss nothing. No detail too small when there are sleepers everywhere. Terrorists, subversives and their many fellow travellers are a constant threat to Irish democracy. Cascade has said so. And Gibbon says little else.

With Claude's letter the mailman has noticed an address written in the anxious hand of a male person in some distress, carved in deep and pressured curls, the fruity blackberry of a cheap ballpoint. Whoever sent it was in a sweat. Someone who perhaps knows where the bodies are buried, or where the banknotes are stashed. Someone who, one way or another, knows too much. Between that, the wonky stamp and the Liverpudlian postmark, the postman reasoned he had several grounds for concern – or for curiosity at least. And so he stepped sideways and crouched between the wheelie bins and opened the letter with the razorblade he carries for this purpose.

Claude's letter was read quickly and once satisfied that it contained news of personal rather than national crisis, the mailman resealed the envelope, sprang to his feet, relocated the letterbox, savoured his power once more and opted, finally, for delivery. At that very instant he felt himself the most potent man in Ireland. He is the final arbiter – the hand outstretched and his wavering thumb the sole focus of the slavering multitudes. Let the letter go! Release the letter! No! No! Deprive Schroeder of his news! Keep the letter! Put it with the rest! It was a very important decision, as are all his decisions in these dangerous days. And in the end he decided to send the head of an English king into a tailspin as the letter headed for the hall floor of no. 28. He let the letter live and he listened with something like love as it hit the tiles.

– I'll report you for this, Schroeder says again.

– Report away. I'm the last line of defence. Anyway, he wants to meet you. What has he done, your friend?

– Fuck you!

And then as the DART begins to slow once more, the mailman who knows everything and suspects even more suddenly leaps to his feet and makes for the doors. Schroeder, shocked and fuming, watches him lope off down the platform like a six-foot kid with a belly full of sherbet. Like a man who has killed the real mailman, stuck his dismembered bits into the Edwardian pillar boxes of Jacobite green and taken to delivering the Dún Laoghaire mail on some insane postal frolic of his own. Schroeder hokes in the bag. He'd better read the fucking thing now. This, says Schroeder under his spearmint breath, is turning out to be one shitty, shitty morning.

Dear Anton,
You will be surprised to hear from me. It is a very long time since we have spoken to one another. Was it my ORDINATION? Yes? A lifetime ago I think so. Have we spoken since then? Yes we have. Just before I went to PERU, which is where "Saint Martin de Porres" is from and Paddington the Bear who loves his marmalade sandwiches and his . . .

Paddington *the* Bear? Saint Martin de Porres? Inverted commas. Block capitals. Schroeder makes an instant diagnosis of basket-casery and tugs at his hair.

. . . hard things. Hurtful remarks I think. Not that I am to "judge" or scold. In no position. I would say. I am trying just to make contact with you. How are you? I am well. I am no longer in the "PRIESTHOOD" as you know. And it's not that I wasn't even called, more that I did not understand what God was asking of me. Or perhaps I received a message meant for somebody else maybe? Wouldn't that be a good one!!! HA HA! But I still adhere to the "teachings of CHRIST." Forgiveness and love the heart of it

all. And I forgive you hurtful words for all of my life and I hope
that you will forgive me too. Of my own sins . . .

Sins? Forgiveness? Not the inevitable, surely? Claude in handcuffs,
in an anorak, led through ranks of spitting trolls with fagbutts and
highlights to be jailed, unforgiven and chemically adjusted. A pa-
riah, a danger, and Schroeder would be thankful that Mr and Mrs
Butler were both long dead and wouldn't have to see their shiny
boy dragged from backseat to courtroom – a hand on his head so
he wouldn't bump it. As if anybody cares. *Mind your head scumbag!*
Father Claude the Good. Father Alpha and Father Omega and all
the fallen clergy in between.

. . . when I left the "PRIESTHOOD" there were many who
thought bad of me. Perhaps you saw me for a "weak man" too. A
man of no principles. But nobody understood "the circumstances"
but me. This I must explain to you. Confess to you. Because here
I am seeking the forgiveness of an old friend which must surely be
the great forgiveness in all human life . . .

Schroeder throws the letter on the seat beside him and tries to dis-
tract himself with a separate rage. What the fuck are you looking at,
King? You warmongering piece of shit. But no good. A more personal focus is needed and he finds it quickly. A huddle of schoolboys
on the platform. School uniform from the waist up and, from the
waist down, shorts, bare legs and the dried rugby-mud of privilege.
Little tadpole lawyers and doctors – perfect crossbreeds between the
cheekboned princesses of Southside Dublin and the gormless gods
from across the avenue. And all of them complicit in what happened. In sucking the soul out of the place. The nation. In capitu-
lating to vulgarity at every turn. In raising the accountant above the
medic, the socialite above the poet, the general above the pianist,
the professional shit above the man who might possibly fix your
head. All these little fuckwits care about is Leinster Rugby and ste-

roids. It's in their genes. All else has been bred out of them long ago. Even the sight of that uniform, almost thirty years later, still makes Schroeder spit. The older boys oxter-cogging him into the jacks, sticking his head down the toilet and then the flush – the air full of male stink and taunts of *Welcome to Guantanamo!* He remembers with shame that he yielded immediately to get it over with as quickly as possible, picturing, as he sobbed, the man he had read about, murdered in a cruel and unusual way, propped upright inside a giant cathedral bell as it rang out across Paris. Decibelled to death, the vibrations disrupting his heart and soul to the point of explosion. That was his terror, his cheek pressed against the sleek sweep of the toilet bowl, his eyes stinging and the vapour of industrial disinfectant eating at his brain. When his head was finally lifted he looked sideways and saw that Claude had been watching the whole thing. Not actually partaking in the cruelty, but present even so. In the vicinity and hovering with a big innocent face and just the twisted hint of a smile.

Schroeder stares at the letter. It looks like a wounded man trying to get up.

. . . possible that you meet me in Dublin? I will be there at the end of the month. For a FUNCTION. I arrive on the 27th. What about Redding's Hotel. 3 PM in the afternoon? There are things I need to tell you about but can only do so "IN PERSON."

– Not a fucking hope, says Schroeder to the coastline view. Not a fucking snowball's.

The DART expires as it enters Blackrock / *An Charraig Dhubh* and stands for a tense ten minutes until a soldier suddenly smashes out a window with his rifle butt, climbs out into the air and disappears down the platform. Even the Spanish students fall silent until, at last, unapologetic as ever, the train slides away again and on to Booterstown / *Baile an Bhóthair* – protected home of the Kingfisher: *Alcedo atthis.* The Halcyon bird. Sign of calm waters and the promise of spring. If you are not lucky enough to see one today, the sign says, don't give up, it may be here soon. Like the train perhaps. Or Father fucking Claude. Or that grinning bastard King still looking up from the newspapers strewn on the floor. *For the comfort and safety of other rail users do not place your feet on the seat.*

Schroeder counts the herons hunched in wait for passing trade – the Charons of Booterstown Marsh in their misted hellscape gurgling on its glacial tills, the culverted Trimelston stream, the Nutley stream bringing in the salt sea – the very salinity that once rarefied the place for plants and birds. Snipe. Teal. Tufted. The sulky shelduck and the shoveller. And over the wall, in the Bay itself, whatever hardy sharks can stand the radiation are chomping on the city's fleshy detritus – murder victims mostly – and maybe the odd mullet.

Schroeder must have been about twelve when the first great white appeared off the coast of Kerry, their outriders having been spotted the year before. Nobody really believed it but soon there was actual footage of seal kills and fins. When that same first shark was killed by a drunken Corkonian genuflecting on the prow of his boat with a high velocity rifle, it was a big news story. Not least because when the man got back to Cork he was mauled by his pet wolf, crazed by the smell of shark all over his master's hands. Every cloud, said Mrs S. A very funny woman when she wanted to be, Mrs S.

. . . we have all made mistakes. Mine was to loose my way inside my "faith" which is deep. Yours was loosing your way inside your "desire" which is dark. Do you not agree with me? But REDEMP-TION is available to all of us if we have the courage for it. And if we can recognise it. This world needs "good people" to live in it like brave people.

To live in it like brave people? Faith. Desire which is dark? Redemption! Courage! Loosing (sic) your way? Maybe Claude wants to talk about how Schroeder did his science project for him? And how Claude got best in the class for it and how he swaggered like a flute band for a full fortnight encouraging Mr and Mrs S to think that the boy from across the street was some kind of genius. And yet it was Schroeder who wrote every word of it. *The Flora and Fauna of Booterstown Marsh.* The little egret.

The mix of freshwater and salt-sea flora – the mad names: bistort, horsetail, sea aster, creeping bent, sea milkwort and the most significant if he remembers correctly – Borrer's grass, then found only in a few places in Ireland. He can still remember most of it. Borrer's saltmarsh-grass.

Puccinellia fasciculata to *Carduelis carduelis* and a flock of gold-finches comes alongside. Schroeder had thought them long extinct and they seem so exotic in the beachy light. Der Distelfink. They remain by the window, astonishing, undulating slightly, before withdrawing the privilege and veering out into the toxins of San-dymount Strand. The train then plunges into the back gardens of Dublin 4 with its tennis courts and deep basement kitchens, orchids and spice racks arranged in windows lined with prison bars. Then it's Sydney Parade / *Paráid Sydney*, a drag act in any language. Alsa-tians patrol the woodbine hedges. They bark at the train and lunge at the rats.

yours faithfully,
your "old pal,"
Claude Butler
P. S. I think that Dublin must have changed? A lot? Do you think so too?

Schroeder gets off at Lansdowne Road/ *Bóthar Lansdún,* crosses the tracks, and, as if to make the morning's movie roll backwards on the reel, undoing all harm done, he heads straight back the way he came. As if the letter might be unread. As if the mailman and the Branchman might be un-met. As if life might be un-lived and these towering anxieties un-felt – anxieties which remind him now of difficult music – a torrent of barely recognisable phrases mutating into pure tension, throbbing with the insistent yet uneven pulse of paranoia. He swallows his last miniature like an cormorant downing a pout.

NINE

– SCHIPHOL is a thundering bitch!

And with that doormat declaration, Francesca Maldini dumps her bag in the hall and charges up the stairs. Schroeder shouts after her but the shower has already powered into life and she steps under its several roasting jets. No legal limits for her. She has the Kronos Quartet on her shower-phones and she'll be there for a while – always the five of them in there together – herself and the strings. Glass usually or Terry Riley.

Schroeder distracts himself with current events on NB1. King's visit is now a fortnight away and the crackdown has begun with Gibbons announcing a series of "strong measures." It seems that anybody considered even the slightest threat to King's visit has already been taken to the Park and left in the care of the Americans – a full-blown orange jumpsuit scenario. It's foreigners mostly – teachers, restaurant workers, students and even a few professional footballers who just happen to come from one of several countries engaged in some kind conflict with the US. Cascade is taking no chances here. Nothing will go wrong on his watch. Certainly not some embarrassing hurl of a shoe or, worse again, some actual attempt on the Presidential person.

I'm watching the same programme and rolling my eyes just like Schroeder. Roadblocks have been set up at all points of entry into the city and long pile-ups of tanks sprouting little tricolours are queuing on the hard shoulder along the inner ring. Search and clear operations are already underway in the most unlikely places and the biggest operation of all seems to be in Ranelagh, named for Lord Ranelagh, Paymaster General to the Forces, where one entire street has been emptied and truckloads of illegal weapons have been found – most of them planted, no doubt, by cuckolded apparatchiks and touts.

There has been activity in Dún Laoghaire too and military vehicles are now clogging up the roads around the harbour and several restaurants, cafés and hookah houses have been closed down with officials citing "health reasons." A barbershop has been raided in Glasthule in broad daylight and everybody in it, all Egyptians, have been deported and for no good reason. A mysterious hole has been dug in the middle of a hockey pitch in Blackrock and something similar has occurred in the grounds of the Russian Orthodox church. The final shot in the report is of a tank parked like a rearing horse right on the Glenageary Roundabout. The Glen of the Sheep.

You OK up there? Schroeder shouts to the landing.

No answer.

He shoves a bottle of Chablis in the freezer for a rapid chill, settles himself on the sofa and speculates. Her eyes will be closed now, her hands clasped about her neck, her mouth half-open, her elbows pressing against herself to make little waterfalls of silver and blue. This is surely the luxurious prelude to one of those perfect nice-to-be-home sessions, fired perhaps by new lacy purchases from the boutiques of the P. C. Hooftstraat. And so he sniffs at his own breath as the shower drones off and wet feet stomp on the floorboards above. Drawers open and close. The sliding doors of the wardrobe whoosh and Schroeder imagines the rustle of paper bags and the brisk clipping of clips. She's in front of the mirror, reddening her lips, teasing her hair, arranging herself for supreme effect. He leaps to the cupboard and downs a sneaky slug of Stoli. Neat. Anticipatory. From the neck.

But when Francesca appears at the kitchen door she's certainly not dressed for sex. She's wearing an Irish soccer jersey, jeans and a pair of bedroom slippers designed as comic Friesian cows. Her face is grey and her hair drips like kelp as her mouth seems to prepare itself for some deadly announcement. He looks into her eyes. Like chocolate still but no lustre now and certainly no lust. No sign of anything other than business to be done and a grim mission to be accomplished. And just as her lips begin to form the words, Schroeder looks down at the two grinning Friesians and Maximillian retreats like a kicked dog.

– Schroeder, we need to talk.

Schroeder wheels away. He has witnessed such scenes in the movies and he knows how this one goes.

– This is difficult, she says.

Schroeder clutches a clump of hair on the crown of his head.

– For you or for me?

She takes a long slow breath.

– I'm leaving. I'm sorry.

Schroeder feels his mouth suck dry and he watches Francesca circle slightly as if to inspect the extent of the wound she has inflicted. Then she takes to the sofa and gazes up at the chandelier, tears now bleeding from the corners of her eyes and rolling into her ears. Inexplicably, Schroeder almost smiles.

– What are you saying?

Francesca sits up, hugs her knees and looks to the corner of the room as if to watch the blank television. Schroeder lashes a quadruple measure into a glass.

– You mean you're *leaving* leaving?

– Yes.

– Why? What the hell's happened?

– Nothing's happened.

– So who is it? Do I know him?

Schroeder is disappointed by his lines.

– Stop it, Schroeder.

– I suppose he's some tosser with his jumper stuffed into his trousers is he?

A better line but useless all the same and Francesca rubs her throat with the back of her hands.

– Don't, Schro. Please.

– You're a dark fucking horse, Fran.

– So it would seem.

– Some wanker in PR is he?

– If you must know he's a chef.

– A celebrity chef?

– Just a chef.

She's lying. Schroeder knows it. And I know it too. I am so hopped up on Presbutex that I can spot falsehoods faster than a hawk can clock a viper in a Connemara bog.

– So where did you meet him? The cook?

– Chinatown.

– So he's a Chinaman?

– No he's not a *Chinaman*. He works in Chinatown.

– Chinatown?

– In Amsterdam.

– Does he do Kung Fu?

– Fuck off, Schroeder.

– Cook you some sautéed bullfrog, did he? Or maybe some urinating shrimp?

– What the fuck does that mean?

– It's a delicacy, Francesca. You like delicacies. Dog in a fucking clay pot perhaps?

– He's just a guy, Schroeder. No big deal. He's just a guy.

– Tell you what Francesca. Fuck it. Just go get your stuff.

Now, I accept that this might seem like a strange development. That a character so recently introduced would simply arrive home from Schiphol in Chapter Nine and end a relationship without any signs in the previous chapters that such a twist was likely. But then this is precisely my difficulty in writing this. Real people such as Francesca and Schroeder do not behave in any way as required by editors, publishers and readers alike. Yes, I might well have attempted to invent reasons to justify such actions but that is not my purpose here and I have made this clear from the start. And in any case it is the fact of her leaving which is the crucial part. The reason itself is not, at this stage in the narrative, knowable. Or even imaginable. And so if the narrative is not what you, as a reader, might wish for in your fiction, then let me say again, repeating what I said at the very beginning, this is an honest and faithful record and I will not, for the sake of literary convention, make things up. I regret if scenes such as these are unsatisfying, discombobulating or even fatal to your willingness to persist, but there it is. As I have said repeatedly, real people never behave as expected of them in books and therefore rarely succeed as characters. Indeed it's entirely possible when the doings and sayings of real people are written down they are immediately rendered incredible. And so, all Francesca says is,

– I'm leaving because I have to.

Her exact words and Schroeder actually snorts.

– You mean because you want to?

– No. Because I have to.

And then, with her lips seeming to curtsey slightly, Francesca gathers a few things and walks quietly beneath the skylight of number 28 and closes the door so gently behind her that Schroeder doesn't even hear the click. But when the deep new silence eventually betrays her absence, Schroeder makes himself a large vodka and cranberry – frozen Stoli with clean shards of ice-cap just to sharpen the kick. But when the drink loses its poke he makes another, a bigger one this time, and without the cranberry. There are many more to follow and later, in the swimming twilight, the shock of Francesca's leaving hits him like a mountainside of falling rocks.

Then he mails Walton to break the news. The reply is immediate. (Walton is also plastered and here I have corrected the spelling for them both.)

– *want the loan of something?*

– *the loan of what?*

– *virtual sex with the stars?*

– *are you kidding me?*

– *it'll take your mind off the middle east.*

– *no. thank you all the same.*

– *it's interactive.*

– *i don't care.*

– *are you OK?*

– *grand.*

— there's this english actress the dead spit of Fran. just won an award for best performer in a group scene.

— fuck off.

— she's the head of her. just trying to help.

— and again. fuck off.

Schroeder stays up all night, listening to music, flicking through books and watching his Paula newsflash stash, and when morning comes he rearranges his furniture with extraordinary energy. Then he showers and sleeps, his stomach full of enough mood adjusters to keep him fuelled for a fortnight. When he awakes mid-afternoon, ravenous for spicy soup, there's nothing but throbbing confrontation on his mind. Beyond his curtains he senses a multitude of challenges and delights, threats and opportunities, all lurking in the streets of Baile Átha Cliath. And he knows exactly what he must do. He must place himself at the very heart of it. Headbutt the psycho, eyeball the Gorgon and pin down the vamp. He must put himself directly in harm's way. Stride long and hard into Dublin City and take it all on with fearlessness and verve. He can do what he likes now. Within reason and without. It's either that or lie in bed for a fortnight and cry like a toddler. And so he eats his drugs, drains a tin of soup and exits. I wish I could steady him but I dare not intervene. And here things take a turn.

TEN

WESTMORELAND STREET, named for John Fane, 10th Earl of Westmoreland, Lord Lieutenant of Ireland, and the military is evicting skeletal squatters from derelict buildings. The whole place is bottlenecked by rubberneckers hoping for a bloodbath but Schroeder stays well out of it, lurking among the market stalls, sipping a silty Turkish coffee that could kill a horse but which, due to the magnitude of his hangover, is having little effect. Some explosive fission seems to be at work deep within his ribcage and with each new Francesca flashback, Schroeder fears for his heart. *Palpato. Palpatas. Palpatat.*

I survey the scene. Ratboys sprout from street lamps, spreading sputum and skin disease as they goad the soldiers and jeer at the miserable wrecks being dragged out onto the street. Such cruel, graceless little shits with their forelocks of grease and I can just imagine Schroeder on a rooftop, settling into a sniper's pose and picking them off one by one – dropping them from the streetlamps, on their heads, on their backs, on their Ratboy arses. Unregistered for generations, not one of them would be missed. The great unchecked. As pervasive as pigeons. St. Columb's Columbiformes. The squabs of Columba livia. Up the Doves!

Schroeder is just about to move off (in search of Paula Viola no doubt) when a girl with red shoulder-length hair sweeps by on an old-fashioned bicycle, her appearance entirely a throwback, her clothes as noir as the bike and a black beret suggesting either a pallbearer from the last century or a smoking *chanteuse* from his lost Parisienne dreams. The crimson lips suggest more Paris than Provo and Schroeder immediately savours the charge of the entire package – that big black Triumph gliding along the Dublin streets. A woman of style. A woman of confidence. A woman who makes love only on Louis XIV furniture, red velvet always and enriched with galloon in the Galeries des Glaces. And so with Ms Maldini temporarily forgotten and Ms Viola casually postponed, Schroeder names her Chantal. I have never seen her before and this is an instant worry.

She stops a little further up the street and Schroeder is rendered bloodless as she dismounts and the grey of the shabby thoroughfare is lit by a band of cabaret flesh. He flings his coffee from him and follows, agreeing enthusiastically with himself that such a spectacular stereotype is no more than he deserves. She stalls, turns and yes, she gives him a look – a look, he is almost certain, suggestive of many erotic adventures ahead. But as he begins to catch up, she moves off again, directing her bicycle towards the old Palace Bar, now a strip club called Wilde's, famous for its slogan "Forty-Nine Gorgeous Girls and One Wagon." Schroeder calculates quickly, and with growing euphoria, that the bicycle girl must surely be one of the gorgeous ones. She's certainly dressed for it and why else would she step even a short distance into Temple Bar, an area of such threat and decay, the grass now growing on the streets as it does in the deep American South.

The Temple Bar zone, named for Sir William Temple, Provost of Trinity, was once considered Dublin's entertainment district but, in reality, it was never more than a sinkful of slop, the markings of drunks ascending the walls in jagged graphs of piss. Spit hung on the windows, blood rose in the drains and dried up pizzas of puke spread themselves all over the pavements. When they finally closed the place down, it rotted so rapidly that now there's nowhere in the entire metropolitan area which festers with quite so much danger and disease. The old ruined clubs and bars are now mostly crack houses and the one gang-run saloon that remains open in Meeting House Square specializes only in cheap booze and handguns. Nobody goes near it unless they want to kill somebody, or else have no strong objections to being killed themselves. In short, the place is lethal – murders, beatings, knifings and knee-cappings. Only recently, a gang nailed a teenager to a door and then dragged other teenagers off Dame Street, named for the Church of St. Mary del Dam, to witness the boy's agony. The military eventually came to free him with morphine and a clawhammer and it didn't even make the news.

And yet she turns right, wheels her bicycle right past Wilde's and walks directly into the actual pit itself. Schroeder finds it quite impossible not to follow and he slips a pill from the plectrum pocket of his jeans and crunches down hard, wondering what the Branch would make of him now, undertaking such a perilous diversion. But he has detected just a hint of sexual invitation and it's more than enough for any man for whom things have not been going well in life or in love. A man in such circumstances will chance anything for fantasies fulfilled. And so he follows. Right into Fleet Street, named for a street in London, itself named for a subterranean river audible still in Clerkenwell.

Almost immediately Schroeder senses the junkies skulking in the windowless shells but Chantal leads on and he follows, stalked in turn by a rum scatter of feral cats. The stink gets worse and glancing into the rancid tunnel of Merchant's Arch he sees an enormous greyhound nose at a corpse. A bus driver by the looks of it. But Chantal's heels are click, click, clicking. And the bicycle is tick, tick, ticking and its broad saddle is all burnished and smooth and Schroeder follows on. Ahead of him his quarry is all flank and rump, suggesting to Schroeder the African plains and a haunchy antelope to be taken down by the last of the big cats. Carnal really is the word for it. Of the flesh.

Schroeder has never once followed Paula Viola in this way. In fact he has never actually followed her as such. With her it's more a case of his being in the places she is likely to be – which is not quite the same thing. He is not, after all, some class of stalker. He has never once spoken to her or approached her in any way. Even that day in Brown Thomas. Schroeder, let it be known, is no precision pervert with a checklist of fetishes. Nor has he ever been the lonely voyeur or the sad collector of intimate memorabilia, half sickened, half bored. Any suggestion of same would be to do him a great disservice. In my view. And yet here he is following this voluptuous *aisling* into danger and dare. And in hopes of what exactly? *Carnivore. Carnival.* Carnations in a bucket. Carnations the colour of flesh. I am very concerned.

Turn back, Schroeder. Turn back.

But of course he cannot hear and of course I cannot quite see as the cats scatter like marbles and a half-naked man emerges from a doorway. He is yellow-skinned and toothless and seems no more than a spectre but when Schroeder catches the glint of a hypo, his brain is attacked by a high-pitched tone which he takes to be the very sound of his own fear. Fear in the small of his back. Instinctively he goes for a bluff, reaching for an imaginary weapon, groping in his jacket as if he's packing something confident. Don't even think about it, bud. The man's eyes move to the commotion in Schroeder's pocket and, without any change in expression, he simply fades away again, taking the hypo with him. Schroeder walks on and the cats circle once more. Christ Schroeder, I'm thinking, get out of there. You will die here. And your death will not be a happy one.

Chantal is now walking across open space, avoiding the remains of last night's fires and taking a sharp left towards Dame Street. Schroeder follows, giddy now like a cartoon man in a trance as she enters a laneway which will eventually emerge onto World Bank Plaza at the most shabby corner of the four. She stops halfway up and Schroeder waits as she chains her bicycle to a lamp post all hung with surveillance cameras before entering an internet hub called the Big Star. Illegal. An unapproved venue for sure. Anyone even attempting anonymity these days is considered an obvious risk to the State and raids on these places tend to be brutal. And so Schroeder, not quite knowing what to do next, sits beside two Japanese Goths on a massive concrete boulder and considers his options.

– You got a cigarette? asks one of the Goths.

– Get your own fucking cigarettes.

Then a scream off to the right and, from one of the buildings further up, a teenage boy with yellow hair runs out into the street, taking random diagonals but not getting far. Three other men come after him and knock him to the ground. And as the boy curls up they kick him hard in the ribs and drag him back inside. Schroeder scans the emptiness and listens. Then another scream, sustained and terrible and Schroeder snorts the very thought of it out through his nose. The doings of this parallel universe are best left alone. A place where, almost certainly, he will get his head in his hands. A place where tougher men than him have been disembowelled in the middle of the day.

I like to cite Loeb in such circumstances. Human activity, just like the movements of plants, is governed by tropisms and the very workings of the mind can be explained by way of the physio-chemical. Certainly that's what it feels like to Schroeder as he heads towards the Big Star Internet Café and swings open its battered steel door. He's acting almost in spite of himself and the true sensation, rather than one of courage and nerve, seems to be one of dumb dreaminess. Perhaps some physio-chemical mechanism really is at work, and perhaps everything he has done (and thought) from the moment Chantal flashed by on Westmoreland Street, really has been entirely beyond his control.

In the darkness of the café she is the only customer, her own phototropic face glowing in the cyber-light, her fingers flying delicately as if conjuring Shostakovich from a Steinway. Schroeder sits down at the unit next to her and she speaks without turning from the screen.

– You want a picture or what?

Not French. Irish. Sounds like Galway.

– Do you have any?

– None that you're ever going to see.

– That's a damn shame.

And still she keeps her eyes on the screen, her fingers moving across the keys even faster now, like a hailstorm on a tin roof.

– You've been staring at my arse from the traffic lights at the top of O'Connell Street.

– You noticed?

– I'm used to it. I've got the best arse in Dublin.

Schroeder sneezes.

– I think you might be right.

Her hair, held in place by the beret, is arranged to hang down loose over one side of her face. It's glamour of the old school and in whatever flashes Schroeder gets of her eyes they seem like backlit emeralds, as if her mind, her personality, her very self is directly behind them – permanently and powerfully on. Shamelessly he watches her and yet she continues to type and scroll. And as her fingers fly, her tongue begins to tease her top lip – a tongue pointed and long and capable of anything. This is the sort of danger Schroeder is more than willing to embrace.

– You're a very fast typist.

– Is that your best line?

– Well you *are*. An extremely fast typist.

– My thoughts don't come out of my mouth, she says. They come out of my fingers. Brain to fingertip. Direct. Nothing happens in between.

Schroeder logs on, a risky business in a place like this, but he wants to prolong his time with her. He half reads the news headlines. A bomb has just gone off in Rome. Just minutes ago in fact. At exactly the time he was reaching for a weapon that he didn't have. Seventeen dead on the Via Veneto. More self-immolations in China. Twenty-two more species extinct in the Amazon, a chemical hoax causing commuter chaos in Prague and the Élysée Palace finally admitting that French Marines stationed in Antarctica have been using live penguins as fuel.

– You writing a novel? Schroeder asks.

– Nobody writes novels.

– They write novels in Canada.

– God bless Canada.

– So what are you doing?

– Bits and pieces.

– You'll get yourself killed walking around out there.

– Danger sharpens the mind. It's a form of meditation. It produces a keen sense of agitation. Then I come in here and I write.

– An interesting technique.

– Technique is everything.

– Are you a journalist?

– Designer.

– Clothes?

– Pyramids.

– OK. Well that's certainly an ancient profession.

– Musclemeds over on Middle Abbey Street. I build pyramids of plastic boxes in the window. High protein food for bodybuilders. I just pile the stuff up. In pyramids. And whenever somebody comes in I sell a box and then I fix the pyramid again.

– So you design *and* build pyramids?

She chuckles and Schroeder begins to taste an old confidence again.

– So who's minding the pyramids now?

– Nobody. I just close the place up whenever I feel like it and I come here instead.

– What about the bodybuilders?

– Fuck 'em.

Then Schroeder chuckles. He likes her style. She's the beautiful, wild-card stranger and perhaps there's a little redemption in the darkness after all? An exotic chocolate egg in return for all the Lenten grief.

– I thought perhaps you were a stripper.

– Is that good?

– When you turned into Fleet Street I mean . . . an exotic dancer I mean.

– Sorry to disappoint you. Although I know all the moves.

Schroeder sneezes hard three times in a row and pretends to check his email. All the usual stuff. Updates, circulars, threat assessments and traffic info on King's visit – details of road closures, restrictions and information on how long the airports will be shut. In the middle of it all he notices one from Walton. He's not thinking straight and foolishly he opens it. One simple nudge and there on the screen is a clip (with audio) of an orgasmic blonde in full *Sheela-na-Gig* display. It's Jakki Jack and yes, on this vivid evidence, she really is a screamer. And in this place, alone with the *chanteuse*, it's the most terrible sound. Chantal looks across at the screen and then at Schroeder. Schroeder looks at Chantal and then at the screen. There's nothing he can do but click it off and stare at his feet. Chantal sweeps the hair from her face.

– Something you want to tell me?

– I'm really sorry, says Schroeder. It's my friend. He thinks this kind of thing is funny.

– Hilarious.

– Well, it's not my thing.

– And it was all going so well too.

– No. Look. It's this guy I know. He's in a wheelchair. I think he's an addict. Honestly. And she's famous apparently. Estonian.

– I think you'll find she's Ukrainian.

And with that she logs off with extraordinary speed and before Schroeder can think of anything intelligent to say, she's off into the light. He sits there stunned. He has blown it completely. Or at least Walton has, thanks to his wailing pornstar from Kiev. By now Chantal will be freewheeling towards Trinity, relieved at her very lucky escape from the perv about to pounce. And he doesn't even have her actual name.

On the blinding plaza some kind of new chemical murk has descended and even the Goths are clamping on their surgical masks. To get in out of the stench Schroeder heads for a cramped Dame Street dive, there to curse his luck and wait for what seems like some internal incendiary to explode in his guts. His hangover is back. Headache, nausea and all the trimmings. He could kill Walton for this. He was almost there! With Chantal the *chanteuse* and her desolate songs of old Pigalle. Nothing for it now but a few angry jolts of hooch. He's about four shots in when Roark seems to burst up through the floorboards like a bamboo rat.

– Hello horse. Fancy shooting yourself at all?

– What have you got?

– Glock. Old school. Every home should have one.

– Stolen?

– Jays, clean as a whistle.

– How much?

– Cash only. 150. Dollars are best.

Schroeder peels off three fifties and pockets the pistol.

I appreciate that there are elements of the thriller now creeping into the narrative – a femme fatale, a gun, etc. – and indeed there will be more heightened scenes soon, but again I refer you to my opening remarks. This is not a thriller in any shape or form. I am simply telling the truth as best as I can by employing the methods outlined at the get-go. And again I repeat, this is not about the assassination of Richard Rutledge Barnes King. This is about dysfunction, anhedonia and perhaps, if I can possibly find a place for it, redemption. There seems to be an absolute insistence on it as far as publication is concerned. And if these pages are to get out at all, it will have to be there somewhere, presumably at the end. I don't believe in it but there it is.

ELEVEN

THE DART IS BLACK with people and Schroeder cordons himself off immediately, securing his privacy and hoping that the Murakami will get him as far as Grand Canal Dock / *Dug na Canálach Móire*. But as the city passes by he cannot concentrate and he gazes hard into the high-rise huddles rolling past – the flimsy Dublin-sized skyscrapers where citizens sip wine and twist nightly on futons, listening to their neighbours floss through thin apartment walls. Urban culchies, Schroeder calls them, for he is the most terrible snob when it comes to these apartment dwellers, the interchangeable units of the corporate scheme of things. I know what he's thinking, for it's a very old whine of my own that their ancestors bred in these very same high-rises at the end of the 20th century and at the very beginning of this one, to produce this slow-witted host of drones – identical generations of headhunted cliff-dwellers, auks and puffins, huddling together for warmth and company of sorts.

And yet Schroeder envies them their simplicity, their anonymity and their endless bored promiscuity. Most of all he covets their lack of fear. They do, for a living, whatever it is people do in places like the Financial Centre or any of the other little Manhattans that reach once more into the skies along the quays – redesignated business zones that still look exactly like architects' models, their windy thoroughfares desolate but for the odd figure strategically placed. And then, at close of business, evacuated by Metros and walkways, the auks and the puffins head back to their colonies and abandon all to the sewer rats and the wild cats which eat them. And yet they all seem somehow contented. Well turned out and happy in their own skins. I know what he's thinking. I always know what he's thinking.

I also know what he's doing. He's distracting himself. He's meeting Claude Butler today and he's diverting himself with rage, imagining himself spraying the windows as he passes. Glass shattering. Plaster flying. Culchies dropping. An old sub-machine from the

Raoul Walsh movies. No use popping off the Glock at a target quite so big as this. A question of scale surely. And of suitability. For these people have destroyed the city. Every hotel, restaurant and pub built in Dublin for decades has been designed in their image – without taste, without soul, without history and without real Guinness. And all to facilitate their dullard vows of ambitious obedience. Not one of them knows anything about anything. Not even the slightest clue of the ghosts which surround them as they sleep. De Valera's men armed to the teeth and crouched behind thumping bags of flour in Boland's Mill.

If a revolution was to happen these days, Dev would be as well to give the Mill a miss and maybe go for some superpub in Stoney-batter. Not much point in Connolly smashing out the windows of the General Post Office to take potshots at soldiers all sandbagged in front of lingerie stores – the heads of dummies dressed as porno-nurses exploding behind them. They'd be better advised to go capture Chucho's of Grafton Street or maybe the Bank of Shanghai. Pearse might read the Declaration at the Mountjoy Mall, from the top of a jammed escalator. Or, more symbolically, he might actually be on the escalator, ascending through the ranks of shoppers descending on either side of him with their giant bags from GAP.

Schroeder, God bless him, gets worked up by things like this. He once caught his bedside alarm flashing 19:16 and he huffed for a week because the reference was lost on Francesca. She knows no history either. A trait which situates her on her very own planet and makes her so very good at her job. But that's all for later. Our present scenario sees a somewhat stressed Schroeder arriving in the city centre by DART in order to meet Claude Butler from across the street. And as the train pulls into the bright green and yellow conservatory of Pearse Station / *Stáisiún na bPiarsach*, Schroeder refocuses on the very thoughts he has just been trying to banish. Thoughts of Claude. Of priestly people. Of Holy People. God's chosen people. Come in Father and have a cup of tea.

Somewhere between Pearse and Tara Street / *Sraid na Teamhrach* a dark palm with inky lifelines appears at Schroeder's chin. It's a Roma woman asking for money with a desperate pleading, as if she urgently needs her fortune told as much as any clink of loose coins. Cash has been illegal for years but it hasn't stopped her asking.

– No change, Schroeder mutters.

She asks again and, not even looking at her this time, Schroeder shakes his head.

– No.

He doesn't mind giving a few illicit dollars to the Roma women now and again, or to the limbless vets lined up in Talbot Street, but not every day of the week. Dublin has made him cold (made everybody cold) but why should *he* feel bad? This woman came to him with *her* hand out. *She* to him. Yes, there was a time he would have given her something and made a point of smiling but not any more. He has hardened like an artery. Miserable in the meantime, he's like Frankenstein's monster. Make me happy, he thinks, and I shall again be virtuous.

He couldn't find the letter anywhere this morning but he's pretty sure it said three o'clock. And so he'll show up on time, get it done and get it over. He'll wish Claude well and hope he clears off back to Liverpool and forgets all about him for another decade or so.

Tara Street / *Sraid na Teamhrach* is a crush. Young dopes from all over the European Alliance are massed at every train door, at the top and bottom of every escalator and at every entrance and exit. Dumb-eyed youth adrift with no notion of thoroughfare are hanging onto each other, hands hooked in each other's pockets, talking shite on their cells and clogging up the station with their vacant selves. Schroeder swears through gritted teeth but all they do is stare, their rucksacks and backpacks and bumbags taking a violent pummelling from Schroeder's angry progress. Like the stupidest herd of stupid calves they just gaze in silence as he ploughs through them for breath. Clear the fuckers out. Hurleys and baseball bats. Bus the bastards to the airport and render them high into the clouds over Europe. Whatever it takes.

– Fucksake, would yis fucking move!

The ticket collector is Scandinavian and he has a way of saying thank you that surprises and cheers Schroeder slightly but when he finally pushes his way out into the glare he's hit by the full reek of the Liffey and all the airborne poisons that make the river gloop like platinum. A small boy tap-dances, bottle-tops jammed in his runners, and Schroeder's mood plummets further. A man playing a hornpipe on a concertina stares with sadness at the passing legs of citizens just landed, in no mood for music or the open sea. Addicts trail off for methadone on Pearse Street, named for An Piarsach, aforementioned executed leader of 1916, son of an English stone mason and monumental sculptor of Great Brunswick Street, not far and parallel. Gangs of scurrying hoppers hiss *hashish!* and then come the offers of coke and heroin and Schroeder pretends not to hear. He knows never to raise his eyes from the ground. Not at a deadly junction like this. A black hole. A death-trap.

Another deep breath and he launches himself into the multitude on Burgh Quay, named for Margaret Amelia Burgh, wife of John Foster, speaker of the Irish House of Commons and now the con-stipated gateway to the city, and begins to dodge his way westwards. A fat woman with a two-seater buggy crammed full of tinned dog food seems to have the sidewalk all to herself and everyone has to go around her, taking their chances with the traffic swinging around the one-way system. I know he hates this section of the quays. Everybody does. It's clogged and stinking. Dirtbags, pushers, bandits and the odd brace of cops with their sad-eyed, black and tan dogs.

Across the Liffey, Schroeder sees the phantom Spire shoot cloud-wards. It was of course inevitable that, sooner or later, like the Pillar before it, it would be felled. Not that anybody cared. And sure what was it anyway? A status symbol? A folly? A vanity project built for the Millennium at a time of crazy prophecies from madmen who, as it turned out, were not too far off the mark? So little remains now of the Dublin Schroeder was born into and, in mockery of it all, he blesses himself as he passes the caged parking lot where the old

Abbey Theatre used to be – closed for lack of money twenty-five years ago – a skeletal reminder that Dublin is now neither the second city of the Empire nor the first of the Republic. That in truth this city is just another hub of global dealing – a worn-out commercial capital of a state which is serially bought and sold with one treacherous stab of a keypad after another. A place so deep in debt that all sovereignty has been gone for years. A country which should have changed its very name back in 2010. Rebranded itself in the hopes that the world might have forgotten the details by now. My suggestion back then had been Anhedonia. And it still is.

I watch Schroeder cross O'Connell Street, named for the Liberator, formerly Sackville Street, named for Lionel Cranfield Sackville, Duke of Dorset and Lord Lieutenant of Ireland. He checks himself when a man in a bright red anorak steps out to confront the traffic. Everyone immediately hesitates. An anorak in these desert temperatures immediately marks the man out as a danger and a red anorak (with the hood up) even more so. A bus bouncing southwards over the bridge is refusing, on principle, to slow down and horns are blasted and arms are raised. The man in the anorak stands his ground and pulls at his hair. The bus rumbles on. The driver is getting out of the main strip as fast as he can and nothing will stand in his way, especially some crazy-head wearing a girl's coat. Only at the very last moment does the man twirl his body aside so that the bus can roar on in solemn triumph towards Trinity. It's a very close thing.

Dickhead! somebody yells. But the red anorak just takes a wild look at the sky and wanders on, all traffic now completely stopped, warily watching the man and waiting for his next move. When he finally stumbles onto the opposite sidewalk and vanishes into the crowd Schroeder knows that there goes someone who won't last the day. And Dublin gets going again. Cities are always full of unpleasantries. So many that they simply have to be ignored. If you don't step over people you'll never get where you're going. America has known this for a very long time. And we're no different here.

Schroeder still has half an hour to ready himself and he decides on College Green. If he can find a place which isn't playing retro Austrian techno he'll settle himself and rehearse his response to whatever confession Claude needs him to hear. And whatever it is, Schroeder tells himself, it will not become his problem. He angles towards Purcell's and takes a seat at the bar to sip at a bowl of soup. But he can't relax and soon he's playing with the salt and pepper, clacking the wooden cellars against each other and all the time getting more and more uneasy. A thick Belgian beer goes down well enough – solid, treacly and strong – and with five minutes to spare he pays up and walks back into the chaos of College Green.

Some kind of ruction is happening at the main Trinity checkpoint. Voices are raised but everything ceases very suddenly when a shot is fired, presumably into the air. Probably some student late for an exam has just been too lippy with a corporal. Or perhaps some pap has tried to steal the soul of Princess King. Nobody hurt but gunshot even so. What a people we have become. So terminal now that we're beyond even the salvage of poets. This is Ireland's oldest university after all and there's gunfire in the broad, blank middle of the day. It's just as well Schroeder doesn't work there any more. With so many soldiers around he'd probably be dead by now. These days, when he's drunk he can draw far too much attention to himself and such public shows of emotion can have all sorts of consequences. The times demand, more than anything, that nobody ever makes a sudden move and barking at the wrong dog can get you arrested, sectioned or worse. All such flare-ups need to be firmly, as I like to put it, nipped in the buddleia.

Of course it was the drinking that lost him the job, although it was all done very politely under the cover of mass redundancies. Schroeder was by no means the biggest mess on the staff but his tutorials tended to attract too much comment and even complaint. Consistently attacking the very canon he was supposed to be teaching hardly seemed appropriate, and being a one-novel writer, and one failed novel writer at that, his remarks often seemed bitter and self-regarding. His superiors had their spies in situ and word got back on a daily basis. He was warned twice, then dismissed. A negative presence they said. Bad for student morale.

Anyway, he arrives at the hotel at three on the nose. A crawling dump this past twenty years, Redding's still retains sad traces of when it was a much swankier joint, popular with actors and pop stars and always stuffed in the early evenings with young lawyers on the make. It's a strange choice for Claude, although he probably imagines that it's just Schroeder's kind of place. As it happens, Schroeder hasn't been here since it changed hands all those years ago and they started encouraging the soccer fans by putting TV screens in the bar.

There's no such thing as a quiet room in Redding's – it's almost a boast in fact – but at this time of day, with the guests mostly unconscious, the place is empty but for a bartender who has one eye on Schroeder and the other on a screen where a poker game is being played out by virtual steamboat gamblers who don't strike Schroeder as having very much to lose. There's no sign of Claude and so Schroeder (taking a chance on the ice) orders a vodka on the rocks and sits in the corner with much on his mind and a clear view of the door.

Claude arrives fifteen minutes late, looking much the same as he always did, same red cheeks, dressed like some engineering student uncertain of any colour beyond grey. He's wearing the same soft shoes he always wore in civilian life. Cream coloured. Standard-issue harmless. He might no longer be a priest but he's still the essence of folk-mass dull – the whole ensemble indicating someone who has never heard of The Clash and wouldn't like them even if he did. He walks towards Schroeder with uneasy speed, his hand already out and squeezing the air in front of him. He's sweating heavily. Same mammy's haircut now silvering at the sides.

– I'm very sorry I'm late, he says, there was a poor man in distress and I had to assist him.

– Wearing a red anorak, was he?

– How did you know?

Typical! Claude's obsessive and insistent charity had always made Schroeder queasy and here again he finds his brain curling up at the very idea of it. Claude helping himself to the needy as ever. Claude of Assisi ladling soup, conversing with junkies, visiting sick people he doesn't even know – all essential work experience on the CV of any aspiring priest. But because Schroeder has always regarded Claude's priestly lark as no more than a giant sidestepping of life, he has always found these endless good works more than a little repellent. The nightly excursions with the steaming saucepans no more than an excuse not to deal with his own contemporaries – man, woman or beast – especially woman or beast.

– Poor man. Indeed. In a very bad way.

Claude perches on the edge of the seat, his back straight and his hands clasped in his lap like some principal of a girls' school. Again, here is a signal that he's not like the other boys. Not for him any interest in cool posturings or the boorish sexual energies of men with their instinctive sense of shape and relaxation. I am utterly sexless, he is saying on repeat. I am quite beyond it. My dear people, I don't live in your world. I am merely here to minister to it. Have some warm soup and let me give you my coat. I don't need it anyway. I have another one and it too is grey and cheap and out of date. Nobody will ever admire you in a garment like this, but that's not what life's about, my poor impoverished son. True happiness is only to be found in blah, blah, blah. Drink up, there's a good fellow. It'll do you good. God Bless. God Willing. God Spares Us.

– An unfortunate man, he says. I suspect he had been hit by a car. Didn't speak English. Didn't seem to know where he lived. Didn't seem to know who he was or even where he was. Anything. He was very lost, the poor man.

Only just arrived in Dublin and Claude is already at the old schtick. The crazy in the red anorak. In a city of millions Claude zooms in on the anorak man, the same man who for Schroeder had provided little more than a sad diversion. And wouldn't you just know that Claude the Good would be the one to risk knife and syringe to help him out? Sickening. The inevitability of it. The consistency of his apparently selfless ways. And of course the shame he likes to heap on those who consistently fail to act.

– Thank you very much for meeting me, he says. It has been so long. You look well.

And Schroeder is thinking to himself, get it over with, Claude. Just tell me what's on your mind. Confess it all. Do your worst and let me go again. Release me back into the wild. Back to my hedonistic disaster of a life. Shallow and empty, yes, but at least it's shot through with the actual pleasures and pains of this Earth. Which is, after all, even if you refuse to accept it, the actual place where we all live and die.

– So Claude, what can I do for you?

Claude holds his knees. Lines web out from his eyes. He seems exhausted. Spent. Pig-eyed. Eyebrows brittle as twigs.

I have imagined this conversation many times, he says. So let me see. Perhaps I should begin with when I left Meath and went to Peru. I said that I wanted to make a difference and you said, if you remember, that I might as well because I had made no difference in Meath. Except of course you used a profanity. Well I have to say that wounded me very much. It hurt me for my friend to say such a thing.

Schroeder nods.

– OK. I'm sorry about that. I shouldn't have said it. I didn't mean anything by it.

– Well, I forgive you.

– Anything else?

– You have always thought little of me. And I know that you still do. I'm not like you. You think I'm an inferior man.

– Claude, I never said that.

– Well, in any case, perhaps I'm more of a man than you think. The reason I left the priesthood is because I fell in love.

– Well, that's your business, Claude. Nothing to do with me.

– I failed in my duty as a priest. My order is still a celibate one and when love entered the room it was my duty to flee and I didn't. I stayed there in love's ambience. And the young lady in question, she fell in love with me too. We met and we talked and we met again and soon I was deeply in love with her and I had crossed into a place forbidden to me. I had fallen in love with her and she had fallen in love with me. What do you make of that for a turn-up for the books?

Schroeder shifts in his seat. The caring bog-soft voice that only priests can perfect is making him seasick. *Love's ambience*, wherever he got that from.

– Well that's all great, Schroeder says. Congratulations.

But then Claude suddenly grips the underside of his seat, turning instantly snappy and hard.

– No congratulation! None! I let her down. I withdrew from the love. Finally I did flee, in accordance with my vows, and I hurt her very badly. She was distraught and she plunged into a terrible grief. I might have helped her but, as I was the cause of it, I had to keep away.

– Yes of course.

– She had given me her heart. As they say. And I tried to hand it back as gently as I could but there is no good way to do such a thing. It's terrible. It makes you want to die. A terrible thing to wish for.

– These things happen.

Two hookers take a seat at the bar. They're smiling like weasels and Schroeder doesn't want to be there when they make their offer.

– I'll have to head soon, Claude. Would you like a quick drink or something?

– Tea please.

– I don't think they could manage drinkable tea in here. You want juice of some kind. Or a soda?

Claude shakes his head as if trying to loose some obstruction in his throat.

– Monica. A primary school teacher. She never recovered. Her family wrote to me. Her brother actually threatened me with physical violence. But there was nothing I could do for her. As a man or as a priest there was nothing I could do but remove myself yet further.

– That's the way it goes, Claude. Water perhaps?

Claude isn't listening.

– Some time later I left the priesthood. If I could do nothing for poor Monica I would do something for the world in which we both lived. There was much prayer and meditation. Do you forgive me? God has forgiven me but do you? Do you forgive me my sin?

Schroeder rolls the vodka around in his mouth and swallows hard.

– I'm not sure what your sin is exactly.

– Do you forgive me?

– For what?

– I need you to absolve me.

– You don't need me to absolve you. This is entirely your business. This has nothing to do with me whatsoever.

Claude's eyes narrow and Schroeder recognises that words are needed urgently. A formula however fraudulent is required. He must give Claude what he needs.

– Yes. Of course I forgive you. For all of it.

And Claude smiles.

– Really? You do?

– Yes. Of course. *Ego te absolvo* and all that.

Claude assumes a lopsided, lemon juice expression.

– I'm glad. So glad. So happy about that. Thank you. A friend's forgiveness. It must surely be the greatest.

– Good.

– You really forgive me?

– Yes. I really forgive you.

– Fantastic.

– Well there it is.

Claude claps his hands.

– Do you remember that project we did? At school. The little egret and the shelduck?

The two girls make their move. The more appealing of the two does all the talking while the other one chews her thumb.

– You guys want company?

– No thanks, says Schroeder. We're just having a private meeting.

– You sure about that?

– Quite sure.

– What about your friend?

Claude is staring hard at his own left shoulder.

– He's OK, Schroeder says. But thanks anyway.

– My friend will blow him for twenty.

– No. Really. Thank you. He's quite alright.

– He doesn't look it.

– Thanks again but no thanks.

– Well if you change your mind . . .

The girls return to their perches and Schroeder tries to break the jangly spell they have left behind. He orders another drink.

– So how have you been otherwise?

– I had a little setback there. A scare. But everything is fine.

– Good.

– I have no fear of anything now. Not a thing.

Schroeder looks at Claude and wonders how he can be afraid of nothing when he himself is afraid of even the word *scare*. All those words terrify him. Bowel. Prostate. Oesophageal. *Testicular*, in particular, might, in other circumstances, be quite a beautiful word like *funicular* or *crepuscular*, but *prostate* is altogether ugly like *apostate* or *prostrate*. It reeks of evil, bad news and Holy Orders.

– But you're OK now?

– Right as rain.

– Good.

It was Canon Boran who first explained to the class how a young man might be ordained a priest, demonstrating the procedure by lying on the floor between the desks just as the postulant would *prostrate* himself on the day – lying there in a gesture of submission. Prostrating oneself. It sounded obscene, especially in front of a bishop, cancerous black spots spreading for all to see on the soles of your shoes as you press your innocent nose to the marble.

Schroeder had been cruel about Claude's ordination because, to him, it was all a big joke. Some kind of grim launch as a bottle of holy water was smashed against the side of Claude's empty head and he was shoved off to his parish in Meath. With Schroeder it was always the bitter word because he could never forgive Claude his weakness. Forgive him that smile on his face in the toilets of St. Gavin's. And now he can't forgive him his sins, such as they are, even if he wanted to. And in any case, unlike with Claude, the forgiveness of sins has never been a personal boast.

– And you have no fear of anything?

– Not a thing.

– Nothing at all?

– No.

Claude presses his hands together as if he's about to consecrate the table between them. Melchisedech Claude with his powers to say Mass, forgive sins, bless, preach and sanctify – all subject to the authority of a bishop who looked like Peter Lorre and to whom he promised canonical obedience on the flat of his face. Bishop Lorre beaming as if conducting the very power of Heaven through the point of his mitre and out through the porcelain tips of his fingernails.

– And what are you afraid of? he asks.

Schroeder is not getting into any of this. Not with Claude. He's not about to tell Claude that sometimes it's as if his very blood is on the boil and that the ingredients which are a-bubble within him, apart from the chemical components of old alcohol and drugs, are the very cells of fear itself. He feels them travel deep inside him, moving on the high-speed lines of his unknowable circulatory system, attacking him by the second, sometimes with tiny anxieties, sometimes with actual terror. No. Not with Claude. This is much too serious for that.

– I'm not here for counselling, Claude. You wanted to see me, remember.

– I've met a lot of damaged men.

– I'm not fucking damaged!

Claude blinks and inhales sharply. Schroeder downs the vodka and rattles the shrinking beads of ice in the glass.

– It was good to see you again Claude. I hope things work out.

– So am I forgiven?

– Yes! Yes! Forgiven. Absolutely.

– Good. All is forgiven.

– OK then.

– I have a job now. A most interesting job.

– Good.

Claude grabs his hand.

– I'm about God's business.

Schroeder pictures Paddy Viera and wrings his hand loose again.

– You must know this. You must know what I'm doing. God wants me to continue to preach his Word.

– That's all good, Claude. Now I really have to go. Sorry.

– This is very important.

– Important to you maybe but to be perfectly honest, Claude . . .

Claude jumps to his feet and, pointing at the ceiling, he declares, But this involves God!

The bartender cocks his head. The hookers cross their legs again.

– Sit down, Claude, for fucksake and keep your voice down.

Claude sits down and leans in close.

– I'm an evangelist now. God has a purpose for me. He wants me to make contact with the powerful men and women of this world and bring them towards the path of His love. I'm an old-fashioned evangelist. I write letters. I write epistles. I write to all the great leaders of the world.

– That's great Claude. That'll keep you busy.

– Every day. Without fail. I write my letters.

– I don't suppose you get many answers?

– You'd be surprised. On my wall I have many photographs which have been sent in reply. Some are signed. *Best wishes,* etc. In the person's own actual handwriting. His Holiness Pope Michael sent a picture of the Holy Family.

– It must have been a slow day in the Holy See.

– I'm like an advisor. That's my job. A *spiritual* advisor of course. I know nothing about economics or defence. Can you imagine? I'd have the place ruined.

– Me neither.

Schroeder has tried. He has cooperated. He has played ball. But he will not linger for this.

– Goodbye, Claude. I really do have to go now.

– Some of these people are good men. Honourable men. Women too of course. Some want to end all wars and I am helping them do it. I give guidance. A letter every day. I feel that all good men are open to the Word of God. We can all be redeemed.

Schroeder thinks again of Paddy Viera. The lifeless eyes. The spider-long fingers.

– So people keep telling me.

– Are you a believer? In redemption?

– Only in novels, Claude. Publishers insist on it.

– I'll pray hard for you.

– Goodbye, Claude.

As Schroeder leaves Redding's, he turns to see his childhood friend sandwiched between the two hookers. He's wearing the same gormless face he wore on the day he was ordained. The hookers are stroking his arms and blowing in his ears. They're telling him they have a room upstairs and that they'll do things to him that will take the eyes out of his head. He seems helpless. Stupid. Lost. He's at their mercy now and Schroeder watches as they drag him away. He doesn't intervene. It's nothing to do with him. Not this. And not now. But Schroeder also realises that the sight of his old friend being coffined in the elevator by two vampires isn't the only reason he never wants to see him again. Claude is deranged. As mad as a cut snake.

All of the above, indeed much of the foregoing, may at times seem unnecessary. But this, as I keep repeating, is not some script buffed to perfection to meet the rules of some formulaic plotline. Not one single word and not one single scenario so far is aimed with any accuracy at some overwhelming coitus in the third act. So don't expect it. It will not happen unless it does. For what I am dealing with here, as I have stated from the very beginning, is the actual truth. This is about real people, real events, real thoughts and real behaviour. And do any of us believe that real people ever act as demanded by the conventions of a novel or a script? Of course they don't. And furthermore, the characters I am dealing with here are in many ways unknown, even to themselves, and so my refusal to invent or reinvent them is steadfast. At least in the normal sense of invention. For the root of invention is "discover" and, yes, invention in that sense is ongoing. I'm discovering the thing. I'm discovering it all.

TWELVE

Two DAYS LATER and I discover Schroeder at a sidewalk café on Wicklow Street. Solemn in the shade of an awning, he's handling the cruets before him and savouring the fumes of anise which rise like inspiration from the marble. He's just about to start scribbling on the inside cover of the Murakami when he spies Chantal, in a tight leather jacket, wheeling her bicycle diagonally across from the parking lot and coming straight for him. She's wearing Wayfarer shades and the red-curtain sheen of her hair is heavy and wet as if she's just out of the shower.

– Well, she says. If it isn't the creepy guy.

Schroeder is thrown.

– You look like you're just out of the shower, he says.

– There you go. I rest my case.

Chantal chains her bicycle to the trunk of a rusting lamp post and Schroeder notices the crimson shine of her fingernails. All moulded perfection beneath the smooth, zipped sheen of leather, she sits down beside him and orders an espresso.

– So what gives, creepy guy?

– Are you following me? Schroeder asks.

– You wish.

– What's your name?

– Margaret.

– Seriously?

– You got a problem with Margaret?

– I've been calling you Chantal.

She seems to weigh the name in her mouth.

– I like it. Mind if I use it?

– All yours.

– You gonna buy me a coffee or what?

– Sorry about the other day.

The green eyes flash.

– I'm a big girl.

She unzips her jacket and Schroeder runs the movie of the lost hours to come. Mid-afternoon suntrap, bedroom curtains drawn. All-nighters on a dozen pillows and the purple dawn. Lush life. Sleep until lunchtime with that delicious, physical fatigue one can almost swallow and breathe. He tries to channel some blood flow back to his brain.

– Margaret what?

– Lynch.

– As in mob hangings?

– As in the wine.

– Good answer.

– You been in the Ninth Circle of Temple Bar lately?

– That was a definite once off.

– You did good. I was impressed.

– I liked your theory about the danger stimulating you.

– Did you indeed?

– I mean the writing.

– Oh, it does that too.

– Does what?

– It turns me on.

– What does?

– Danger. It turns me on.

– What do you mean?

– I mean sexually.

– Well, that's a new one.

– No it's not. And what turns you on, Anton Schroeder?

– When a woman calls me by my full name.

– And why do you think that is, Anton Schroeder?

– I don't know. It seems proprietorial somehow. Inappropriately so.

– Interesting. And there was me, Anton Schroeder, thinking it was just the zip.

There is nothing I can do here. This woman, whoever she is, is much too skilled and he is utterly lost in her now. Yes, her Left Bank body is an increasing delight he wants to take home and unwrap, but there's much more to it. In her novel company all the anxieties and humiliations of recent weeks seem to shed like dirty clothes. He takes a deep breath and allows himself to plunge into what looks like sheer possibility.

– Do you think we might go for a coffee sometime?

– We're having one now.

– I mean go for a drink some night?

Chantal looks at her fingernails and smiles.

– It's not a good time to be out in the evenings.

– It doesn't have to be in the city. We could go somewhere quiet.

Chantal flicks her hair.

– Bit too much on my plate at present.

Schroeder makes a clown's sad face.

– No, she says, it's not like that at all. In fact I think we'll be seeing plenty of each other.

– You do?

– It's starting to look that way. Yes.

With Schroeder's pen, she scribbles on a napkin, folds it in four and pushes it across the table. When Schroeder reaches for it she slaps her hand on his.

– Not here.

– All a bit cloak and dagger isn't it?

– Well, at this stage it's mostly cloak.

She squeezes Schroeder's hand very slightly but breaks away suddenly when two truckloads of soldiers roar up Exchequer Street. The trucks empty and the soldiers (Irish) trot to each side of the street and begin to seal the place off. Chantal stands, zips up her jacket and nods to the napkin in Schroeder's hand.

– Put that away, like a good man.

Schroeder closes his fist around the napkin and pushes his chair back.

– You sure about that drink?

– I'll be seeing you.

Then she bends over, puts both her hands low on his hips and kisses him on the cheek – an electrifying brush of spearmint breath shooting across his ear.

– Anton Schroeder, she says, I think that really is a gun in your pocket.

Schroeder sneezes three times as he watches Chantal unlock the bicycle, step sideways into it and steady herself on the kerb. He is now actually trembling a little as she looks over her shoulder with a final burlesque smile before diving off into the traffic, her sleek leather back up and down like a dolphin in the waves. The soldiers are shouting now but Schroeder just stands there hypnotized like some willing stooge who knows well that Chantal's seductive performance (whatever it is) isn't quite over yet and that soon he'll be scoffing raw onions and pretending to be Elvis.

The soldiers herd everyone along the sidewalk and into Grafton Street, named for Charles Fitzroy, 2nd Duke of Grafton, wayward son of the illegitimate son of Charles II. And from there they are marched in total silence in a slow parade towards the Green. All except Schroeder who ducks out at Duke Street, named for the very same reprobate, slipping the throng and exiting left through the Garda checkpoint with some improvised yarn about diabetes, low sugar and what would happen if he went hypo. He needs the chocolateria on Dawson Street, he says, and they let him pass.

Once safely at the far end of Duke Street he stops in front of a liquor store and unfolds the napkin now all damp and inky in his palm. He's hoping for a phone number accompanied by some provocative scribble just to keep him on edge until the next time – accomplished tease that Chantal most certainly is – and yes there is indeed a number. But the message which comes with it, in backward leaning capitals, is something he has to read three times before it goes in.

YOU MAY BE IN DANGER. USE THIS NUMBER.

The cell shudders on cue, hard in his groin. The Galwegian voice again. Chantal.

– Don't do anything stupid, she says.

Schroeder looks up and down the street.

– Where are you?

She hangs up and Schroeder crosses the street and sits on the sill of a store specializing in cod history for tourists – family trees, maps and coats of arms. He reads the note again and he thinks about that day in the ruins of Temple Bar and suddenly he's not quite so sure about who exactly is following who. He feels as if the scenery is being shifted all around him, as if props are being silently carried off stage and replaced by pieces from an altogether different production. In the window he sees a trinity of helmeted heads in profile proper, visors snapped closed like space warriors. He gazes at their sinister duplication. The motto reads *Avise la Fin*. The clan is O'Cinneide. A second later the cell shudders once more.

– Fucksake, Chantal, what's going on?

– Chantal? Very fancy.

Francesca. She has forgotten a pair of boots and wants Schroeder to leave them for her on the doorstep. He hangs up quickly and tries to compute. Francesca calls back.

– Don't you dare hang up on me!

– Not a good time, Fran.

– Chantal, eh? You've always wanted a Chantal.

– Seriously. This is not a good time.

– Is she French?

– I don't know anything about her.

– You don't hang about, do you?

– Look Fran, call me later.

– Chantal what?

– I don't know.

– Where does she live?

– I don't know that either.

– Where does she work?

– I have to go.

Half an hour (and several drinks) later Schroeder is standing among the giant iron bins of Middle Abbey Street. Musclemeds is locked and grilled and even though there are three of Chantal's bespoke pyramids in the window, the place looks as though it hasn't been open in years. Either that or Chantal doesn't take much pride in her work. The place is a dump set in a dump, and Middle Abbey Street, as usual, reeks of danger and worse.

Go home, Schroeder. Go home.

And he's just about to leave when he senses a sudden sun's eclipse. A shadow rises behind him and he turns to see a man the size of Croagh Patrick, his acned neck suggesting a beefhead out to score illegal protein within the Musclemed pyramids of Chantal. But when he makes a bouncer's gesture with his outstretched arms, Schroeder knows that the man has only one true purpose here. It's a classic move which signifies that Schroeder should either move away from the area immediately or have his neck snapped like a stale baguette. Schroeder steps backwards, then sideways, like a man about to convert a try and, once satisfied that he's on his way, the giant turns and walks silently into the traffic, his back obscuring the full width of a passing truck.

Jump on the LUAS, Schroeder. Go home.

But Schroeder isn't done yet. Chantal says that she works in this place and yet, evidently, nobody works here at all. And he realises that she has directed him here for a purpose and that he must now find out what this place actually is. And if he really is in danger, then he must confront it. Seek it out. Bring it on. So speaketh the Pernod and the Presbutex. And so he finds his way into Musclemeds through the old Scientology building about five doors down – the first in a parade of derelict shells without any kind of front door. Everything smells of dead cats and carbon and, once inside, he walks up a ribcage of stairs which creak like a long funeral beneath his feet. He hauls himself up into the attic and then makes his way back through the roof-spaces – a well known squatters' trick, not that he's ever tried it out until now. And not that, come to think of it, he has ever broken into a building either, and certainly not with a pistol in his pants.

The roofs have been opened and stripped like the hull of a salvaged ship and the fragile space is full of sky and pigeons, their nests, their carcasses and their shit. So many slates are missing that Schroeder gets a terrifying sense of being adrift, as if he's actually walking in the sky itself and that he'll be blown out into the street at any minute. It's worse up here than in any basement dungeon and yet, whether it be *déjà vu* or the fragmented remembrances of old nightmare, much of it seems recognisable. Below him, what seems like miles below, the sounds of the city are so intense and clear, it might be the exotic audio of Beirut or Bangalore.

Once directly above Musclemeds, he lowers himself through the ceiling and drops to the floor – the thud of his landing seeming to make the whole building shake. Now locked inside the bleached whalebones of the street, the Glock obscenely in his hand, he walks down three flights of stairs and with every creak he squeezes the gun a little tighter, expecting at any moment a web of ricochets to strap him to the wall.

In the store itself there's nothing but a counter and scattered tins of protein. But there's also a back room and Schroeder pushes the door, imagining what it feels like to fire at some shadow figure which has already taken him down in a shower of lead. He takes a deep breath and, gun-first, he enters. Light leaks from the room, the Glock glows in his hand and his finger tightens on the trigger as he peers into the half-lit room.

A man sits motionless at a table. A tiny figure with silver gaffer tape stretched hard and deep across his mouth. Yet more tape winds around his upper arms, his torso and his wrists. The man doesn't move and Schroeder tries to focus, trying somehow to bend his vision beyond the concealing darkness. He steps towards the table, flicks out at an anglepoise and suddenly there's a little still life with bottle of Stolichnaya and two tumblers. As for the figure, Schroeder recognises at once the terrified Chihuahua eyes of Roark – all trussed up like a battered, silver, tout cocoon.

Schroeder puts the gun on the table and starts to ease the tape from Roark's mouth. Roark sucks in air and his head rolls back and there's a whole new stench of urine. There's a lot of blood too. Dried and fresh. And teeth are missing. Everything is mashed, split and hanging, and when he tries to speak, all Roark can manage is a groan as his eyes sink to the gun resting between them. Perhaps he thinks that if this is a game of spin-the-bottle then the turn is now Schroeder's and he leans away as if to present his cheek to a bullet. It has been coming for years. The typical tout's demise and it looks as if Schroeder is the one to do the deed.

– Who did this to you? asks Schroeder.

Roark moans.

– Big guy? Bald head?

Roark nods with his eyes.

– Was there a woman? Red hair?

Roark stiffens and his moans go all gurgle and choke.

Schroeder looks around the room. Bare boards. Dust. And another door to his left. This one iron, barred and padlocked. This is exactly the sort of place where people get hung up by their heels and made to confess to all manner of recent atrocities. It's a place where that very anglepoise is used to illuminate the truth in a terrified pair of eyes. A place where people disappear completely. And now Schroeder feels like he's in the middle of some terrible trial. Some kind of practical exam where he must behave as is expected of a man with a loaded gun. He has been brought here as surely as Roark has been, and perhaps his task really is to shoot this tortured tout in the back of his rolling head. That certainly seems to be the picture. What else could it be? The hog-tied maggot. The back room. The loaded Glock.

Minutes pass. Many powerless, clueless minutes with Roark spluttering and Schroeder trying to think straight. It all comes back to Chantal and so he smooths out the napkin on the table and rings the number and waits for the connection. And as he's waiting he sees that Roark's eyes are growing wider and then, in that same instant, his heart bumps when he hears a ringtone in the very air behind his head – the opening bars of "Amhrán na bhFiann." Roark twists in pure terror and Schroeder turns to find Chantal – her tight leather torso gleaming in the light. Schroeder clicks off his cell and the national anthem stops.

– Give me the gun, Schroeder.
– What's going on here?
– Give me the gun.
He hands it over. It makes no difference.
– What the hell is going on?
Roark sounds like he's choking to death. Chantal ignores him.
– So you made it?
– What is this place?
– It's where I work. I told you.
Schroeder gestures to Roark.
– And is this the kind of work you do?
She shrugs.
– So you're UIA or what?
– Oh please!
– No. Really. What exactly are you? Exactly.
– I'm a civil servant. Exactly.
Chantal pours two vodkas.
– You know, Anton Schroeder, you've more balls than I thought.
– Just the two. Same as you.
Chantal takes a long drink, swallows without a wince and then, looking hard at her empty glass, she sighs in approval at the vodka's kick. Then she sets the glass down again, precisely on the ring she had raised it from. Schroeder reaches for his drink and looks around the room.

– The clearer the spirit, says Chantal, the better it is for you.
– Cut the crap, Chantal.
– OK, she says. Here's the beef. I've been following you. For

quite some time as it happens.
– You? Following me? I don't think so.
– For quite a while.
– But I followed you.
Chantal smiles.
– Anton Schroeder, I've been on that DART so many times, in and out of the city, backwards and forwards. Jesus you really don't know if you're coming or going, do you?
– I don't believe that.
– There are different ways of following people, she says, flicking her hair. And my preferred method is to have the person follow me. More fun that way. For me at least. And the mark never suspects anything if he believes that the initiative is all his.
– So I'm a mark, am I?
– Yep.
– And how come I never saw you?
– Flat shoes. When I didn't want you to see me I wore flat shoes. When a woman is in flat shoes men like you don't notice them at all. I know your type. And so then when I wanted you to follow me through Temple Bar all I had to do was become someone you'd be certain to follow. I replaced the flats with heels. I became a little French. Red lipstick. Existentialist Hibernerotic chic. That endless promise of detached and confident sex is something men like you just can't resist. You've been reared on pornography.
– As simple as that?
– You followed me, didn't you? And anyway I have eyes in the back of my ass.
– The best arse in Dublin blah, blah, blah.
– Indubitably.
Then the Man Mountain enters and Roark winces and slumps. He knows he's surplus now and Schroeder watches with a swelling nausea as Roark's mouth is taped up once more. The man then picks Roark up like a rolled-up mat and throws him over his shoulder. Then he carries him, fireman's lift, out through the iron door.

Schroeder stands up.

– Where's he taking him?

– Don't concern yourself.

– Where does that door lead to?

– Under the street.

– Under the street to where?

Chantal strokes the table as if it were an ancient fur.

– The Liffey.

Schroeder imagines Roark, not quite dead, wrapped in black plastic, bound hand and foot and the splash and the cold water and the darkness and the nothingness and the bursting lungs. And Schroeder fears that this Man Mountain will soon be back for him, this time with a medical bag full of gear to be employed on his fingernails and testicles. He sees the beatings on his feet, the waterboarding, his own gun shoved down his throat.

– So am I next? he asks.

Chantal shakes her head as a mother would.

– Relax.

– You're telling me to relax?

– I've a question for you.

– I'm all fucking ears.

– It's the same question you asked me. Why *am* I following you?

Schroeder recognises this as the sort of question a schoolteacher might ask. Designed to humiliate and trap – the answer, any answer, will be the inevitable proof of his stupidity. And in this case the guarantee of his doom.

– You're asking me why *you* are following *me*? How the fuck would I know! I thought I was following you!

Chantal joins her hands and leans her chin on the summit.

– Mr Schroeder, she says, I've had you under surveillance for some time and I have absolutely no idea why. It's not always my job to know these things but, in this case, I'm totally at a loss. Can you think of any reason, any reason at all, why I might be following you?

– Just tell me what's going on.

– Schroeder, I don't know what's going on. And so I'm asking you. Why am I following you? And why was Mr Roark following you?

– I have no fucking idea.

– What's your view on President King?

– I think he's an asshole.

– You do?

– That's not really an opinion though, is it? It's more of a fact.

– Would you describe yourself as anti-American?

– Have you seen my record collection?

– Yes.

– You have?

– I told you. I have you under surveillance.

– Well, as you've seen my record collection then how the fuck could I be anti-American? Johnny Cash, Bruce Springsteen, Duke fucking Ellington. Americans all. And I'm guessing you've been through my books too.

– I have.

– I rest my case.

– How do you feel about President King's visit?

– I don't feel anything about it. I plan to ignore it. Watch some decent movies all day long. American movies by the way.

– Claude Butler. Tell me about him.

– Never liked the guy.

– He's an old friend of yours.

– When I was eleven. He lived across the street. I hardly even know him.

– You were a guest at his ordination.

– I couldn't say no, could I?

– You met him recently.

– Yes.

– What did you make of him?

– He's not well.

– In what sense?

– In every fucking sense.

– Look Schroeder, I'm on your side.

– And what side is that exactly?

– Those women in the hotel. They weren't hookers.

– Well they walked like hookers and they talked like hookers and they sure as hell looked like hookers.

– I want you to go home now, Schroeder. And lie low for a while.

– Lie low? Am I in a gangster movie?

– Perhaps you are.

Chantal screws the top back on the bottle.

– When you get home, Schroeder, take a look around. And be thorough about it. Maybe go see your pal Walton. I think you should pay him a visit.

– And why would I want to do that?

– It would be the neighbourly thing do.

And then she stands, hands Schroeder back his gun, leads him out of the room, unlocks the front door and looses him once more into the middle of Middle Abbey Street. Pigeons pick at what's left of a fish supper, a ginger cat is doing yoga on top of a burned-out car and Schroeder, his eyes adjusting to the sunlight, jumps a passing LUAS to Connolly. From there, with his heart banging like a Dutch nightclub, the DART sucks him back out to Dún Laoghaire where the skies are almost blackened now by swarms of ants in their nuptial flight and by the hurricanes of silent gulls in off the waves to eat them up.

Back in Hibernia Road I'm hammering my heel into the floorboards hoping for a response from Walton. Usually when I do this I hear his wheelchair roll like a marlin dashing for a guacamaya lure but, so far, there hasn't been a sound. I walk from room to room stomping on the floor and rapping the radiators with a broom handle but still no response. I prostrate myself on the floor with my ear to the boards but again nothing. This is not good. And this is what awaits Schroeder as he descends to Walton's flat where the door is open and stale air lingers. And it comes almost naturally now to draw the Glock and hold it out before him.

He nudges the door with his elbow and steps inside the hallway, pricking the darkness with the muzzle of the pistol, entirely ready for the sight of blackening blood pooling on the tiles. The place stinks of unflushed toilets and the very silence warns him not to call out, not to make a sound of his own as he opens the living-room door, anticipating a body unconscious or worse. But there's no one there. Just bin bags full of congealing clothes and leaning towers of pizza boxes topped with ancient socks.

Upstairs, inches away, I have my ear to the floorboards, wincing every time Schroeder calls out Walton's name. He calls over and over but there's no answer. And, mirrored by me directly above him, he looks in the kitchen. Then he checks the toilet. Then under the stairs and under the beds. He searches everywhere. But nothing. Then he tries the back garden. The junk. The barricade. Behind the hedges and in my dacha. But again. Nothing. Walton isn't here and given what Schroeder has just seen happen to Roark, he fears the worst. I also know that something bad has taken place and, to my growing horror, I know that it has happened, not just under my nose, but under my very floorboards and in my very house. Me who misses nothing has missed something at last.

Schroeder goes back inside and stares at the customized bed with its systems of handles and pulleys and wonders if there can be any reasonable explanation for any of this. The house has not been damaged, the open door has not been forced and there's no sign anywhere of either break-in or assault. He sits at Walton's desk and shuffles a few pieces of paper, looking for any kind of message or note but again nothing – just the slim lifeless unit, a paperweight, nail clippers, a camera, chewing gum, Kleenex and the plastic bags of painkillers. He looks out the window and scans the strange new view of my garden. The rotting heirlooms. The vixen's labyrinth. Something, we both know, is very badly wrong.

But then a clue. A ball of glossy paper on the floor. Skin of course. The inevitable Walton smut and Schroeder throws it on the desk and watches it unfurl. It's a flier for an event in South William

Street – a personal appearance by "sex superstar" Jackie (sic) Jack at a place called Paradiso and it's scheduled for today. So that's where he is! The sad bastard has gone to worship at the constantly arched feet of Jakki Jack on a State Visit of her very own. He has actually gone out! Progress for him surely, even if it is to Paradiso. Even if it is to bear witness to Jakki Jack – her hair expansive, blonde and hard, her skin thick with tan and chalky make-up coating a faceful of spots, some of them bleeding slightly at the corners of her mouth.

Right now he will be seated before her glistening torso as it makes a comedy of a pink vest. She is hunched over a pile of product, a huge silver marker moving with wildly inaccurate speed as men leer in silence and Walton is there before her. In Paradiso. He is giving her honour and respect. Hoping for a rub of the relic, desperate to inhale some miraculous perfume which will have him walking again. Wheeled before her now he will bow and tell her everything. And she will look right through him and someone will tell him to move along.

Schroeder pockets the Glock and he's just about to leave when he accidentally tips against the screen and the unit powers up. The screensaver, predictably enough, is all herself – the Jackster – in her customary high-gloss environment of leather furniture and yucca plants. An anxious double tap consigns her endless nudity to darkness once again but what appears in its place hits Schroeder like a haymaker. It's the beautiful smiling face of Francesca and, in panic, Schroeder taps again and whoosh! Twenty or so visible folders scatter across the screen. Most are titled *JJ* and some plain *JAKKI* but there's one in particular which attacks Schroeder with a sudden sickness and dread. The file is named *Francesca* and it opens to Fran's beautiful face and then deeper again he finds yet more – shots of Francesca in the garden and Francesca on the street. All are taken in secret and with a zoom and each one – every last one – is a close-up of her laughter and her eyes. No body parts here. No leopard skin or Lycra. No spaghetti-strap dresses of silver lamé. No fishtail bustiers and polished glutes. For these are portraits. Portraits proper. Head and shoulders. And all are taken, from a distance, with love.

Even Schroeder doesn't have such images in his head. And of a woman he might have loved. And so I know what he's thinking. That he will never forgive this trespass. That Walton will be rightly called on this. And that for violations of this nature, this intimate nature, the transgressor must be made to pay. And then he notices that hidden yet deeper, quivering like a queen bee, is a file named simply *S*. And when he taps on that one, he forgets all about Francesca and her beautiful, captured face. Because everything in this one is about him.

In several frantic seconds Schroeder discovers something that I, of course, already know – that Walton has the entire contents of Schroeder's computer buried deep within his own. Every note, pic, email, article and download. He has the lot. In fact, same as me, he has Schroeder's entire hard drive patched directly into his.

At first it occurs to Schroeder that perhaps, so long out of sight, Walton has gone entirely mad – his mind now just as broken as his limbs and somehow stupefied beyond all reason by Jakki Jack and her pals. But when he clicks on yet another file he discovers that this is more than just the deranged curiosity of a self-confessed voyeur. For this one is a file which even I haven't seen. Titled *LMCH26501K*. It contains full details of Schroeder's every move over the past six months. His comings and goings, a list of the websites he has visited (mostly legitimate but even so) and even a detailed reference to Francesca leaving. This stuff is actual surveillance, and in many ways it's even more detailed than mine. Less discriminatory by far and much more mechanical.

Schroeder reaches for Walton's whiskey. Why would anybody be interested in this sort of detail, and again, why would Walton have it on his unit? And how could he even know these things in the first place? He's house-bound after all. Chair-bound and porn-bound too. And when Schroeder clicks on a photograph of himself leaving the house he gets an even worse jolt. The photograph could only have been taken from one position. Not from Walton's basement but from upstairs – from my place, from the upstairs window of (and I know what he's thinking) that putrid old bastard with the sleekit eyes. There's two of them in it! He tells himself, Walton *and* Monk – his ancient old fuck of a landlord. They're *both* watching him. And they're pooling their intelligence. He's wrong of course, but that's what it looks like.

Something like a stroke begins to develop deep in Schroeder's torso, the tectonic plates of his heart seeming to shift in a growing panic. He grips his thighs and the entire movie of his mind begins to slip its reels and spill around his feet. His cell thuds. Chantal/ Margaret.

– You OK?

– So Walton's a tout.

– You work fast.

– He's spying on me!

– He's not a nice man.

– And the old guy too.

– Don't worry about him.

– There are photographs on Walton's computer which could only have been taken by him. From upstairs.

– Look, Schroeder, they're hooked into each other's computers. Neither of them knows that the other is doing it.

– Is Walton in the Liffey now too?

– He's an informer *and* a voyeur and that's a dangerous combination. He's been monitoring you for years but for no particular reason. He knows nothing about what's going on here.

– What the fuck *is* going on here?

– We don't have the full picture. We questioned Roark and he didn't know why he was following you either.

– You questioned him alright.

– Look Schroeder, Walton is your business. Do what you like. These people are never missed.

– What does that mean?

– Whatever you want it to.

– Who the fuck *are* these people? And who the fuck are *you*?

Line goes dead. Loud buzz.

Schroeder takes another slug of the whiskey and tries to blank his wide-eyed nightmare of touts and gunshots. The cut of the liquor helps him focus and it occurs to him that if a man has already read his own file then he might well have something of an advantage. And that if a man knows the source of all treachery simmering all around him, then he's sure to be ready for it when it finally starts to spit. And that if a man knows there really is a rat in his kitchen then at least he can do something about it.

And then as the whiskey spreads further within his chest, Schroeder decides that the only sensible way to deal with rats is with smoke, viciousness, and plenty of bullets. But in his own good time. No point in sitting here in the filth and the dust. He'd be better off waiting in his own gaff – alert, prepared, listening out for the rattling sound of wheels. And, in any case, there's no way Walton can get down the steps without him.

Back at no. 28, on vigil, Schroeder resorts to a pill salad and passes the time with an image search for Paula Viola. He finds her at a charity do. A dress of gold. Plunge-line front and back. Heels. Her hair up. Bling. Meanwhile I'm trying to figure out what to do next, weighing up whether or not Schroeder has it in him to point a gun at Walton. I think it unlikely. But then of course Schroeder, just like the rest of us, has enough anger in his guts to do just about anything if the wrong ingredients should happen to mix.

And of course I'm angry at myself. I have been ignoring Walton for a very long time, underestimating him and ruling him out. A serious error on my part, for once, and now there is much catching up to be done. And so on this night of some torment for the both of us – Messrs. Schroeder and Monk – we both sit up all night. We watch and we wait. And as the night goes on and Walton fails to return, our instincts start telling us the very same thing. Either he has scored with the world renowned fellatrix Jakki Jack or he's already dead.

THIRTEEN

NEXT MORNING Schroeder steps from the DART at Pearse / *Stáisiún na bPiarsach* and takes the connection to Stephen's Green / *Faiche Stiabhna*. A huge sprawling underworld modelled on Gare Montparnasse, it's strangely silent today without the sonic chaos of snake-oil salesmen, evangelical Africans and assorted buskers in assorted disciplines. In fact whenever the city's tunnels are cleansed of anybody considered unpredictable, it's the buskers who are always the first to go – the pan pipers, the didgeridooists and finally the harpers, the tin whistlers, the box-players and the scrapers. As a result, apart from an increased military presence, the station is much less clogged than usual and the effect is unsettling as Schroeder walks briskly through the enormous concourse and steps into an elevator big enough to carry horses. As the doors close four Guards start beating some howling crazy-head with nightsticks and fists. Dull thuds, groans and thwacks.

Emerging into raging sunlight on the only corner of the Green still open to the public, Schroeder grunts at the psychedelic tableau of geraniums and teenagers arranged with care around O'Donovan Rossa's rock. He can remember (and so can I) the feel of that same erratic against his own back, not so very long ago, when he too was expelling smoke through his nose like some sleek and muscular stallion, so full of longing and hope. Of course, he had no idea then that life would one day ambush him precisely at the point where it was too late to do anything much about it. Life's cruellest joke of all, he believes, and he'll never forget the dull shock of its revelation. That sheer gunk of too-latedness. Of course I'm much older and know that life's cruellest jokes are saved until the finale but I can't really blame him. After all, nothing of his present was ever to have been his future, no more than this run-down wreck of a capital was ever to have been Ireland's.

As he crosses into King Street South, passing the old Gaiety Theatre, now enjoying its reputation as the largest sports bar in the European Alliance, a text leaps in Schroeder's pocket. It's Francesca hoping he's OK but Schroeder just swears in a whisper and turns into Clarendon Street, named for Henry Hyde, 2nd Earl of Clarendon, then along Chatham Row, named for William Pitt, son of the 1st Earl of Chatham and finally, in what seems like a jackknife into another micro-climate altogether, into the swill of the wrong end of South William, named in 1676 for William Williams, about whom I know very little. The place stinks like a desert sewer, a stench I can still remember from the last days of Bourbon Street, that flat daytime miasma of heat and disinfectant – booze, piss and puke evaporating in the Gulf sun.

He walks with feigned assurance. On either side of the street, tall purple weeds – loosestrife is it? – and wrought iron steps which lead to the basements of places barred with neon signs made up mostly of the letter X. Threatening eyes lock on him immediately. He is being assessed. Sussed out. What is his business here? His drug of choice? His proclivity of choice? Is there a long-term profit in his presence on this rancid strip or is he simply to be bludgeoned and robbed? Doomed-looking men (with knives, he is certain) begin to tug and point, urge and threaten – all trying to get him to enter whatever den they're promoting. Cat-houses, strip clubs, massage parlours, pleasure-domes and little kiosk cinemas right on the footpath where you can watch the choice of your choosing all by yourself. Schroeder feels the Glock throb in his pocket. Walton was here yesterday. A soft target for hard tickets. The question is whether or not he got out alive.

There's a queue outside Paradiso and people are slipping in through a narrow door half-blocked with a torn curtain of faded blue velvet. Today's congregation is for someone called Kitty Killarney and even the thought of it makes Schroeder shudder. He's not exactly sure what a public appearance involves in these very particular circumstances but it all seems very grim indeed. Everything is much too silent. Much too tense to be wholesome. He recognises a few shifty local fixtures, and one cokehead who used to be in a band called The Hypnic Jerks recognises him back.

– Heeeeyy bud.

Schroeder clenches his fists. He doesn't expect to be known in a street like this. Surely he is well beyond the orbit of this sad conclave. Surely there can be no overlap here between this guy's life and his? This is some parallel universe after all and certainly not some dirty corner of his own.

– Schroeder, says the Hypnic guy. Fucking hell man. Sweet.

– Yes. Hi. I'm looking for Walton. You remember Louis Walton? You seen him anywhere?

– Off the TV Louis Walton? Haven't seen him in years, man.

– Were you here yesterday?

– Ooooh yezzzzz!

– Did you see him?

– Wasn't paying much attention to the punters. Jakki's a ledge. Know what I mean bud?

– You must have seen him. He's in a wheelchair.

– Sorry man. Can't help you.

– You sure? Wheelchair?

A bouncer pounds up the quivering steps like a Tongan prop. Schroeder's throat is drying up but he gets the question out.

– Was there a guy here yesterday in a wheelchair?

– Fuckin' right there was. Banging on about wheelchair access. Had to give the fucker a fireman's lift. As if this gig isn't shitty enough.

– When did you see him last?

– When I threw him out on his ear. Started shouting at yer one. Saying she was an imposter. *You're not her! You're not her!* Had to carry him out screaming and dump him back in his wheelie machine. The little bollix went ballistic.

– Where did he go after that?

– No fucking idea, pal. But he better not come back anywhere near here. Or he'll need two fucking wheelchairs.

There's a ripple in the queue and all heads turn to face two identical men with tattooed faces crossing the street towards them. Between them is a miniscule girl with camogie legs of titanium white. Her hair is orange and it matches her hot pants. She wears cracked, white, calf-length boots and a sparkling halter top of emerald green. The queue grows even quieter.

– Howayiz? says Kitty Killarney (an evident Dub) as she descends into Paradiso. Wit' yis in a minute.

Schroeder scans the facade of Paradiso. So Walton *was* here yesterday. And made a show of himself too, probably drunk or fried on painkillers. At least that's something, although he could be anywhere now. The Liffey most likely. Gone the way of all touts, his wheelchair upended in some rat-shit alley.

– You coming to see Kitty? asks the Hypnic guy.

– Not my type.

– Not mine either but sure fuck it.

Schroeder moves, trying not to breathe, up and down off the curb as he dodges hustlers, dealers and pimps. A man with an eyepatch puts a many-ringed hand on his shoulder but he squirms out from under it and heads for the Wicklow Street barrier which marks the end of the strip. And for all the crowds both loitering and in motion, there's barely a word said. These men who linger here, staring up at windows, have only one purpose and their focus is intense – as addicted to this squalor as much as any junkie on the DART needs his smack. He speeds up. The place, and the scenario, is starting to physically sicken him. He had never entrusted his fantasy life to the jaded imagination of others and although this soul-eating world is always just a curtain swish away in any man's life, it had never yet lured him in.

– Get out of there, Schroeder. Go. Go now. Good man. And shake the dust from your feet.

Schroeder limbos underneath the barrier, takes one of the sidewalk seats at Reed's and orders a double espresso from a wholesome-looking Australian in a yellow t-shirt. After the false disinfectant promise of what he's just passed through, he's glad to see something real, to witness the actual carnival of real beauty on the move. Here on Wicklow Street, so close to Paradiso and the rest, is perhaps his favourite spot in all of Dublin – the very crossroads of the city's parading actual gorgeousness and he perches there often. A man after my own heart. I often used to sit there myself, my face tilted towards the sun.

The coffee arrives but, after South William, he's far too wired to even look at it. He's thinking about Walton, trying to figure out what happened. Walton carried down the steps and deposited at a table in front of Ms Jack and his expression suddenly falling away like a mudslide when he realises that it's not her. And he leans forward to examine closer her tumbling eyes and he whispers something which nobody else can hear. And then Ms Jack's head jerks backwards and, as if writing an urgent message in thin air, she begins to signal wildly with her magic marker. Security moves in and Walton is lifted off the table again and dragged, legs trailing, through the throbbing assembly. He is carried upstairs and planted back in his wheelchair on the street outside. His upper body is heaving and his breath is short. That's not her! He is shouting repeatedly. That's not her! She's a fucking imposter! That's not her!

And then Chantal appears. Hippy dress. Like a fortune teller and not to Schroeder's taste.

– You must be wearing flat shoes, he says.

– You're getting the hang of it.

– So who was following who today?

– Slumming, weren't you?

– I went to Paradiso. Walton was there yesterday.

– He was.

– Would you have any idea where he might be now?

– Not a clue.

– There was trouble.

– There was. He got out of hand.

– Seems our Ukrainian friend is an imposter.

– He was right about that.

– I'm not really interested in that part of it. I just want to know where he is.

– That was her sister. But with all the surgery she's had by now she's a ringer. Does all the public appearances and soon she'll be doing all the movies too, once the backlog is cleared.

– Not for the first time Chantal, you have me bewildered.

– Seems there's about ten features not released yet. They don't want the word to get out until they've been marketed.

– What word?

– That she's been dead for a year and a half. Remember that bomb in Frankfurt? She was caught up in that. She died. Along with lots of other people. Her real name was Aleksandra something. I forget what.

– Frankfurt? That was a UIA job.

– The UIA doesn't exist.

– Well for people that don't exist they're pretty fucking lethal.

– Whatever you say, Schroeder. Anyway, she's dead and you can appreciate the damper that sort of information would put on her latest adventures. And on the solitary pursuits of her followers.

– And these people don't even notice?

– Walton noticed.

– She's been sending him her underwear.

– Somebody has.

Schroeder stretches his arms skywards.

– There's not much you don't know, is there?

– No conspiracy too small, Schroeder. And anyway, you can't monitor a man like Walton – or any man come to think of it – without picking up all manner of crap.

– So are you watching Walton too?

Chantal nods. Schroeder looks into her eyes.

– So where is he then? Tell me. You know. And I know you know.

– And you know what he was up to. He was a tout, Schroeder.

– Was?

Chantal flicks a crumb across the table.

– Can I ask you, Schroeder, what you were planning to do to him if you found him?

– Call him a prick, probably.

– I thought perhaps you were going to shoot him.

Schroeder folds his arms.

– So tell me then. Where is he?

Chantal reaches for Schroeder's coffee, downs it and tells him what she knows. That sometime yesterday Walton went to the quarantined end of Sandymount Strand. That in his lap was a litre of gas and a disposable cigarette lighter and that there, on the damp sand of Dumhach Trá, he poured the gas over his head and set himself ablaze. To the folks on the Strand Road he was no more than a distant little bonfire.

And then the tide came in and put him out.

FOURTEEN

I'M ON THE SOFA, a Stoli in a highball, minding my own cheese biscuits. On Channel NB1 a panel is discussing the day's events so far – looped images of presidential progress through the streets of Dublin City, the beetle-black Cadillac and Richard R. King slouched invisible within, tanked-up as ever on Kentucky Straight Bourbon and cookie jars full of happy pills and extra-strong mints. In a hazy longshot, the cavalcade moves like a flashing reptile and studio experts marvel at the Elite Presidential Guard, swinging their machine guns like garden strimmers – a sinister, dark cohort in helmets and shades walking, mostly backwards, up the middle of Dame Street. There's no mention of Walton the human fireball spurting flames like a monk in a mall. There's no mention either of Roark, rolling in a bin liner at the bottom of the Bay. Nor is there even the slightest reference to Schroeder laid out on his own sofa, agitated, and waiting for Paula Viola to do her thing live on the national airwaves.

– A logistical nightmare, says the anchor over and over again. A security headache.

Ireland is represented on this "historic" day by a screeching flock of sugared-up schoolchildren – embassy kids and army brats shaking their tiny flags at the top of Parliament Street. Green, white and orange. Red, white and blue. No actual Dubliners of course because people know the drill by now and they're all at home with the burgers and the beer. And yet no matter how jarred and apathetic the people of Ireland become, the threat level will remain jammed at a constant orange as gangs of silhouetted men scrutinize an entire population's absence. Perched like puffy birdwatchers, they scan the empty streets while high above them, among the swifts and buzzards and kites, half a dozen helicopters from Shannon are hung with menace and poke. Should a sudden glinting window suggest some bazooka potshot at the President, they're all set to make smithereens of Georgian Dublin. Or what's left of it.

The panel has long ago run out of things to say and once the State Visitor himself is sitting down to the State Dinner there's nothing left but wild speculation about whatever comes next into the anchor's muscular head. Does the President have a special affinity with Ireland? Did he enjoy his round of golf? Will he be feeling tired by now? Has he spoken to his daughter yet? How is she getting on at Trinity? Isn't Princess a delightful name for a President's daughter?

Schroeder is moaning as if his head is crammed with nails and screws. It's as if the last few days have scooped out his insides, and so he swallows two more Presbutex and sips at a tumbler of Smirnoff. The coverage is deadly and dull and he swears at a social diarist now spoofing on about food, reacting to some desperate query about the menu. Atlantic prawns, he's suggesting, to be followed by Wicklow lamb. The wine list, he pretends to know, will be exclusively Californian. Santa Inez and Sonoma. But then eventually with Schroeder in near despair, the longed-for newsflash arrives. Schroeder starts to tingle. And so do I.

– I'm sorry, I'll have to stop you there . . .

The arrested social diarist, miffed at the interruption, begins to whimper loudly at the bad manners of it, but the anchor raises a hand as if to repel a mosquito.

– We are getting reports that . . . We are hearing . . . I'm told we are now going live to our reporter Paula Viola who's at Dublin Castle . . .

A flick of a switch and there she is, the colonial cobbles shining all around her. Schroeder flares and crouches forward as Paula's face is suddenly blanched by a spotlight which leaves her blinking. She's unsteady and not like herself at all. There's something seriously wrong and she seems to be struggling to arrange the words she's about to say. And then she sighs and swallows and Schroeder stops breathing, both of them now caught in the very same flash flood of adrenalin – both of them focussing on the silence in front of her lips.

– A major incident has occurred tonight here at Dublin Castle.

Only moments ago we witnessed chaotic scenes and it appears that President King has been shot.

She pauses. Her swimmer's shoulders heave.

– The incident happened just moments ago at the conclusion of tonight's State Dinner. It appears the President was in a side room, preparing to leave the building, when he was shot. It would seem fatally. Or quite probably fatally.

The anchor butts in.

– Fatally or quite probably?

Paula's fists tighten. She begins to speak very slowly.

– It has not yet been confirmed but I *can* tell you that I witnessed the body being stretchered out of the Castle. And yes, President King appears to be deceased. I can confirm that his head was covered. And that there was a lot of blood.

I go upstairs immediately and start herding information from every source available. Schroeder leans even closer to the screen.

– Early reports are suggesting an Irish national although this is unconfirmed. And again, according to initial reports, it is my understanding that the assassin is dead at the scene.

– Paula, for the moment, thank you.

Paula's image snaps from the screen and Schroeder pours himself several large drinks. As newsflashes go, this is a big one. He can tell that Paula is deeply aroused just to be there, breathing in the sheer drama of the deadly. And he knows exactly what she's thinking. That some American network will snap her up in the morning. That she's a made woman now. That she'll go global after this. And that fuckwit anchor is thinking the very same thing as he swings towards his audience, slides his glasses on, then slides them off again.

– Dramatic and distressing news from Dublin tonight. If you've just joined us, it would seem that President Richard King has, this evening, been assassinated while leaving a State Dinner in his honour at Dublin Castle. It would appear that . . .

Then the roar of fighter planes carving through the salty heat above Dún Laoghaire. I move to my skylight and I can tell that they're heading for the Park – still the largest park in the European Alliance, once home to a strung-out herd of fallow deer that nibbled the clover from 1662 until St. Patrick's Day five years ago when every last one of them was taken out by an off-duty marine off his head on mushrooms. And as I watch I remember how Schroeder used to visit that zoo with his mother. And how she would hold his hand as he threw bits of apple to the last surviving rhinoceros in what was then called the EU. That old boilerplate rhino had always seemed to him so monumental and solitary, always so invincible in his African daydream, but now all that can be said is that it is utterly extinct. No more than matter and mush. Like beech leaves in a bin liner, as Schroeder once wrote in his school magazine.

And then Paula is live again. And there are pictures of King under a sheet and most of the blood is where his head is supposed to be. So Wicklow or not, Santa Inez or Sonoma, what is certain is that unless a Dublin Bay prawn has exploded like a pink grenade in the Presidential mouth, it isn't the dinner that killed him. And whatever it is, whoever it was – King's casket is sure to be a closed one.

And then more breaking news.

Deep in the stainless steel kitchen of a Georgetown restaurant, Vice-President Delmore Flame is sworn in. A still appears simultaneously on screens from Baghdad to Bogotá – the vital signs of continuity. And barely ten minutes later he's live from the Oval Office swearing to bring to justice whoever is responsible. Yes, the assailant is dead. Yes, he's possibly an Irish national but all options are being kept open. Every avenue will be explored. Freedom has many enemies, and until he better knows the facts of the case, all of freedom's enemies are prime suspects and will be given no quarter. There will be no hiding place, etc. etc.

Schroeder has by now swallowed so much vodka that he is staggering around the room, stumbling over chairs and talking in a drunken falsetto. He's as horny as a three-balled tomcat but Paula keeps appearing and disappearing just as quickly. This rolling series of newsflashes is no respecter of anybody's performance – hers or his. Stop cutting her off, you fuckers! Let her finish! Let her fucking finish! And so Schroeder's last conscious act on the night that President King is shot is to trickle the last drops of vodka onto his tongue and suck it all up into the tingling roof of his mouth. And then, with the world in genuine crisis and the television at full volume, he passes out – on his knees, humiliated, his ankles shackled by his jeans.

When he awakes, five armed men in black balaclavas and boilersuits are standing in the room. One of them is pointing a gun directly at his face and another is binding his hands with plastic ties. That gun is the last thing Schroeder sees as a sack is twisted down hard around his head and he's dragged out into Hibernia Road and put in the back of a truck with hard seats of busted leather and foam. He can feel the intimate, pressured heaviness of male shoulders tight on either side of him and he knows that they have come for him at last.

And what am I doing while all of this is happening? I am trembling. Military or Branch or UIA, they have finally landed and now they're taking Schroeder to the Park where aircraft host on a pentagram of missile-lined strips, and itch like pipistrelles about to swarm from the concrete ruins of the zoo. Richard Rutledge Barnes King has just been assassinated in Dublin and Schroeder is now en route to his end. And I am watching from the window. I have lived in the manner I live for eight long decades and now I am impotent at last.

FIFTEEN

HOODED AND ALONE, Schroeder is held for three days – a period he estimates simply by the number of meals he is slipped and the feel of his beard whenever they lift his hood just enough to let him eat. The food also suggests Fort Phoenix – meat substitute in a tube and breakfasts of coffee and something approximating cornbread. And although he has seen no insignia, he is more and more certain that his captors are American. The total refusal of anyone to open their mouths suggests even further that, were they to speak, their accents might well be the Cumberland Gap. But then again, even if they are Americans, he still has no way of knowing who exactly they are. Exactly.

The good news is that he hasn't been drugged and this would appear to rule out the UIA. Their favoured method is to seize people on the way back from the pub, inject them with some knock-out serum and then drop them off in another country altogether, so pumped up on drugs that they can't even remember who they are or where they have come from, condemning them to spend the rest of their lives bewildered and homeless on the streets of some provincial town in somewhere like Norway or Poland. But right now, as far as Schroeder can tell, he has been spared that one. At least he still knows who he is. Anton Schroeder of Hibernia Road Dún Laoghaire. No. 28. And he has some idea of where he is. Or, at least, where he might be.

But what confuses Schroeder is that he's still in his own clothes and his hands are no longer bound. The Yanks would surely have him in serious shackles by now and he'd be all dolled up in orange. And even stranger again is the fact that he hasn't been questioned – something which soon begins to worry him more than anything. Because if he's not being questioned then why is he being held? Perhaps they already have all the answers they need? Intelligence culled from his diaries and his notes, ripped from his hard drive and delivered to them by Walton? Or by Roark? Or by that old goat at number 26? Or maybe they're just killing time? Waiting for some expert torturer to fly into town with his tools.

What unsettles him most of all is that his anxiety (and it's never amounted to any more than that) seems to come and go in gentle waves, sometimes diminishing to almost nothing as he lies and waits in the dark sterility of his cell. Eventually he starts to understand that he's sleeping through most of it, slipping into a dreamless state which while seeming brief, might well be lasting for hours on end – a sensation a bit like dying perhaps. But, that said, dying quite comfortably. In a monitored hospital bed in some deluxe departure suite.

On what Schroeder guesses is this third day, he is brought into another room and lowered, almost with tenderness, onto a wooden stool. When the hood is removed, he is facing three men seated at a fold-up desk. They wear suits and ties and all three are fiddling with broken pencils. The one in the middle seems more human than the other two and Schroeder decides to concentrate on him. He's about fifty with blue eyes and sandy hair scattered meagrely on a bright-red scalp. His teeth are bad. He's a smoker. And Schroeder now recognises him as the man with the giant fists who searched his bag on the street. The Beetroot Man.

– Why am I here? Schroeder asks.

– I'm not authorized to answer that.

Yes. The accent is Irish. Derry. Donegal. Inishowen. Buncrana. Maybe Culdaff. Maybe Muff.

– Are these two Irish as well? Schroeder asks.

The Beetroot Man sighs.

– No more questions. Thank you.

– They look like Mormons to me.

No reaction from the Mormons. They're not the type to rise to ridicule. They're the type to shoot you in the forehead. And the Beetroot Man continues.

– Mr Schroeder, he says. You are to be released later this morning.

– What was I in for?

– I'm not authorized to discuss that.

– Well I didn't kill the President of the United States if that's what you think.

– Nobody said you did.

– I was watching it on the telly. Surely you know that.

The Beetroot Man glances at one of the Mormons.

– I'm not authorized . . .

– Authorized by who? says Schroeder. These guys? UIA are they? The Mormon Branch?

It's at this point that Schroeder understands just how much he's been drugged. He is obviously far too composed given the situation. Here he is, face-to-face with at least two UIA operatives, possibly three, and he's being a smart-arse. And the only explanation for that is that they have him stewed on something potent yet selective in its effects. It would certainly explain all the sleeping, all the missing time and, most especially, all this unwarranted calm.

– So where exactly am I? he asks.

The Beetroot Man is clearly the designated speaker.

– That should be obvious enough, he says, when you're released.

– So I'm in the Park?

Schroeder looks at the other two. First one and then the other.

– And the last rhinoceros in Europe. What became of him? And you two fuckers have probably eaten all the squirrels by now too.

The Beetroot Man scratches his eyebrow.

– You will be released in an hour's time and I must inform you, sir, that when you return to your home you will find members of the press outside your door. It would be very advisable that you do not talk to them under any circumstances. And I mean *very* advisable. That you make no public statement.

– Statement about what? That I've been here for at least three days and nobody has even spoken to me?

– You have not been arrested, Mr Schroeder.

One of the Mormons stands up without a word and signals with his pencil that the conference is over. Then the other one rises and Beetroot Man nods. As they leave the room the Beetroot Man turns and fixes Schroeder with a stare.

– Don't be a prick, Mr Schroeder. Under no circumstances whatsofuckingever make any reference to your time here.

An hour later Schroeder is released into the Phoenix Park. He's well beyond the perimeter of the base now, on a road which leads directly to the Parkgate Street entrance. Unsteady and unshaven, he begins to walk beneath the beech and the lime and breathe the new air untainted by leather, plastic and disinfectant. It's a bright morning and busy too – joggers, cyclists and rollerbladers enjoying as much of the land as is still open to them, ignoring the dull rotors of choppers which regularly fill the air with whacks and thuds.

To Schroeder, who has now actually been *inside* Fort Phoenix and has just faced at least two of the really heavy guys, there seems to be something extremely naive about all this recreation, something brainwashed even with life in the Park seeming to go on as if nothing has changed. As if King has not been killed at all, as if Walton and Roark are still alive and as if Schroeder himself has not been lifted and released unscathed.

Obviously I am not a witness to any of this, but the following and indeed all the prior detail on Schroeder's incarceration are taken – verbatim for the most part – from his own notes. Horse's mouth and, as ever, I must insist, even if his actions or reactions seem to you unlikely or out of character, that no other account is possible. There is no other account to go on and so I'm working with what there is and uncovering only what I may – in this case a very confused Schroeder, released from Fort Phoenix and scuffing along the grass, trying to gather himself, to assess what has just happened and work out just how drugged he might still be.

He stares high up into the sunlit leaves and closes his eyes tight, trying somehow to squeeze his mind into action. And just as he opens them again a rattling black streak of bicycle flashes past, almost knocking him over a low chain fence. It's Chantal. Margaret

Lynch. Whoever Chantal is. Whoever Margaret Lynch is. He's about to call out but as he steps forward he realises that she's dropped a rolled up copy of *The European* at his feet and that she's definitely not stopping to discuss it.

Schroeder looks around to see if he's being tailed, but he knows that if he is being followed, then there's nothing much he can do about it now. They will already have seen Chantal cycle by. And they will already have seen the newspaper drop and, in any event, they will have read (and possibly written) whatever is in it. And so, with all the appearance of a regular citizen in the Park, Schroeder sits down under a swirling ash and unrolls the newsprint. He's ready for anything but even so, he takes a very deep breath. The headline is blunt. You couldn't make it up.

PREZ ASSASSIN IRISH PRIEST

And then Schroeder sees a photograph of a grinning young man in a clerical uniform and he feels as if his brain is being pulled out through the top of his head. He shakes the pages hard and tries to focus on a snap taken at an ordination many years before when that same face had pressed itself against the cold marble and smiled at the very thought of being called Father Claude. Prissy little Claude Butler from across the street prostrating himself and making rash priestly vows he would never be able to keep.

. . . a forty two year old former priest . . . born in Dublin . . . an address in Liverpool . . . not known to have any connection with any terrorist group . . . acted alone . . . close range . . . turned the gun on himself . . .

Schroeder's guts start to writhe and nausea rises in his throat. He closes his eyes and drops his head between his knees. *Turned the gun on himself.* Jesus. *Dead at the scene.* Schroeder's heart thunders and a freezing sweat breaks across his back and his lungs start to pack up as he eats the air around him for even the slightest drops of oxygen. And then, turning the page, what he sees next is a bigger shock again – his own impassive face staring out from the newsprint. His author's pic from the so-called promotional campaign for *Lucky's Tirade*.

According to Pat Rogerson, a mailman in the area, the killer had been in recent contact with his childhood friend . . . Hibernia Road, Dún . . .

The paper is full of it. Father Assassin they're calling him. On the very same page in history as John Wilkes Booth, Charles J. Guiteau, Leon Czolgosz, Lee Harvey Oswald, Stefan G. Huffman and Mike Bradley Hanley. Assassins all – or so they say – and now Schroeder is himself forever linked to them all. Page after page of it. More horseshit from the mailman, then profiles of Claude stuffed with details Schroeder neither knows nor believes. The priesthood, the exit, an affair with a married woman, a spell in a mental hospital, heavy drinking, living in Belfast, drug problems – Benzedrine of all fucking things – and all of it traced back to a "normal" childhood on Hibernia Road, Dún Laoghaire. And then a sample of what is definitely Claude's handwriting. The full details of his endless letter writing to the White House. Deluded nonsense with Claude convinced that the President now relied on him to do the right thing. The letter published here is all about King being a good man and "the true revelation of the Kingdom of God" being his only purpose in life. Mad stuff. Garbled guff. The word RIGHTEOUS everywhere in blocks.

Schroeder bins the newspaper and hails a cab in Parkgate Street. The driver clocks him immediately.

– They seek him here, they seek him there.

– What the fuck does that mean?

– I said you'd be in the Park. They said you were in Shannon but I knew you'd be in there.

– Just drive, will you?

– You going home?

Schroeder puts the window down.

– Yes. I take it you already know where that is.

The driver turns up the radio and some hypocritical rent-a-gob is singing King's praises, saying he was less of a hawk than people realised and that, in fact, he might well have been on the verge of adjusting foreign policy towards a more conciliatory position. He was a product of his time, says some other dose. A man of principle. Tough but also, it seems, a doting father with a keen sense of humour. A pianist like Nixon. A golfer like Clinton. A gardener like Ramirez.

– Would you turn that shite off?

The driver obliges and begins to whistle something by Mozart, eyeing Schroeder all the time.

– The funeral's on Friday. That'll be a big affair.

– Which funeral? says Schroeder to himself.

– What's that, bud?

– Just get me home, will you.

– Can I just say one thing to you, bud. There's no way he done it. Your friend. You can't just kill an American President. It's impossible. There's no way he could walk up to the President of America in Dublin Castle. Carrying a gun? No way, bud. Another shaggin' stitch up if you ask me.

Schroeder says nothing. It's a long road home. The inside of his head feels like cotton wool, somehow squeaky and soft. His lips are numb, his eyes dart in circles, his heart rumbles like apples in a bucket and as the cab turns into Hibernia Road, it seems to stop altogether when he sees the size of the crowd at the gate. About fifty people with cameras and booms squeezed between vans all sprouting dishes and cables. And as the cab comes into view, the whole thing explodes into chaos and they attack like baboons at a safari park. They're all over him as soon as he opens the car door and questions start firing all around him.

– Why were you arrested?

– Were any charges put to you?

– Why did he do it?

– Were you involved in any way?

– Will you condemn the assassination?

– Were you and the assassin close?

– Were you in contact with him on the day of the shooting?

– Will you be making a statement?

Without a word Schroeder burrows his way through the heaving bodies, now moving like crabs on either side of him. It might be the drugs or the shock or both, but when he finally makes it inside and stands alone in his silent hallway, he realises that he's flushing with adrenaline. It takes him a moment to settle but after a quick shot of Stoli he starts to look around the kitchen. No sign of any search anywhere. No evidence of disruption, however subtle. And it's the same in every room, as far as he can see. Things are exactly as he left them and even the Glock seems undiscovered. But surely they must have searched the house? Surely every trace, digital or dust, has been examined, catalogued and analysed? Surely every floorboard has been lifted? Every jar opened, every tube squeezed and every sock unrolled? Surely they've scanned this place down to the very last silverfish and microscopic mite? They must have. Surely. He lies three-quarters prone on his bed and tries to think. This makes no sense. None of it. If they haven't searched the house and if they haven't questioned him, then why not? And before he can advance even a basic theory, he slips like a gentle avalanche into total darkness.

But I will not sleep now. And maybe I will never sleep again. I know that when the drugs wear off Schroeder will awake with some of the truth of his situation pounding hard in his brain and, without any mystery balm to soothe him, the dark lizards of paranoia will crawl all over his face once more and chew at the rash of his four-day beard. Outside he will hear a ratchety magpie, a car door slam, an ignition and zoom and the scatter-call of a spooked blackbird bolting for another hedge and he will be shaken by every second of it.

He will realise then that there are two new arctic bodies out there in the world – one friendless on a slab in a Dublin morgue, the other lying in repose in the East Room of the White House. At first he will think he has dreamed the whole thing, but when he lifts the blind and peers into the sunshine, he will understand so very clearly that this is all very real indeed. He will see the microphone people outside his door like dogs at a kill. And one of them will point right at him and steaming coffees will be dropped at the sudden sight of the spectre in the window – Schroeder unsteady like an ailing Pope.

And he will crawl back into his bed, pull the covers around his throat and stare up at the light bulb as if it were some agent of good counsel. But because this is not some nightmare of his own design he will have no idea of how to even begin to assess its components. He will swipe at screens and keyboards, and everywhere breathless reporters will be standing on the very same cobbles where Paula Viola had stood, and they will all be telling the world, in all the world's languages, that President King is to be buried in Arlington Cemetery with full honours and that many world leaders are expected to attend.

On the European networks questions will fly about who exactly was behind it. Is there a history of any organized group in Ireland likely to assassinate an American president? What of the reports that the assassin, a former cleric, was actually dressed as a priest when he fired the shot? Has the Vatican commented yet? Is it some kind of extremist Catholic thing? And then theories, one as wild as the other, will be offered and rejected as American accents of booming authority attempt to clear the way towards a global consensus. Claude Butler was crazy, Claude Butler was writing insane letters to the White House and Claude Butler killed the President of the United States because Claude Butler was nuts. No further questions.

And eventually Schroeder will recall the letter. The letter. *I will be there at the end of the month. For a FUNCTION. I arrive on the 27th.* And he will realise that this letter is something which can connect him directly to what happened and a total panic will set in as, naked and wrecked, he will search his own house for that handwritten invitation to meet the assassin just days before the hit, but he will not find it anywhere. And then he will slump again as Claude's face appears once more on the screen and there's news that a search of his flat in Liverpool has uncovered Bibles and guns and small explosives and it will get worse by the minute and Schroeder will need to talk to someone. He will need somebody to make sense of it, someone to somehow straighten everything out, get him re-tuned and re-balanced, fixed and reassured. He will need a sober-headed saviour to make everything alright again. A redeemer. And a large brandy. And yet another special slumber-cocktail of pills, like the one he discovered by chance on St. Patrick's Day last. A green one, a white one and an orange one.

But the only person who can really look after him simply cannot intervene. This protocol is sacrosanct but I will be ready even so. There when he awakes and there, after a fashion, when he finds dozens more messages on the answering machine and something similar in his email. I will urge him on as he deletes them all with an angry cluster-chord of keys, and I will sigh along with him when the instant he clears them another bunch slots in to take their place. And I will console him as he glances through the last batch quickly and, one by one, makes them disappear. Delete. Delete. Delete. Until, that is, he gets to the very last one and I am powerless again. This message he will never delete. It's from the desk of Paula Viola. She will call him again once the funeral is over. She is up to her neck right now but meanwhile he is not to talk to anyone else. She wants an exclusive. And she will make it worth his while.

SIXTEEN

WITH THE SQUARE-JAWED ANCHOR now planted in a baking Washington park, Paula Viola is behind the desk in the studios of NB1. It's her very first time as anchor and she's taking full advantage in a blue silk top which has already popped its buttons. Schroeder, tipping away at the vodka, gazes at her like a dog, his head at an angle, his breathing slow and deliberate. At this stage the coverage has mostly been reruns of interviews with Cascade and Gibbon, intercut with the odd vox-pop from desolate Americans amazed to be on Pennsylvania Avenue, temporarily open for the first time since the last big funeral. Paula has been doing really well. Unflustered. Unhurried. The tone just right. Not much mention is made of Claude Butler today, out of respect for people's sensitivities no doubt, although they'll all return to him soon enough. Father Assassin. The Killer Padre. The Bloody Priest. But yes, she's doing really well.

– And now I hand you back to Washington . . .

I'm getting tired of the same shots. The Capitol Rotunda. King's casket lying on a catafalque of pine boards. And I find myself repeating the word to myself. *Catafalque. Catafalque.* So too is Schroeder, for whom the images of the day are already becoming disordered. Such a great word, *catafalque.* The pine boards. The black cloth. The bier made up so hurriedly for Abraham Lincoln in 1865. Of course I've seen all this before but Schroeder will learn several new words today, as well as something of the disrupted geography and ancient ways of Washington. A *caisson* drawn by six black horses with three riders, while a section chief from the Old Guard Caisson Platoon rides another. The casket transferred at Pennsylvania Avenue and then a caparisoned horse – riderless with boots reversed in the stirrups – from the days of Genghis Khan. Or even before that. Buddha. Afghanistan perhaps. Not a patch on the funeral of Lord Clare when the good people of Dublin lined the streets and flung dead cats at the hearse.

The Irish contingent in Washington led by An t-Uachtarán O'Connor, who seems to have lost about three stone in the space of a week. More than likely he hasn't eaten since that lamb dish at Dublin Castle and he probably didn't manage very much that night either. Beside him, Domhnach of the Cloven Head and Gibbon of the Clenching Sphincter look like they have been kidnapped. They have the demeanour of two men who are getting the blame for the whole thing. Nobody nods in their direction, nobody shakes their hands and most just look at them crooked, like they're planning to swat them once the funeral is over. The First Lady seems particularly flammable and Princess, bored by the looks of it, is chewing a miniscule piece of gum and looking good in a black cloche hat. Sophisticated. She looks as if she's running late for class and doesn't especially care.

Schroeder watches closely as all manner of crooks and villains come strolling in. An American commentator with a voice like an ad for Budweiser is naming their names out loud. Presidents, prime ministers, kings, queens, sheikhs, dukes, princes, judges, generals, ambassadors, movie stars, dictators and admirals. And then a tsunami of dignitaries in suits of jet black, their creases sharp, their ties perfect, the order of it all interrupted by bright regalia from Africa, Arabia, Libya, Jordan and by those deluded European characters typically overdressed on occasions like these – people with medals and sashes, swords and epaulettes – like that Groucho Marx clown from the Commission. Just one big suicide belt, thinks Schroeder, and it would finish the whole thing off. Strapped around some startled archbishop perhaps and the whole caboodle could all be finished in a flash. *Novis ordo seclorum.*

Swallowing a handful of pills, he sets the bottle on the floor at his feet and before long he's not really sure what he's looking at. What is live and what is recorded, what is happening now, what has already happened and what might well be happening tomorrow. And to think that little Claude is the cause of it all. The boy most likely to be beaten up has somehow managed to stop the entire planet. And still the mourners wander in.

The phone buzzes. Schroeder downs his drink and checks the number. Chantal.

– Ms Lynch. Thought perhaps you'd vanished.

– You been drinking?

– How dare you.

– The press still outside?

– Not as many.

– Have you spoken to anyone?

– I have nothing to say and I'm not saying it.

– Are you drunk?

– That's entirely possible.

Schroeder hears Chantal sigh long and hard into his ear. Very intimate. An unexpected erotic bonus.

– We need to talk.

– OK. So what are you wearing?

– Listen carefully, Schroeder. Meet me in half an hour. Seapoint. The DART car-park.

– So it's dagger now as well as cloak?

– I know why I've been following you.

– Is it good?

– Half an hour.

In the corner of the room, Washington hands back to Paula, who looks like she's planning on unzipping the cameraman. Then she hands back to Washington again and a striking close-up of Princess King, and Schroeder sinks a couple of coffees. He washes his face, exits at speed and the scattered journos jump on him immediately.

– Just going to get milk. Be back in five minutes. I'll make a statement then. Five minutes.

They seem satisfied and start calling their editors.

No trains are running, Seapoint is deserted and crows wander at their ease. Schroeder stands in the shade waiting for Chantal's bicycle to sweep down the slope, but half an hour passes and still no bicycle. He's just about to phone when a gleaming blue car turns in from the road and circles once, and then again. It's some kind of Lexus, sleek and sinister, and as it begins its third circuit of the car-park, Schroeder pulls the Glock from his pocket and steps back against a tree. When the car finally comes to a stop beside him, the window steadily descending, Schroeder finds himself pointing the gun directly at the profile of a woman he has never seen before. A blonde in shades. She's a total mystery to him. Until, that is, he catches the sly burlesque smile.

– Get in, Anton.

Schroeder leans over and stares in wonder. Chantal looks good as a blonde in a trouser suit. Nothing of the Bohemian in her now and not a hint of the *chanteuse* behind those impenetrable shades. Not a sniff of the girl on the bicycle. And her legs look so long in the trousers, it's as if she now possesses a different body as well as a different passport.

– What are you doing? What's with the hair? With the wheels?

– Get in.

But Schroeder keeps staring and it's not until she tells him to put the gun away before he hurts himself that he even begins to understand. It's her voice. Her accent. No Galway in it now. Not a trace of it. She sounds like an American.

– Why are you talking like an American?

– Because I am a goddamn American. Get in the fucking car.

Schroeder pockets the Glock, gets in and waits to be spoken to as she takes the old coast road towards Sandycove. Out in the harbour Schroeder can see the *Barry* and a marina full of yachts all barred from sailing while it's there. He aims an accusing finger but Chantal doesn't react. With most people watching the funeral, the roads are quiet and the car glides southwards unmolested. The world seems somehow suspended. King will be in the ground soon and the new man – Flame – is no doubt already swinging around some new global bag of cats by which he might, in turn, be remembered when *his* end comes but such matters don't concern Schroeder for now. He's just trying to work out who exactly is driving the car.

Finally, as they near Dalkey and still look dead ahead, she speaks.
- So Schroeder. We need to discuss a few things.
- I think we probably do.
- I know this must seem a little strange.
- So you're American?
- You betcha.
- You're lucky I didn't shoot you.
- Schroeder, why exactly *do* you carry that gun?
- It's for decoration.
- Neat.
- Neat? Jesus. You really are American.
Schroeder's head starts to hurt and he rubs his temples hard.
- There's water in the glove compartment.
There's also a gun in the glove compartment and Schroeder recoils.
- Standard issue, Schroeder. And I'm not planning on using it.
- So who are you? UIA?
- My name is Taylor Copland and I'm not UIA.
- Taylor?
- Taylor Mary-Kate Copland, as in *Fanfare for the Common Man*.
- And this is your real accent?
- Sure is.
The car turns left at Sorrento Terrace and begins to climb the Vico Road, named, as I could tell her, whoever she is, for Giambattista Vico – he of the cyclic theory. The sky seems huge over the glittering sea and kites circle high above the mansions and piles. Naval vessels bead the horizon and a sudden chopper angles low along the cliffs.
- You like the beach, Schroeder?
On the crunching radioactive pebbles of Killiney Beach, Schroeder and Taylor Copland look just like any other couple, walking thoughtfully, passing the time of day in each others' company – the woman classy and sophisticated, the man scruffy and awkward in the open air. She's doing most of the talking and he's stopping

occasionally and waving his hands around. To passing joggers and dog-walkers they might be talking about the movies or home decor, or discussing some minor romantic dispute which the gentle waves will surely resolve.

– Your name just kept cropping up, she says. *Schroeder. Schroeder. Schroeder.* But nothing ever made any sense because we could see that you were no threat to anything. And yet somehow it seemed that for some reason you were being watched.

– I *was* being watched! I had a tout living next door! Not to mention J. Edgar fucking Hoover out pissing in his garden.

– Forget about him.

– And what about Walton?

– A low-level informer is all. Internet surveillance mostly. He was just another rat searching for dirt on anybody he knew. For blackmail purposes probably. And for him it was just something he could do all day long. Speculative but easy work. The net's just one giant honeytrap after all. Which of course is why they haven't shut it down.

– And Roark? What about him?

– Someone like him would have no idea what the big picture was.

– And the big picture is what exactly?

– Well I'll admit, we had no idea until the wild card showed up.

– Claude.

– Yep. It seems that your friend was the actual mark. That's who they were *really* watching. And so you were a sort of subsection of the operation. These people are always thorough. They cover all bases. And that meant that you were somehow in the picture.

– And who exactly are *these people*?

– I'm only authorized to tell you a certain amount.

– Yadda yadda yadda . . .

– Someone else will fill you in on the rest. But I can tell you this. Claude Butler did not kill President King.

– Of course he fucking did! People saw him do it!

– He didn't kill him and they know it. Why do you think you weren't even questioned in the Park? There was no need. They already know all there is to know.

– But he was writing mad letters to the White House. He was a basket case. His flat was full of guns and explosives. And Bibles.

– *Officially* yes, the assassin is Claude. But trust me, he didn't do it. And anyway it can't be done. Not like that. Think about it. *Numquam perit solus Caesar.*

Schroeder grips the bridge of his nose between finger and thumb. Taylor Copland does exactly the same thing.

– Look Schroeder, the official line is that the President was assassinated by Claude Butler and that he acted alone. At first this was all pretty straightforward, but then a certain mailman showed up and reported seeing a letter in which Butler asked to meet you just a few days before it happened.

– The skinhead.

– That was problematic. One of those loose ends that make these people very jumpy. That letter should never have reached you. But of course these are always the things that get missed. Something as simple as a letter. It was unfortunate because you were never part of the plan.

– What fucking plan? Are you saying that I'm part of some plan now? A conspiracy, is that it? Is that what this is all about? That the letter makes me part of it?

Taylor Copland looks out towards the Sugar Loaf. She takes her time, as if rehearsing every word in advance.

– They never saw that letter because it was destroyed before they could find it.

– But that letter was at my place. Nobody had any access to it. Who could possibly have destroyed it?

Taylor glances skywards and Schroeder hears her reply just a split second before she actually says it.

– Francesca.

Schroeder stops dead. Taylor Copland doesn't blink.

– She took it before she left and she burned it.

– Why would she do that?

– Because she knew it would implicate you.

– In *what* for fucksake?

– The assassination.

– But how? It hadn't happened yet!

Taylor Copland plays with her watch.

– Schroeder. Listen to me carefully. Francesca is not exactly in public relations. Yes, she works for your government but it's not in PR. And that's the reason she left you. I know she dressed it up, fed you a story and gave you reasons and made excuses about meeting someone – but there was nobody. It wasn't like that at all. It was more a case of a sudden and unexpected conflict of interest and, well, she chose her career. Destroying that letter was probably some kind of parting gift.

– What career?

– Schroeder, she's intelligence.

– Not a chance. If Francesca was involved in anything like that I would have known about it.

– Actually, Schroeder, you wouldn't have known about it. And you didn't.

– This is bullshit.

– She was recruited a year ago. By your own government at first. But the thing is, I think she might be working for more than one government. Or perhaps no government at all.

Schroeder waves a warning finger.

– No. Not a chance. No fucking way!

– I know this is hard to believe.

– UIA?

Taylor Copland nods.

– You sure we're talking about the same person?

She nods again.

– Chantal or Taylor or Margaret or whoever-the-fuck you are . . . you're out of your fucking mind!

– She's in Beijing as we speak.

– No, she's not in fucking Beijing. I happen to know that she's not.

– She's in Beijing, Schroeder. Nobody learns Mandarin for nothing.

Schroeder recalls Francesca sitting on a bollard outside that Blackrock restaurant. T-shirt and jeans. And how whenever they kissed in front of the bathroom mirror, he would watch her as if they were in a movie of their very own, because he had always preferred to believe that she existed only to a certain extent and that she was, in fact, as virtual as any Jakki Jack. It was one of his favourite theories after all – that she might be no more than a crucial, erotic and beautiful vision. That she was the fabulous Francesca Maldini – curious, fascinating, attentive, sensitive and understanding. And yet, throughout all the time they were together, it had always been her *realness* that he had skirted around. While some men unpacked their virtual lovers from boxes or fondled lap dancers on worn velvet seats, Schroeder had to himself a real, live, actual woman and yet he had preserved the conceit that she was otherwise. Could it have been possible that all this time she was flying back and forwards to China doing God knows what?

– Look, is this some kind of test? Some stupid role-play thing?

– No, Schroeder, it's not.

– So what does she do?

– We're not sure.

– Well let's see now. Does she, and let's just pick an example from the top of my head, does she kill people?

– There's no evidence for that.

– Good. Well that's something at least.

– But then of course there wouldn't be.

– What?

– Evidence.

– Jesus!

– Ever wonder why Walton set himself on fire?

– It was a suicide.

– But why did he do it?

– I don't know. He had a bad experience in Paradiso. Jakki Jack wasn't Jakki Jack. He lost the plot. How do I know?

– It was Francesca.

– What?

– Francesca.

– Why?

– Maybe she didn't like the pictures?

– So she what? She set him on fire? And anyway, I thought you said she was in Beijing.

– She is. She did it by proxy. She told Walton that Jakki Jack was dead. Blown to pieces in that Frankfurt bomb. And, somewhat traumatized by this, he did what he did. She didn't set him on fire herself. He did.

Schroeder takes the Glock from his pocket and holds it up to the light. He hops it a few times in his hand, feeling the weight of it in his palm, staring at it as if it were small dead pet. Then he hurls it spinning high into the air and out over the waves. He watches it rise, then stall, then plummet, and then he waits for it to land in the soup with a suck and a plop.

– So much for fucking Chekhov, he says. I seem to be a little out of my depth here.

– That's a fair assessment, says Taylor Copland, and she turns as if to resume her stroll. But Schroeder is going nowhere and he hunkers down on the stones.

– Why should I trust you on any of this? I mean, you're not a Galway girl on a bicycle, you're an American with a fuck-off weapon in your glove compartment.

– I'm telling you what I know.

– Well tell me this then. Why would Francesca destroy the letter? Why?

– Use your head, Schroeder. To protect you from any association with Claude Butler.

– But this was *before* King was killed. She's not a clairvoyant for fucksake. She didn't know Claude was going to do what he did.

Taylor Copland purses her lips and flicks her hair.

– Let's wait in the car, Schroeder.

– Wait for what exactly?

– Let's just wait in the car.

– I don't imagine I've much choice.

– Not a whole lot. This goes well beyond you and me.

Schroeder and Taylor Copland sit together for an hour, saying almost nothing and looking out at the swelling smog on the horizon. Walkers and joggers continue to bob along the shore. Three teenagers in wetsuits take off towards Dalkey in canoes. Crows mob a raggedy heron and pair of yellow dogs mate miserably in the grass. Taylor Copland closes her eyes and Schroeder tries to pinpoint the moment when his life stopped being his own. He can't do it.

– What exactly are we waiting for? he asks eventually.

Taylor straightens up and Schroeder follows her eyeline out towards the little tub of tower on Dalkey Island. She gets out of the car, rests her arse on the bonnet and they both look out into the waves. A rigid hull inflatable is bouncing across the water, fins of white water in its wake. Taylor signals Schroeder to get out and together they walk down towards the shore. The inflatable is coming straight for them and Schroeder can make out three men in black waterproofs. Schroeder's breath catches as the boat hushes onto the beach and a lifejacket lands at his feet.

– I guess your ride's here, says Taylor Copland.

– Where am I going?

– The Garden of Ireland.

– I'm going to Wicklow? In a boat?

– The roads are blocked, Schroeder. Go with these men. You'll be met. You'll stay in a safe place for a couple of weeks and then we'll take it from there.

– And what am I going to do in fucking Wicklow?

– You do nothing. You stay there. You'll be safe.

– I'm not going anywhere. I don't believe any of this crap. It's all bullshit. And anyway I have to do an interview.

– You won't be doing that. I've already spoken to Ms Viola.

– I'm doing that interview! And you can't stop me.

– What is it with you and her, Schroeder? I've been following you and you've been following her. OK she's an attractive woman, but jeez Schroeder that thing in Brown Thomas was just a little too creepy.

– She wants an exclusive interview and she can have it.

– At this time, Schroeder, an interview is not a runner. Absolutely no way. Go to Wicklow. Lie low. It'll give me time to sort things. In any case you were seen leaving Dublin Airport two hours ago and soon they'll be tearing up Paris looking for you.

– So I'm in Paris, am I?

– Misleading intelligence from an impeccable source. And one other thing. When you get to Wicklow. Shave your head. And keep it shaved.

– So now you're telling me to shave my head?

– And grow a beard.

– You want me to shave my head and grow a beard?

– Just do it, Schroeder. I'll explain next time I see you.

– This is just bullshit.

– Get in the boat, Schroeder.

Schroeder steps back.

– And how do I know these guys aren't going to kill me?

– Because I've told them not to.

SEVENTEEN

THE PALE NOW EXTENDS well beyond Dublin but the Garden of Ireland lies beyond it still. A sparsely populated county, Wicklow is home to tiny settlements of outsiders and outcasts – environmentalists, potters, marijuana farmers – and the crusty remnants of the aristocracy. The rest are a scattering of lost and lawless crews which, for the most part, exist like kernes in the oily muck of its forests and valleys. It's a place where a man might easily merge with the hedges and dissolve in the ditches and this, of course, is why Schroeder has been delivered here – to a charred cottage in one of the county's farthest corners – a deep, plunging valley shot across by occasional jays and lorded over by buzzards anticipating a corpse of some kind – perhaps even that of Schroeder himself. Quite the thought for his thanatophobic self.

But Schroeder, by his own account, is treated well and is free, within reason, to experience the many strange and exhausting flavours in the Wicklonian air. The steady supply of vodka helps. The pills too (even Presbutex), and whenever he requests something specifically to help him sleep – *really* sleep – this is also provided. It passes the time and Schroeder takes it as a better class of oblivion than dead drunkenness or resorting to anything with even trace amounts of opiate. The difficulty, of course, is that after a few days of uninterrupted slumber, Schroeder has absolutely no idea of exactly how long he has been there, and with time now twisted beyond even the understanding of his chunky Swiss watch (the first mention of this accoutrement), all he can be sure of is that it has been weeks rather than days. Not that it matters much anyway. There's nothing he can do about any of this. This is the back of beyond and it cannot be escaped.

In those first few days all questions are stone-walled and all anxieties are casually dismissed. Sometimes the Beetroot Man makes the odd remark about his growing beard, but the others – seven of them in all – are utterly silent and seem to float like phantoms, concealing themselves in various positions around the rocks and lanes – watching, waiting and guarding against some mystery which Schroeder has yet to understand. The only real moment of panic comes when the Beetroot Man takes Schroeder around the side of the farmhouse and asks him to stand up against the gable wall. Schroeder imagines Kilmainham bullets but all the man does is take his picture. A mugshot, it seems. The ragged beard and the shorn head all lumps and bumps like a bowl of alabaster eggs.

At night he stands at the window, raising his arms like a magician conjuring himself. Sometimes he is Vitruvian Man, Leonardo's perfect man, the geometric algorithm, the circle squared. But, at thirty-nine, the perfect lines and proportions are hardly credible and he becomes some desperate sidekick, starfished with leather manacles to a turning wheel, awaiting the rotor of hurtling steel. The blindfolded knife-thrower is spun and pointed vaguely at the revolving, rickety wheel, and Schroeder hears the daggers hurled at the crucial gaps between his limbs and feels the blood run from the side of his head, the thud of steel into cork and board and the audience gasping as one – the cold knives whacking against the heat of his ears and the curried sweat of his armpits. No place to be, he tells himself, pinned to a wheel in Cill Mhantáin, and he squirms and strains to free his ankles, wrists and neck. To get down off the cross and fly.

At times he can barely recognise himself. The lumpy head. The beard darkening on his jaws and every delta of leathery skin seemingly trapped within rivers of corkscrew veins that pulse and strain with crazed cells and messages. He holds up his arms and makes a Y of himself, allowing his hands to droop like a dancer's and, admiring his new and languid shape, he bends one knee over the other and hangs his head low to one side – a three-step transfiguration from shorn magician to Vitruvian Man to knife thrower's assistant to Jesus Christ himself. Same ribs, same stretched muscles, same sinews in the neck.

He tries, at times, to figure things out, but always in the end he realises that there's nothing sensible he can surmise or even reasonably speculate upon. And as a result he gets a little monkish – meditative even – contemplating the smallest things. A beetle making its way across the flags, a spider on the ceiling, a slater under the mat. The only thing he doesn't dwell upon – thanks be to medication and booze – is the body count back in Dublin. The President whacked, the priest popped, Walton cooked to blackened jerky on Sandymount Strand and that shit Roark nibbled by three-eyed mackerel as he bobs his way to Wales.

And to think that he could be at home in his front room with Paula Viola sitting right in front of him and willing to do anything – anything – just to get the story. Unbuttonings and loosenings, clips and straps, fingernails and tongues. And he knows that he will, if he ever gets away from here, make sure, no matter what, to give her that exclusive. And while he's thinking of her, I'm thinking of him. And I confess that I'm worried sick. I'm not a believer. How could I be when I've studied so much human nature in my time? But in this latest crisis I pray a little even so. To all the many gods of my childhood. In the hope that maybe one of them might remember me. Ah, you again. The little heretic . . .

When I was eleven years old I believed so fervently in a higher power that I simply couldn't accept, as was expected of me, that there was only one. And so I figured, in an imaginative heresy of my own, that there was a multitude of gods – billions of them – and that each person on Earth had a god all to themselves. One each. For the most part these deities got on well enough with each other, but whenever they fell out, that was when trouble started either for the individual or for the country in which he lived. Things might well remain local if you were lucky, but if enough gods got drawn into the row then you had a war. Maybe one god would take it out on another god or perhaps even a group of gods would gang up on another group, the consequences for mankind depending on the severity of the dispute. It was a dangerous theory for an eleven year old and they tried to make me recant. But I never did. Not formally anyway. And so, for want of anything more constructive to do, I now pray to them all. And I pray for Schroeder's safe return.

And then, early one morning, Taylor Copland shows up and asks Schroeder to join her in the kitchen. She settles herself against the sink and looks him up and down.

– You look like the Taliban.

– Not a good look, is it?

– Not in my home town.

She indicates that Schroeder should sit, and pours him a coffee.

– Good news, Schroeder. You're in the clear.

– In the clear with who?

– With everybody concerned. I'm sorry it took so long. But it's sorted.

– How long have I been here?

– Too long, I know. But you owe me big time.

– For what exactly?

– For convincing certain people that you're no danger to anybody. That you had no prior knowledge of the President's assassination. That you know nothing much about anything.

– But I *didn't* have any knowledge of it! I *don't* know anything!

– Sure. And in the absence of the letter there's no reason to believe otherwise.

– And what about him? The mailman? He knows what was in it.

– He's out of the picture.

– What does that mean?

– It means he's out of the picture.

– Jesus!

– The important thing, Schroeder, is that nobody can connect you to Butler.

– And what about Redding's Hotel? Those hookers weren't hookers. You said so yourself.

– They were watching Claude. Not you.

– But they must have found out who I was?

– Of course they did. But they were ordered to forget about it. And they did that.

– Ordered by who?

– By the people who give orders.

– And the bartender?

– He wasn't a bartender.

– Is anybody who they fucking say they are?

– Probably not.

– And who am I now? With my fetching new look?

– Go freshen up, Schroeder. We're going to Dublin.

And so this especially elastic stretch of narrative snaps back once more. The characters like yo-yos. The action up and down like a hoor's drawers and the plot condemned by the powerful-altogether suck of Louisiana sinkholes. So then what's to be said of this Wicklow diversion? This uneventful sojourn in the Garden of Hibernia, this almost Edenic idyll under armed guard in the lawless, distant hills beyond? Has it, in any way, transported or enraptured us, and if so, to what degree? But then to ask whether the story has been pushed along, as is customarily demanded, would be to ask the wrong Q. For the A is not concerned with plot and its devices and my feelings on same are known. My sole issue, I repeat, is the truth. *Verum ipsum factum*, as per Vico of the Vico Road, Killiney, County Dublin. So bear with me. I'm almost done.

Half an hour later, in some dead man's suit and sipping vodka from a flask, Schroeder is on his way back to Eblana, Deblana, *Dubh Linn*. Taylor looks focussed and severe, her gun breathing heavily in the glove compartment.

– But won't they come after me anyway? Schroeder asks. To be sure to be sure?

– No need. Everyone has bought the Claude story. It's plausible after all. And nobody wants to fire up a conspiracy theory by taking out the guy's school pals for no good reason.

– And you're still saying he didn't do it?

– He didn't.

– And you're saying I can go about my business as normal?

– Not quite. Not yet.

– I've got the feeling there's something you're not telling me.

– Look, Schroeder, I'm looking after you.

– I'm not convinced.

– And to think there was a time when you'd have crawled across cut glass for me.

– That was Margaret Lynch. She was an Irish girl on a bicycle.

Schroeder angles his face into the breeze.

– And I need to contact Paula Viola.

– Told you, Schroeder. Not a runner. Not at this juncture.

– So this is a juncture, is it?

– Be patient. We're getting there.

Taylor drives with one hand on the wheel, clicking gum against her teeth. There are battleships in the bay. One of them Irish. The rest American.

– What's in the vodka? Schroeder asks.

– Nothing dangerous. But it'll keep you calm. You've had a tough time.

– Well, whatever it is, I like it.

– You know, Schroeder, I'm thinking. You sure have a lot of women in your life. Paula, Francesca, the late great Ms Jack. And then there's me, and variations on the theme of me. You must be quite the man.

– Men born of women.

– Well, we certainly seem in charge of your particular tale. What there is of it.

– I need to contact Paula Viola. She's expecting a call.

– All these women, Schroeder. You must be quite the guy. If I wasn't a vagitarian, I'd try you out myself.

Schroeder drops the flask in his lap.

– What did you say?

Taylor Copland reaches over and picks up the flask.

– I'm just saying I wish she'd interview me.

Schroeder starts sneezing violently. Seven or eight wild sneezes in a row.

– Oh, Schroeder, you're so damn easy.

Taylor Copland hands Schroeder a laminated pass which bears his Wicklow mugshot. Schroeder stares at himself, bearded, anxious and bald.

– Put it on, please.

Schroeder rubs his eyes with his knuckles and angles the laminate to the light. He reads his name aloud. Professor Cosmas Rafferty. Department of English. Trinity College Dublin.

– Who the fuck is Cosmas Rafferty?

– You are. For the next few hours anyway.

– And where are we going exactly?

– You're going to work. Exactly.

– There's no Cosmas Rafferty in the English Department.

– He started a year ago. Irish-American. Does that whole Northern writer schtick.

– Another one? Spare me.

The front of Trinity looks like a thronged Jerusalem marketplace, a brightness of t-shirts and tops set against the grim sulk of military couture. Olive-drab and baby-shit brown. Students gather at the first checkpoint, their laminates swaying in the sun. Above it all, set in copper permanence, Edmund Burke surveys the sangars with distaste while Goldsmith, stuck on a page, ignores the whole thing – the silent scholars passing through metal detectors and funnelling into the cool of the courtyard. Trinity College Dublin. Coláiste na Trínóide, *Collegium Sacrosanctae et Individuae Trinitatis Reginae Elizabethae juxta Dublin.*

Schroeder gazes up at the blackened facade and tugs at his beard. Taylor Copland addresses him via the rear-view mirror.

– Your name is Professor Rafferty. That's all you need to remember.

At the barrier, looking dead ahead, she flashes a pass and a jarhead in Ray-Bans waves her through without a word. The car moves slowly across the cobbles of Parliament Square and then diagonally, still at a crawl, toward the Narrows and the lawns, all concreted over, and then through yet another barrier which rises and falls at the discretion of heavily armed men. Her magic pass is waved again and, after taking the merest squint at Schroeder in the back, another soldier nods.

– You have a good day, he says.

Taylor Copland parks the car, opens the door for Schroeder and leads him towards a corner block.

– Professor Rafferty. Prof Raff to your students. You got it?

– I got it. Although I've no idea what I've got it for.

– Just try to look intelligent.

– I look like a fucking idiot.

– Will you please just walk like a professor.

The entire block seems deserted. No shouts in the stairwell, no whistling caretakers and no slamming doors – just the crack of Taylor's shoes ricocheting around the walls. On a third-floor corridor they approach a door. On the door is Schroeder's new name. Prof C. Rafferty.

– This is you, says Taylor Copland.

The room smells of leather and damp wood. Apple smells and dried books and, through the window, Schroeder can see a thousand rooftops – slate-grey Dublin the same as it ever was. On the wall there's a portrait of Wolfe Tone in the uniform of a French officer.

– If only that man had succeeded, he says, you wouldn't be here at all. We'd all be living like decent Frenchmen by now.

– If I'm not mistaken, Professor Rafferty, that man cut his own throat. Please, take a seat.

Schroeder sits. Taylor Copland exits and then returns a moment later with a man who is obviously security. Crew-cut, clean-shaven and expressionless, his shoulders set in a navy-blue suit. Ignoring Schroeder completely, he glances around the room, nods to Taylor Copland and leaves. Taylor Copland then stands in silence with her back to the door and Schroeder looks up at Tone again, admiring the nose, the ponytail, the epaulettes.

– The French are on the sea, says the Shan Van Vocht.

And then there's a gentle knock and Taylor turns, opens the door and leaves. Schroeder peers up from the desk. Into the room, in jeans and a hoodie, walks Princess King.

– Good morning, she says. Thank you very much for coming.

Schroeder hears himself gulp. He stands up, stumbling slightly, and the first thing that comes out of his mouth is something about being sorry for her loss. She thanks him with swift efficiency and suggests that they both take a seat. And so they sit, the President's daughter and the assassin's childhood pal, face-to-face across Professor Rafferty's ancient pockmarked desk. A slight cough and she begins.

– I apologise for the fact that you've had to alter your appearance so drastically, she says, but it was essential if we were ever to meet like this. Prof Raff is my tutor and this seemed like the only way. For the two of us to meet alone, that is. I hope you understand. Actually you look just like him.

– So where's the real one?

– Moscow. A symposium.

– Don't tell me. Sectarianism in the Short Story?

– Something like that.

She is even more beautiful than Schroeder remembers. The hood frames her face and makes a holy picture of her. Bereavement seems to agree with her.

– Actually we met before, says Schroeder. Briefly.

– I know. You were very kind.

– I'm surprised you remember.

– Mr Schroeder, we don't have much time so let me get right to it. Your friend did not kill my father. I thought you should know. And I thought you should hear it from me.

– People keep telling me that.

– Well, it's true.

– Look, to be honest I didn't really know the guy at all.

Princess King takes off her hood and begins to play with the toggles. Her eyes are green. Piercing.

– Do you believe in coincidence? she asks. In real life I mean.

– Well yes, in that it exists. So yes, I suppose so. Fate no, but coincidence yes. Sure.

– Have you ever heard of Edwin Booth?

Schroeder shakes his head.

– There were three brothers – Edwin, Junius Brutus Junior and John Wilkes – and they all starred together in a production of *Julius Caesar.* Then, three weeks after the end of that run, John Wilkes turned up at another theatre and shot Abraham Lincoln.

– I'm not sure that's a *coincidence*, exactly.

– No. But this next part is. Just a few months before Lincoln was shot, Edwin Booth pulled a young man from the path of an oncoming train at a Jersey City railway station. The man was Robert Lincoln. Abraham Lincoln's son.

– Well I guess that really is a coincidence, yes.

– And if you made it up, nobody would believe you, right?

Schroeder strokes the marble smoothness of his head and shrugs.

– Ms King, I still don't understand why I'm here.

Princess puts her hood back up and goes over to the window.

– There are people who think my father's administration was run by the Devil. I mean *literally* by the Devil. That it was all some sort of Satanic cult. And fair enough, I suppose. Some of those people he was in bed with would kick off a war without a second thought. I mean there were people who came to dinner who made me physically ill. Do you believe in the Devil, Mr Schroeder?

– No. But I know a man who does.

– I'd like to meet him.

– No you wouldn't. He's a very rude bartender. You can probably see the place from here.

– I don't imagine I'll ever meet him then. My social life is somewhat limited.

– Well, you're not missing much.

Princess smiles but the smile soon drops away again.

– My father wasn't a bad man, Mr Schroeder. He certainly wasn't a killer. Not by nature anyway. Sure, he made the decisions, but in the end, and to his credit in a way, he couldn't actually live with them. The drink. The pills. We all know about that. I guess you could say he was a man very much violated by experience.

– I really am sorry about what happened. It must be tough for you. This whole thing.

– Thank you.

– I don't suppose you get a lot of sympathy.

– No, I don't. But you know it would be a great mistake to assume that my father's politics and mine were the same. We were not the same person. We were father and daughter and that's all. I loved him as a father because he was a good father. Although after a while, he sort of stopped being my dad and became something else. And it wasn't about power either, it was more the attention. He liked that a lot. And once he became Vice-President and then President he was sort of carried through life like a groom at a wedding. And he liked that too. I lost him somewhere in there. And he lost himself. I'm telling you this, Mr Schroeder, because you were kind to me that day when we met in the tutorial. I appreciated the way you spoke to me. And I liked your book too.

– You read it? I'm very sorry to hear that. It didn't make a lot of sense in places.

– Well, yes. In places. And perhaps the tone was a little seedy for my taste but yes, I thought it was good. And you seemed to me to be devoted to the truth – whatever that may be.

She stares up at Wolfe Tone and bites her thumb.

– Look, Mr Schroeder, I know who killed my father. I was there when it happened.

– They said you weren't there.

– Oh, I was there alright.

– Are you sure you should be telling me this?

Princess sits down, and once again down comes the hood. Then another little cough to clear the way.

– My father was not a well man, she says. He drank. People know that. But the truth is that he was often depressed. And I mean *extremely* depressed. And this, as you will appreciate, is something which had to be handled with the utmost secrecy. I mean, he was Commander-in-Chief after all. Not good for morale, or indeed global security, to have the most powerful man on the planet crying into his pillow, is it? And so they watched him as closely as any human being has ever been watched. His pills were counted out for him, belts and ties were taken off him and he was never once allowed anywhere near a weapon. There was always the fear that, just once, he might get around his own security and do something stupid. Something unthinkable.

– Look, Ms King, I think you're getting into areas here that I really don't need to know about. And I'd really rather you didn't.

Schroeder tries to focus on an abstract pattern of gouges in Professor Rafferty's desk. He can make out what looks like the Colorado River, the Grand Canyon and the Hoover Dam. Then the canals of Mars. But when he lifts his eyes again she is staring right at him, her eyes now moist with tears.

Princess exhales loud and hard and straightens up.

– There were only a few times each day when my father was ever alone and that was when he went to the bathroom. As he left the dinner that night, he said he needed to go. Secret Service checked the room as they always do, and then they stepped aside and my father went in alone. He was the only person in the place who hadn't been thoroughly searched. And get this for the Wild West, he had a pistol in his boot. In his fucking boot. An antique. A Deringer. A collector's item. And here's another coincidence for you. It was the same kind of gun that killed Abraham Lincoln.

Schroeder reaches across the table and takes the hands of Princess King. She strokes the tops of his with her thumbs and her voice cracks at last.

– Mr Schroeder, she says. These things are always inside jobs and what happened in Dublin was the ultimate inside job. Your friend didn't shoot my father. My father shot himself.

Schroeder's hands are sweating now. The hands of Princess too.

I have said many times that this is no thriller. My exact words were – *this is no thriller or makey-up tale of suspense. Nor is it some titillating, investigative reconstruction of events which may or may not have happened. It is, rather, an honest and faithful record of breakage and distress at a time when dysfunction – personal, local, national, global, cosmic and whatever lies beyond that again, beyond even the farthest pricks of our increasingly desperate little probes – pervaded all. A time when everything was already broken and when, in many ways, the shooting of a President (the actual detail that is) was neither here nor there.*

But even so, we appear to have landed (for all my resistance to the undoubted thrills and spills of it) at some class of denouement. A resolution of a doubtful series of events. A twist. A surprise perhaps. Even a shock. But then, at the heel of the hunt, a denouement forgettable enough in its way. OK, so he killed himself? I get it. Any further business? An anticlimactic climax perhaps and one with, for all its drama, a short-lived pulse. But then as I've said, this has never been about the assassination of Richard Rutledge Barnes King nor its actual details, which are neither here nor there.

– I don't understand why you're telling me this, says Schroeder.

– I owe it to your friend. He was the D. A.

– I don't know what that is.

– Not many do. Anytime my father went anywhere outside the White House there was always somebody in the vicinity known to the inner circle as the D. A. The Designated Assassin.

– Designated?

– Look, my father was basically on permanent suicide watch – a suicide which, if it ever happened, could never and would never, ever, be acknowledged. If anybody was going to kill a US President it certainly wasn't going to be the President himself. So there always had to be someone present who would take the fall if my father tried anything and natural causes just wouldn't fit the facts. And that's what happened in Dublin. Too many people heard the shot. Too many people saw the blood.

– So Claude was a patsy?

– He was the D.A. He was brought into play.

– But why was he even there in the first place?

– He'd been invited. By no less than the President himself. At least he thought he'd been invited. Your friend was a fairly typical D.A. He'd been writing to the White House for a long time, so they had him in place should the need arise. And the need arose. When they opened the door of the cubicle and saw my father's . . . condition . . . the plan went into action immediately. Your friend was asked if he would like to meet the President. He said yes of course he would, that he'd be honoured and, I'm very sorry to tell you this, Mr Schroeder, they took him away and shot him in the head. That way the assassin was dead too. He had turned the gun on himself, etc. etc. No loose ends.

– Dead at the scene.

– Dead at the scene. Look, Mr Schroeder, these people are a different species.

Schroeder can't seem to locate a single word in his head. He pulls his hands away, rubs his eyes, caresses the bumps of his head and then with his knees literally bouncing up and down, he attacks the old Protestant upholstery with his fingernails. Princess takes a deep breath, waits for him to stop, then continues.

– Things are rotten, Mr Schroeder. I know they are. But we have to believe that the next guy will be a good guy. We make our own choices. We are not our fathers. None of us are. But you must never reveal that you spoke to me. That would be very bad for both of us. I'm sure you understand.

– But why are you telling me all this?

– I haven't told you anything. I'm one of only about twenty people who know what really happened and they're all fanatics – all loyal to the institution at all costs. They will never reveal anything.

Ever. And neither will I.

– So what is it you want from me?

Princess King stands up and offers her hand.

– I'm sorry for your loss of your friend. Goodbye, Mr Schroeder. Then she pulls up her hood, taps the door and it opens. She steps out and Taylor Copland steps in.

– Let's go, Mr Schroeder.

In silence, Taylor drives Schroeder back to Hibernia Road. She pulls up at the corner and turns off the ignition.

– You OK, Schroeder?

Schroeder can't get it out of his head. A large restroom in Dublin Castle. The room spacious and plush with blue tiles and a white panelled door centrally positioned. There are gilded mirrors and large white sinks with gilded fittings. There's a line of cubicles of dark wood. President King enters smiling, but once inside the restroom his expression changes. He walks around, getting more and more agitated. He looks in a mirror. He produces a flask from his jacket and takes a long hard swig. He turns and looks to the cubicle. His expression darkens further. He approaches it slowly and enters. He closes the door and then silence. And then a gunshot and a red mist and King slumps forward, his falling body forcing open the cubicle door as he falls, face-first, onto the restroom floor. A small gun skitters across the floor as the President hits the ground. The secret servicemen burst into the room, weapons drawn, and it's all motherfucker this and motherfucker that. Then the D. A. comes into play and Claude Butler is taken away and shot.

– Why did she tell me all those things?

– She didn't tell you anything.

– Oh fuck off! Are we done now?

– Look Schroeder, Ms King wanted to speak with you. I facilitated the meet. It's a meeting which never happened. So yes, I guess we're done.

– Schroeder shrugs.

– You know, I really fancied that *chanteuse*.

– You're an interesting guy, Schroeder, but you're not *that* interesting. If you were a book I'm not sure I'd finish you.

– So that's it then? Mission accomplished? Whatever the fucking mission was? All of this Professor Rafferty stuff was just so you could smuggle me into Trinity so she could tell me stuff that she would immediately deny. I mean seriously? Is that it? I mean there's bodies all over the fucking place and I'm sitting here looking like Arvo Pärt. What exactly was all of this about?

– Ms King likes you, Schroeder. Don't disappoint her.

– What do you mean disappoint her? Disappoint her how? What exactly am I supposed to be doing?

Taylor Copland hands Schroeder a yellow manila folder.

– Ms King asked me to give you this.

– What's this?

– I wouldn't know.

Inside is a typewritten manuscript. Two hundred pages. Or thereabouts.

EIGHTEEN

SIX MONTHS LATER and I'm seated at my kitchen table. Before me is a dark chocolate muffin speared through the crown by a burning red candle. Schroeder, still asleep, is forty years old today and I raise my mug in his honour. The Big Four-Oh people call it, winking at each other as if they're about to enter some secret velvety room for a new kind of sex. As if landing at forty means something that only other forty year olds understand but must never disclose, some delicious new reward for the inductee, something too luscious, too ritualized, too specialized to even talk about aloud. But when Schroeder's clock struck midnight last night, nothing wondrous happened at all and he found himself utterly alone. And with nobody, not even Taylor Copland, to call.

The vodka teased like a kiosk stripper but sober now for half a year, he resisted well. He made another pot of coffee and sat up late, proofing his typewritten manuscript (now heading for two hundred and something pages) for the very last time, running the final red pen over his tale of extremophiles, assassinations and the inadequacies of men. No title yet but he's thinking of *Everything Is Broken*. Or *Catafalque*. Or *Dead at the Scene*. Or maybe *We All Know What Happened*, which was once the opening line. A bigger question still is his pseudonym – last night he decided on Prosper something, as in St. Prosper of Aquitaine, a follower, as I could have told him, of Augustine of Hippo.

As I gaze now at the candle's flame, I recall the morning of my own fortieth birthday. There I was flexing my biceps at the mirror, watching them shrink back into nothing, convinced that a deep physical decay had commenced almost overnight. And only recently flabby about the waist, I became suddenly afraid of my life (and more so of my death), and all I could see was one of those men who strip themselves daily and wade into the caged-off shallows of Seapoint. The old men of the rocks out from first light, every day of their lives, stripping off within spitting distance of Sellafield and the oozing sewers of Swiftian Dublin. The ancient, hairy-eared, horny-toed cormorant-men of Dublin Bay with their saggy chests pointing earthwards in wobbly little W's that were once matters of pectorals and pride. As a dangerous little treat, I had vodka and orange for breakfast that morning and then I did something I had solemnly promised I would never do again.

For years, as agreed, there hadn't even been eye contact. Now, temporarily deranged by vodka, Weetabix and crisis, I broke all my own promises and knocked at the door of no. 28. Mr S was at work and the boy was at school. Mrs S didn't say a word. She just turned and walked back down the hall, me floating behind her into the sitting room. I stood there, literally shivering as she moaned a theatrical moan and, with two lightly trailing fingers, dragged her sparkly red slippers from under the sofa and guided her red toenails towards them. It was a simple action but it made something instantly marvellous of her legs – sheer, perfect shapes no matter where you looked, the points of the prima ballerina, the calves of the cellist, the thighs of wild-haired Carmen rolling fat cigars on flesh the colour of coffee. Mrs S was a beautiful woman who well knew her beauty, understanding every last twist of her toes.

– We had promised, she said, examining her fingernails. And it was working well.

– I know, I whispered, visibly trembling now.

– So why today? she asked. We have managed for years.

– I don't know, I said. But it's my birthday today.

– Ah! smiled Mrs S. The Big Four-Oh.

I nodded with mock sadness.

– We have an hour, she said. Then we must never, ever speak to each other again.

– I'm sorry for turning up like this.

– You're just lucky I'm in the mood.

And so I prayed very urgently (to all the gods of my childhood) that I might still look passable in a certain light. In candlelight perhaps? Or the demure tilt of an anglepoise? Surely in the flattering chiaroscuro of the Caravaggisti I mightn't look too bad for forty? At least in some flickering golden glow which might give me some illusory definition and a little waxy contrast and tone. Perhaps even a touch of warmth and sparkle? But what an imposter I was! What a deluded interloper! To even consider standing in all my wreckage before the astonishing nakedness of Mrs S.

The bedroom was out of bounds for many reasons, and so Mrs S tapped the blinds and the living room darkened in a pre-performance hush. And then, with Mrs S making the definite first move, we made urgent love on the sofa and seriously damaged the coffee table. It was all over very quickly and when I moved in for dessert she gently pushed me away, telling me to leave by the back door and, if I could at all manage it at my age, climb over the wall. I smiled a grim smile and saluted. Mrs S saluted back. This had been a pleasant but extremely dangerous slip and all vows were solemnly re-sworn on the spot.

And then I watched as Mrs S closed her eyes. She really was so very, very beautiful, and I could have kissed her again as a lover might, but I had promised. There would be no more. And in any case, she was perhaps already in her dream, in her turquoise lagoon with some fruity drink with rum and sugar served in a coconut with a purple parasol, weightless in a golden haze that fizzes with emerald hummingbirds, zigzagging back and forth among palms and droplety ferns, her shiny brown skin all nut-smelling and slippery with factor 55. And almost as if within that lustful tangle of black Medusa hair Mrs S could still feel my eyes upon her, she stirred and said something that sounded like a very firm no. Spoons would have been perfect but I had to scarper like the Pimpernel. I blew a final kiss and watched it loop towards the hot salty flesh of her throat and I left. The boy hadn't been mentioned once.

And here, of course, another denouement of sorts. And this perhaps more interesting than the last and certainly more faithful to the French. An untying rather than a wrapping up. Schroeder. The boy. His father's son. Ah yes, the secrets of paternity always sure-fire dynamite in fiction and in life. The contacts and near-misses. The resemblances uncommented on. The cragginess, the thinning hair, the ridges of potato drills on his skull. And now that boy is forty. A man as I was then.

And so, on this his birthday, Schroeder shaves, showers and slaps on aftershave which was a present from Francesca two Christmases ago. He buttons up an Italian shirt, also a gift – linen, grey and faded but fragrant still with memories of holidays and rich meals of Chianti and wild boar. But today he's not thinking of Francesca Maldini – he's thinking of Paula Viola, and Maximillian has already been given a talking to. Nose hairs have been plucked, shoes have been spat upon and three dusty bottles of Brunello di Montalcino face off on the sideboard. Everything conducive and copacetic. And, a full hour ahead of the crew, she arrives bang on time.

Dressed as a vampy librarian, the body of Paula Viola moves beneath her blouse in ways that make Schroeder instantly dizzy. Her hair is longer now, gathered up in a scrunchie, and to see her sitting in the very armchair in which he has so often imagined her is, to Schroeder, almost unbearable. Everything about her is perfect. Even her teeth make him horny.

– So why now? she asks. It's been six months.

– It's my birthday.

– I left a lot of messages. You never got back.

Schroeder's brain is working very hard. He can hear it chunder with the sheer effort of trying to sound impressive.

– I needed time. I was taking stock. I was getting fit. Writing again.

– About what happened?

– Partly that. But mostly about extremophiles.

– Terrorists?

– No. They're not terrorists. They're a sort of microbe and they'll outlast everything else on Earth. Think of a place where nothing can possibly live.

– Like Limerick?

– Worse. A stalactite, say, in the deepest, darkest cave on the planet. Or inside a rock in the hottest desert. Or in polar ice. Or in the sulphurous springs of Hell. Anywhere you can think of. That's where you'll find an extremophile. The worse the conditions, the better these little fellas like it.

– Sounds interesting.

– Well we'll see. It'll need a few more drafts.

Paula Viola's hand rests on her thigh. Maximillian rages and I monitor everything with growing dismay.

– So what have you got for me? asks Paula Viola.

– I'd like to discuss it further.

– In what way discuss it? We agreed on the phone.

– I'm not so sure, now that I . . .

– We have agreed on an interview, Mr Schroeder. The crew is on its way.

And so what can I do? So close and yet unable to act. Short of Navy Seals bursting through the walls, nothing will get in the way of what will happen next. Schroeder has imagined this day for years, day after day, night after night. And for six months now he has struggled with the enormous fact that he has the power to make his fantasies come true, that he has the very information which would bring Paula Viola right into his home.

– Ms Viola. How much do you much you want this interview?

– I'm here, aren't I?

– I know who killed King.

– Claude Butler killed King.

– He didn't.

Paula Viola blinks. She takes a breath.

– OK, then. If, for the sake of argument, Claude Butler didn't kill King, then who did?

Schroeder smiles.

– Don't do it, Schroeder, I'm saying to the muffin on the plate.

– Don't do it, Schroeder, says Taylor Copland to the gun in her glove compartment.

– Don't do it, Schroeder, says Francesca to the kites above Tiananmen Square.

– Don't do it, Schroeder, says Princess King to the portrait of her dad.

But before Schroeder quite realises what he's doing he reaches out and touches Paula Viola's damson hair, slipping his fingers deep into its strands and gripping slightly, tenderly. She leans her head back but Schroeder brushes a fingernail along the side of her neck and his fingers move to her cheek.

– Mr Schroeder, what exactly do you think you're doing?

– Ms Viola, I want you to come upstairs.

– Let's just pretend I didn't hear that, shall we?

– Come upstairs with me now. And I'll tell you exactly who killed Richard King.

Paula Viola pulls away.

– This is bullshit. Claude Butler killed him. Everybody knows that.

– He didn't. And I know who did.

– Give me a name.

– I will.

– You mean in exchange for sex? Is that what you're saying? You'd go that low?

– I would. The question is would you?

– Oh yeah, it's the story of the century. I forgot.

– Governments will fall, Ms Viola. I guarantee it.

Paula Viola stands up and smoothes her skirt. Schroeder sneezes.

– You're lying.

Schroeder stands up.

– I don't lie.

– OK then, who's your source?

– I can't say.

– Tell me who your source is right now or this goes no further.

– I can't tell you that.

Paula Viola suddenly grabs Schroeder by the buckle of his belt and pulls him close. His breath catches as she stares hard into his face, searching for flickers of falsehood or truth. She presses herself against him.

– Who's your fucking source?

– I can't say.

Paula twists the buckle tight.

– Who killed Cock Robin, Mr Schroeder? Tell me.

– It wasn't Claude Butler.

She yanks the buckle hard.

– You sure about that?

– He was stitched up.

She exhales deep and hard right into his mouth.

– You better not be playing me with this.

– I'm very serious.

She grabs his hair with her free hand.

– Tell me who your source is.

– No.

And then Paula Viola stands back, arches an eyebrow and flicks at a button.

– Tell me who your source is.

Schroeder stares at the open button.

– Someone very close to the President. That's all I can say.

– Nobody close to the President would talk. Especially to you.

– My source *is* someone close to the President.

Paula Viola opens another button with one hand and waits for the sneezing to stop.

– How well did you know Princess King?

– She was a student of mine at Trinity. That's all.

– Is she your source?

– My source is someone very close to the President.

Another button.

– And you'll go on record?

– Yes.

Another button. Another sneeze.

– And you'll tell me everything. On camera.

– Yes.

– Everything?

– I'll tell you everything.

Schroeder sits back on the sofa and watches Paula Viola strip down to stilettos and a G-string. Then her hair comes down and she tousles it just as he imagined she would.

– You'd better hurry up, she says. The crew will be here soon.

Paula Viola turns and walks out of the room and although Schroeder watches and lusts, he stays exactly where he is. And whether or not he ever really considers following her upstairs is a secret he will never share. Perhaps he just wants to see how far she will go? Or how far he will not? Paula Viola, to whom he is utterly addicted, has just presented herself at last and he is saying no. He hears her stilettos cracking like bullets on the bare stairs of no. 28 and Schroeder, at forty, is saying no.

And so, on the morning of the Big Four-Oh, Schroeder quietly gives thanks for Francesca Maldini and her parting gift, for Taylor Copland and her ruthless sleight of hand, and yes, for Paula Viola too, as naked as he's dreamt her, her heels now digging into his brand-new goose-down duvet. But most of all he gives thanks for Princess King – a President's daughter who rejected all dysfunction and moved, in one generation, from lost to decent soul and entrusted him with secrets which might, one day, clear the way for who knows what and when. So no. He will not disappoint her. Not now. He must not.

But this, no more than any previous denouement is no way to end things. To either wrap, or more correctly, untie. Not with this soundtrack. A wah-wah, bump n' grindy jazz setting of "Unlaceable You." No. Not with an unconsummated sex scene (contains some nudity) which might, at best, be seen as rather obvious commentary on the treachery, venality and general unseemliness of the media. Or perhaps on the dull predictability of sexual desire and the limited vision of the male gaze. Or, then again, having said that, on the time-less allure of the stiletto. Not the kitten heel, of course, but a proper dagger. Invented by Leonardo, they say. And which, as any school-boy will tell you, can inflict more damage on your metatarsus than an elephant. But there it is. *Dénouement pour Alto Solo. Smorzando.* Next door at no. 26, I pout at the flame, extract the smoking candle and raise the muffin before me. I bite down hard and reason as I chew. Yes. Everything is indeed broken now. Without question. Presidents kill themselves, innocent men get executed in their turn and touts and handlers play out their several games. Unhappy men addicted to booze, sex, information and power stupefy themselves with drugs that unblock their brains on one side and then eat right through them on the other. And yes. I am, in ways, one of them myself. But today, on Schroeder's fortieth birthday, it seems that stranger things are happening. Somehow. Up above my head.

There are tiny spits of rain as I watch Schroeder disappear along Hibernia Road carrying the yellow manila folder. For months, this same folder has been a source of some torture for me, every night listening to Schroeder tapping away, sometimes slowly, sometimes with what seems like rage. But for all my surveillance skills, for all my instinct and experience, even I can't hook into a Hermes 3000. And whatever is in that folder, only Schroeder knows for now. He stands at the corner under a cordyline, stuffs the folder underneath his shirt and watches the rain come down. This is a good day, he tells himself. And a day which is now his own. All this rain, he's thinking to himself – if he's anything like me at all – is as thrilling as a snare drum.

Or perhaps he is just now realising that, based on what he knows, he must concentrate entirely on the assassination. On the conspiracy and the cover-up. And nothing else. No pandiculation, no Borgnine reveries, no retromingent dogs, no historical asides, no ornithology, and as little taxonomy and toponymy as possible. No Latin, Irish or Greek for sure, and in my opinion certainly no comic interludes, sousaphones and words like fuck and fucksake. Most of

all, and this is crucial, he must leave himself out of it entirely. And
me too. At all costs. And then he'll have some story on his hands.
I'm an old man now and the best I can do is bequeath him all I
have. He will have everything at his disposal, including, for what it's
worth, this shirt-box full of hurried pages. After I'm gone, of course,
as per my instructions to Blood, Tobin & Fry Solicitors.

And so I leave things here, with Schroeder under a cordyline, me
at the window and Ms Paula Viola – broadcaster and succubus – arranged like some vicious odalisque on Schroeder's bed. She's trying
to figure it all out. That if, for the sake of argument, it wasn't Claude
Butler, then who? And if, for the sake of argument, it wasn't Claude
Butler, then how would Schroeder be aware of same? But then of
course, as I have said on more than one occasion, there is nothing which cannot be known. Not a thing. And as I descend to my
garden to inspect my dacha and my barricade and see what gilded
finches may have landed in my hedge, I can still hear her summons
through the walls. Shouting up at the chandelier. The general thrust
of her vociferation – from the Latin *vox* and *ferre* – being that Schroeder get his skates on and that, whatever it is, it had better be good.

And now the rain comes down in sheets. In over Dublin Bay.
The drops and the droplets and the dropletíns blackening the sand-
banks and the quays, the hardware and the hulks from San Diego,
Everett and Norfolk, VA. Washing clean the bones of Eblana, the
pots of the Norsemen, the Thingmote and the Liberties. Strongbow in Christchurch my eye! Fitz-this and Fitz-that and all that
follies – the rickety remnants of urchin, junky and hoor. The fallen
houses of merchants and nobles, ecclesiastics and Lords Lieutenant,
statues and plaques to rebels and laureates, shoulder to shoulder
with skanger and sangar and dazzle-painted checkpoints all nets
and puffs of smoke. And the Four Courts and the Custom House,
and the bits of broken bridges nosing in the Liffey's shallow trough.
Trolleys, lorries, bodies, old silver barrels from James's Gate. Expo-
nential distribution is what it is. *Bendita lluvia. Báisteach.* As per the
Marshall-Palmer Law. A Poisson Process? I forget. The position of

errors. Bogholes in a plotlet and such. Characters and the like. Charcuteries such as your one, presently shouting at the Seán D'Olier. But just to think of it. The fluid dynamics of it all. The Tolka gurgling. The Dargle in spate. Flooded culvert and catacomb. The steamed-up windows of the empty DART, the retro chippers and the charnel houses. Cascading gutters at government buildings. Guttersnipes and gulpins. Dams of dead pigeons, the wringing Guards. *Obedientia Civium Urbis Felicitas.* And oh, that Monsieur Fish and his fine weather for the Peking ducksworths in the wet windows of Chinatown. For the spires of San Patricio, for the flag (upside down this long time) on the GPO, and for the watchtowers of Ballywashington in the treetops of the Park. Fresh water. Precipitation. *Fionn Uisce.* Not the fabulous bird at all. The landmarks removed. The rhinoceros dead.

And while we're on the subject of phoenix and fishery, I ask you, what's your venom now? Stochastic, is it? For mine's a Stoli in a highball and it's all probability in the wind-up. The random variables. The hand-grown vegetables watered by Pluvius the Previous. Agapanthus pissed upon. As the Gods made Orion. As Dublin made me. And as I made the boy. The cub and the pup. Schroeder caught in it now, off on his travels, the high Hibernian wind in the shoulder of his sail, and him in his shirtsleeves too.

But ho! Here's a bird in the hedge. African oriole by the whacks of him. Finch that is, not Golden, for this lad is finchy in all respects. Passerine. And lookee yonder! What's that sheltering in the foxes' barricade? It's only one of my long lost pals! Pluviophobic. And them by all accounts extinct. A bee! *Apis mellifera* who should, by rights, be *mellifica.* Maker not carrier. Manufacturer not stevedore. But then, in all fairness, in those dark Linnaean days, a body couldn't know all there was to know. Not like now. These pornisophical (not my word) and rigorless days.

So no Colony Collapse Disorder in my back garden, then. In Dún Laoghaire, Dún Laoire, Dunleary, briefly Kingstown. Honey pie. Honeytrap. Honeybunch. 9.65 km ESE of the metropolitan hub. In my gargoyled home, with thanks to Bleach and Ammonia, in this blasted old port and resort. Number 26 Hibernia Road, in the lashing rain, where I do what I do with a modicum of love. Hawk clocking viper. On the constant *qui vive*, you might say, for every sight and sound. For every last dysfunction and blip. For the crying of souls. For the arse of the fatherless. For the vintage of the wicked. For the groaning of men from out of the city.

MICHAL AJVAZ, *The Golden Age.*
The Other City.
PIERRE ALBERT-BIROT, *Grabinoulor.*
YUZ ALESHKOVSKY, *Kangaroo.*
FELIPE ALFAU, *Chromos.*
Locos.
IVAN ÂNGELO, *The Celebration.*
The Tower of Glass.
ANTÓNIO LOBO ANTUNES,
Knowledge of Hell.
The Splendor of Portugal.
ALAIN ARIAS-MISSON, *Theatre of Incest.*
JOHN ASHBERY & JAMES SCHUYLER,
A Nest of Ninnies.
ROBERT ASHLEY, *Perfect Lives.*
GABRIELA AVIGUR-ROTEM,
Heatwave and Crazy Birds.
DJUNA BARNES, *Ladies Almanack.*
Ryder.
JOHN BARTH, *Letters.*
Sabbatical.
DONALD BARTHELME, *The King.*
Paradise.
SVETISLAV BASARA, *Chinese Letter.*
MIQUEL BAUÇÀ, *The Siege in the Room.*
RENÉ BELLETTO, *Dying.*
MAREK BIENCZYK, *Transparency.*
ANDREI BITOV, *Pushkin House.*
ANDREJ BLATNIK, *You Do Understand.*
LOUIS PAUL BOON, *Chapel Road.*
My Little War.
Summer in Termuren.
ROGER BOYLAN, *Killoyle.*
IGNÁCIO DE LOYOLA BRANDÃO,
Anonymous Celebrity.
Zero.
BONNIE BREMSER, *Troia: Mexican
Memoirs.*
CHRISTINE BROOKE-ROSE,
Amalgamemnon.
BRIGID BROPHY, *In Transit.*

GERALD L. BRUNS,
Modern Poetry and the Idea of Language.
GABRIELLE BURTON, *Heartbreak Hotel.*
MICHEL BUTOR, *Degrees.*
Mobile.
G. CABRERA INFANTE,
Infante's Inferno.
Three Trapped Tigers.
JULIETA CAMPOS,
The Fear of Losing Eurydice.
ANNE CARSON, *Eros the Bittersweet.*
ORLY CASTEL-BLOOM, *Dolly City.*
LOUIS-FERDINAND CÉLINE,
Castle to Castle.
Conversations with Professor Y.
London Bridge.
Normance.
North.
Rigadoon.
MARIE CHAIX,
The Laurels of Lake Constance.
HUGO CHARTERIS, *The Tide Is Right.*
ERIC CHEVILLARD, *Demolishing Nisard.*
MARC CHOLODENKO, *Mordechai
Schamz.*
JOSHUA COHEN, *Witz.*
EMILY HOLMES COLEMAN,
The Shutter of Snow.
ROBERT COOVER, *A Night at the Movies.*
STANLEY CRAWFORD, *Log of the S.S.*
The
Mrs Unguentine.
Some Instructions to My Wife.
RENÉ CREVEL, *Putting My Foot in It.*
RALPH CUSACK, *Cadenza.*
NICHOLAS DELBANCO,
The Count of Concord.
Sherbrookes.
NIGEL DENNIS, *Cards of Identity.*
PETER DIMOCK,
A Short Rhetoric for Leaving the Family.
ARIEL DORFMAN, *Konfidenz.*

COLEMAN DOWELL, *Island People.*
Too Much Flesh and Jabez.
ARKADII DRAGOMOSHCHENKO,
Dust.
RIKKI DUCORNET,
The Complete Butcher's Tales.
The Fountains of Neptune.
The Jade Cabinet.
Phosphor in Dreamland.
WILLIAM EASTLAKE, *The Bamboo Bed.*
Castle Keep.
Lyric of the Circle Heart.
JEAN ECHENOZ, *Chopin's Move.*
STANLEY ELKIN, *A Bad Man.*
Criers and Kibitzers, Kibitzers and Criers.
The Dick Gibson Show.
The Franchiser.
The Living End.
Mrs. Ted Bliss.
FRANÇOIS EMMANUEL,
Invitation to a Voyage.
SALVADOR ESPRIU,
Ariadne in the Grotesque Labyrinth.
LESLIE A. FIEDLER,
Love and Death in the American Novel.
JUAN FILLOY, *Op Oloop.*
ANDY FITCH, *Pop Poetics.*
GUSTAVE FLAUBERT,
Bouvard and Pécuchet.
KASS FLEISHER, *Talking out of School.*
FORD MADOX FORD,
The March of Literature.
JON FOSSE, *Aliss at the Fire.*
Melancholy.
MAX FRISCH, *I'm Not Stiller.*
Man in the Holocene.
CARLOS FUENTES, *Christopher Unborn.*
Distant Relations.
Terra Nostra.
Where the Air Is Clear.
TAKEHIKO FUKUNAGA,
Flowers of Grass.

WILLIAM GADDIS, JR., *The Recognitions.*
JANICE GALLOWAY, *Foreign Parts.*
The Trick Is to Keep Breathing.
WILLIAM H. GASS,
Cartesian Sonata and Other Novellas.
Finding a Form.
A Temple of Texts.
The Tunnel.
Willie Masters' Lonesome Wife.
GÉRARD GAVARRY, *Hoppla! 1 2 3.*
ETIENNE GILSON,
*The Arts of the Beautiful.Forms and
Substances in the Arts.*
C. S. GISCOMBE, *Giscome Road.*
Here.
DOUGLAS GLOVER,
Bad News of the Heart.
WITOLD GOMBROWICZ,
A Kind of Testament.
PAULO EMÍLIO SALES GOMES,
P's Three Women.
GEORGI GOSPODINOV, *Natural Novel.*
JUAN GOYTISOLO, *Count Julian.*
Juan the Landless.
Makbara.
Marks of Identity.
HENRY GREEN, *Back.*
Blindness.
Concluding.
Doting.
Nothing.
JACK GREEN, *Fire the Bastards!*
JIŘÍ GRUŠA, *The Questionnaire.*
MELA HARTWIG,
Am I a Redundant Human Being?
JOHN HAWKES, *The Passion Artist.*
Whistlejacket.
ELIZABETH HEIGHWAY, ED.,
Contemporary Georgian Fiction.
ALEKSANDAR HEMON, ED.,
Best European Fiction.

AIDAN HIGGINS, *Balcony of Europe.*
 Blind Man's Bluff
 Bornholm Night-Ferry.
 Flotsam and Jetsam.
 Langrishe, Go Down.
 Scenes from a Receding Past.
KEIZO HINO, *Isle of Dreams.*
KAZUSHI HOSAKA, *Plainsong.*
ALDOUS HUXLEY, *Antic Hay.*
 Crome Yellow.
 Point Counter Point.
 Those Barren Leaves.
 Time Must Have a Stop.
NAOYUKI II, *The Shadow of a Blue Cat.*
GERT JONKE, *The Distant Sound.*
 Geometric Regional Novel.
 Homage to Czerny.
 The System of Vienna.
JACQUES JOUET, *Mountain R.*
 Savage.
 Upstaged.
MIEKO KANAI, *The Word Book.*
YORAM KANIUK, *Life on Sandpaper.*
HUGH KENNER, *Flaubert.*
 Joyce and Beckett: The Stoic Comedians.
 Joyce's Voices.
DANILO KIŠ, *The Attic.*
 Garden, Ashes.
 The Lute and the Scars
 Psalm 44.
 A Tomb for Boris Davidovich.
ANITA KONKKA, *A Fool's Paradise.*
GEORGE KONRÁD, *The City Builder.*
TADEUSZ KONWICKI,
 A Minor Apocalypse.
 The Polish Complex.
MENIS KOUMANDAREAS, *Koula.*
ELAINE KRAF, *The Princess of 72nd Street.*
JIM KRUSOE, *Iceland.*
AYSE KULIN,
 Farewell: A Mansion in Occupied Istanbul.
EMILIO LASCANO TEGUI,
 On Elegance While Sleeping.

ERIC LAURRENT, *Do Not Touch.*
VIOLETTE LEDUC, *La Bâtarde.*
EDOUARD LEVÉ, *Autoportrait.*
 Suicide.
MARIO LEVI, *Istanbul Was a Fairy Tale.*
DEBORAH LEVY, *Billy and Girl.*
JOSÉ LEZAMA LIMA, *Paradiso.*
ROSA LIKSOM, *Dark Paradise.*
OSMAN LINS, *Avalovara.*
 The Queen of the Prisons of Greece.
ALF MAC LOCHLAINN,
 The Corpus in the Library.
 Out of Focus.
RON LOEWINSOHN, *Magnetic Field(s).*
MINA LOY, *Stories and Essays of Mina Loy.*
D. KEITH MANO, *Take Five.*
MICHELINE AHARONIAN MARCOM,
 The Mirror in the Well.
BEN MARCUS,
 The Age of Wire and String.
WALLACE MARKFIELD, *Teitlebaum's Window.*
 To an Early Grave.
DAVID MARKSON, *Reader's Block.*
 Wittgenstein's Mistress.
CAROLE MASO, *AVA.*
LADISLAV MATEJKA &
KRYSTYNA POMORSKA, EDS.,
 Readings in Russian Poetics: Formalist and Structuralist Views.
HARRY MATHEWS, *Cigarettes.*
 The Conversions.
 The Human Country: New and Collected Stories.
 The Journalist.
 My Life in CIA.
 Singular Pleasures.
 The Sinking of the Odradek.
 Stadium.
 Tlooth.
JOSEPH MCELROY,
 Night Soul and Other Stories.

ABDELWAHAB MEDDEB, *Talismano.*
GERHARD MEIER, *Isle of the Dead.*
HERMAN MELVILLE,
The Confidence-Man.
AMANDA MICHALOPOULOU, *I'd Like.*
STEVEN MILLHAUSER,
The Barnum Museum.
In the Penny Arcade.
RALPH J. MILLS, JR., *Essays on Poetry.*
MOMUS, *The Book of Jokes.*
CHRISTINE MONTALBETTI,
The Origin of Man.
Western.
OLIVE MOORE, *Spleen.*
NICHOLAS MOSLEY, *Accident.*
Assassins.
Catastrophe Practice.
Experience and Religion.
A Garden of Trees.
Hopeful Monsters.
Imago Bird.
Impossible Object.
Inventing God.
Judith.
Look at the Dark.
Natalie Natalia.
Serpent.
Time at War.
WARREN MOTTE,
Fables of the Novel: French Fiction since 1990.
Fiction Now:
The French Novel in the 21st Century.
Oulipo: A Primer of Potential Literature.
GERALD MURNANE, *Barley Patch.*
Inland.
YVES NAVARRE, *Our Share of Time.*
Sweet Tooth.
DOROTHY NELSON, *In Night's City.*
Tar and Feathers.
ESHKOL NEVO, *Homesick.*
WILFRIDO D. NOLLEDO,
But for the Lovers.

FLANN O'BRIEN, *At Swim-Two-Birds.*
The Best of Myles.
The Dalkey Archive.
The Hard Life.
The Poor Mouth.
The Third Policeman.
CLAUDE OLLIER, *The Mise-en-Scène.*
Wert and the Life Without End.
GIOVANNI ORELLI, *Walaschek's Dream.*
PATRIK OUŘEDNÍK, *Europeana.*
The Opportune Moment, 1855.
BORIS PAHOR, *Necropolis.*
FERNANDO DEL PASO,
News from the Empire.
Palinuro of Mexico.
ROBERT PINGET, *The Inquisitory.*
Mahu or The Material.
Trio.
MANUEL PUIG, *Betrayed by Rita Hayworth.*
The Buenos Aires Affair.
Heartbreak Tango.
RAYMOND QUENEAU, *The Last Days.*
Odile.
Pierrot Mon Ami.
Saint Glinglin.
ANN QUIN, *Berg.*
Passages.
Three.
Tripticks.
ISHMAEL REED, *The Free-Lance Pallbearers.*
The Last Days of Louisiana Red.
Ishmael Reed: The Plays.
Juice!
Reckless Eyeballing.
The Terrible Threes.
The Terrible Twos.
Yellow Back Radio Broke-Down.
JASIA REICHARDT,
15 Journeys Warsaw to London.
NOËLLE REVAZ, *With the Animals.*
JOÃO UBALDO RIBEIRO,
House of the Fortunate Buddhas.

JEAN RICARDOU, *Place Names.*

RAINER MARIA RILKE,
The Notebooks of Malte Laurids Brigge.

JULIÁN RÍOS, *The House of Ulysses.*

Larva: A Midsummer Night's Babel.

Poundemonium.

Procession of Shadows.

AUGUSTO ROA BASTOS, *I the Supreme.*

DANIËL ROBBERECHTS,
Arriving in Avignon.

JEAN ROLIN,
The Explosion of the Radiator Hose.

OLIVIER ROLIN, *Hotel Crystal.*

ALIX CLEO ROUBAUD, *Alix's Journal.*

JACQUES ROUBAUD,
*The Form of a City Changes Faster, Alas, Than
the Human Heart.*

The Great Fire of London.

Hortense in Exile.

Hortense Is Abducted.

The Loop.

Mathematics: The Plurality of Worlds of Lewis.

The Princess Hoppy.

Some Thing Black.

RAYMOND ROUSSEL,
Impressions of Africa.

VEDRANA RUDAN, *Night.*

STIG SÆTERBAKKEN, *Siamese.*

Self Control.

LYDIE SALVAYRE, *The Company of Ghosts.*

The Lecture.

The Power of Flies.

LUIS RAFAEL SÁNCHEZ,
Macho Camacho's Beat.

SEVERO SARDUY, *Cobra & Maitreya.*

NATHALIE SARRAUTE,
Do You Hear Them?

Martereau.

The Planetarium.

ARNO SCHMIDT, *Collected Novellas.*

Collected Stories.

Nobodaddy's Children.

Two Novels.

ASAF SCHURR, *Motti.*

GAIL SCOTT, *My Paris.*

DAMION SEARLS,
What We Were Doing and Where We Were Going.

JUNE AKERS SEESE,
Is This What Other Women Feel Too?

What Waiting Really Means.

BERNARD SHARE, *Inish.*

Transit.

VIKTOR SHKLOVSKY, *Bowstring.*

Knight's Move.

A Sentimental Journey: Memoirs 1917–1922.

Energy of Delusion: A Book on Plot.

Literature and Cinematography.

Theory of Prose.

Third Factory.

Zoo, or Letters Not about Love.

PIERRE SINIAC, *The Collaborators.*

KJERSTI A. SKOMSVOLD,
The Faster I Walk, the Smaller I Am.

JOSEF ŠKVORECKÝ,
The Engineer of Human Souls.

GILBERT SORRENTINO,
Aberration of Starlight.

Blue Pastoral.

Crystal Vision.

Imaginative Qualities of Actual Things.

Mulligan Stew.

Pack of Lies.

Red the Fiend.

The Sky Changes.

Something Said.

Splendide-Hôtel.

Steelwork.

Under the Shadow.

W. M. SPACKMAN, *The Complete Fiction.*

ANDRZEJ STASIUK, *Dukla.*

Fado.

GERTRUDE STEIN,
The Making of Americans.
A Novel of Thank You.
LARS SVENDSEN, *A Philosophy of Evil.*
PIOTR SZEWC, *Annihilation.*
GONÇALO M. TAVARES, *Jerusalem.*
Joseph Walser's Machine.
Learning to Pray in the Age of Technique.
LUCIAN DAN TEODOROVICI,
Our Circus Presents...
NIKANOR TERATOLOGEN,
Assisted Living.
STEFAN THEMERSON, *Hobson's Island.*
The Mystery of the Sardine.
Tom Harris.
TAEKO TOMIOKA, *Building Waves.*
JOHN TOOMEY, *Sleepwalker.*
JEAN-PHILIPPE TOUSSAINT,
The Bathroom.
Camera.
Monsieur.
Reticence.
Running Away.
Self-Portrait Abroad.
Television.
The Truth about Marie.
DUMITRU TSEPENEAG, *Hotel Europa.*
The Necessary Marriage.
Pigeon Post.
Vain Art of the Fugue.
ESTHER TUSQUETS, *Stranded.*
DUBRAVKA UGRESIC,
Lend Me Your Character.
Thank You for Not Reading.
TOR ULVEN, *Replacement.*
MATI UNT, *Brecht at Night.*
Diary of a Blood Donor.
Things in the Night.
ÁLVARO URIBE & OLIVIA SEARS, EDS.,
Best of Contemporary Mexican Fiction.
ELOY URROZ, *Friction.*
The Obstacles.

LUISA VALENZUELA,
Dark Desires and the Others.
He Who Searches.
PAUL VERHAEGHEN, *Omega Minor.*
AGLAJA VETERANYI,
Why the Child Is Cooking in the Polenta.
BORIS VIAN, *Heartsnatcher.*
LLORENÇ VILLALONGA,
The Dolls' Room.
TOOMAS VINT,
An Unending Landscape.
ORNELA VORPSI,
The Country Where No One Ever Dies.
AUSTRYN WAINHOUSE,
Hedyphagetica.
CURTIS WHITE,
America's Magic Mountain.
The Idea of Home.
Memories of My Father Watching TV.
Requiem.
DIANE WILLIAMS,
Excitability: Selected Stories.
Romancer Erector.
DOUGLAS WOOLF, *Wall to Wall.*
Ya! & John-Juan.
JAY WRIGHT, *Polynomials and Pollen.*
The Presentable Art of Reading Absence.
PHILIP WYLIE, *Generation of Vipers.*
MARGUERITE YOUNG,
Angel in the Forest.
Miss MacIntosh, My Darling.
REYOUNG, *Unbabbling.*
VLADO ŽABOT, *The Succubus.*
ZORAN ŽIVKOVIĆ , *Hidden Camera.*
LOUIS ZUKOFSKY, *Collected Fiction.*
VITOMIL ZUPAN, *Minuet for Guitar.*
SCOTT ZWIREN, *God Head.*